# THE AFTER-LIVES OF DOCTOR GACHET

First published in 2018
by Eyewear Publishing Ltd
Suite 333, 19-21 Crawford Street
London, WIH IPJ
United Kingdom

*Graphic design by* Edwin Smet
*Author photograph by* Vedran Strelar
*Cover image by* Vincent van Gogh
*Printed in England by* TJ International Ltd, Padstow, Cornwall

Set in Bembo 12 / 15 pt
ISBN 978-1-912477-18-0

**WWW.EYEWEARPUBLISHING.COM**

# THE AFTER-LIVES OF DOCTOR GACHET

## SAM MEEKINGS

EYEWEAR PUBLISHING

# THE ELIXIR
## May 1890

'It wouldn't help you.'

He tapped his pipe against the table to dislodge the last grey knuckle of ash, before tipping the mangy contents onto the grass. Then he reached into his left jacket pocket – raising a quizzical eyebrow when he found it empty – and, next, his right, retrieving the little pouch of tobacco and measuring out a good pinch. He began to fluff it up between his jittery fingers, then started to pack it into the bowl of his pipe.

'Why ever not?' his companion asked. 'I've tried everything else.'

'Ah, you see, you're too sharp, my friend,' the doctor said, keeping his eye on the pernickety task in hand. His fingers shook occasionally these days, and he found it harder than ever to do those fiddly jobs that required a steadiness he could not always muster.

'And that will stop it working?'

The doctor looked up. 'No, don't be absurd. It won't work because you won't believe it will work.'

'That really matters?'

'That is the only thing that matters. I wish I could tell you otherwise. But it is nothing more than a placebo, my friend.'

'I don't believe you. I've heard people talk about it. The famous herbal elixir of the venerable Doctor Paul Gachet.'

'Less of the venerable, please.' The doctor smiled, spreading creases across the deep craters of his face. 'Now, listen to me: the best way to heal the body is to heal the mind. I suspect you know that as well as anyone. All this concoction contains is a few herbs, a little spring water. But if you really believe…'

'Then you admit it is a type of magic – or rather a kind of trickery!'

'No. It is a form of mercy. People want to believe they are cured. Sometimes I can grant them that.'

The younger man rubbed a hand over his bearded chin. His hair was strawberry-blonde and sunblushed, and he wore an old white shirt and a straw hat big enough to obscure the mottled petal of curled and ruined skin that scarred the left side of his face where his earlobe should have been.

'I wish for that above all else.'

'I know,' the doctor replied, setting down his pipe for a moment to concentrate on the subdued young man in front of him.

'But you think it is beyond hope.'

'No, not at all. Don't be so defeatist. But I do not think you would be able to convince yourself that all your troubles had been miraculously cured by a hokum potion from an old provincial quack. And if you were then – heaven forbid – to suffer from another attack, then you would feel more hopeless than ever.'

The younger man nodded. 'I see.'

His tone was one the doctor recognized. He knew that place: the giddy hinterland between hope and hopelessness.

Above them, dun clouds were slowly being unspun by the southeast wind, and the cornfields beside the garden were beginning to shake off their rain-sparked vestments. The doctor struck a match to make the charring light, then tamped the tobacco back down into the pipe's bowl. He looked across at his new friend, who was staring up at the sky while his top teeth worried at his lip. He had been there too, had touched upon that other shore. At last the doctor made the true light, taking a series of shallow puffs before raising the pipe from his mouth to use the stalk to itch his brow.

'I am confident that, given time, you will begin to feel like yourself again,' the doctor said, not because it was true, but because both men knew it was better to pretend than to admit defeat. 'Now, I have a few homeopathic remedies that may do you some good, but really, these attacks – they are the product of an agitated mind. You must try and get some rest, take a long draught of the country air. Let it blow away the cobwebs, eh? And above all, keep painting. Distract yourself. That is the key. Do not fixate yourself on purgatives and miracle cures. That is not a dependable way to deal with the melancholy.'

'You speak from experience.'

The doctor did not reply. He merely sucked on his pipe.

# A QUESTION OF DEPTH

We have been here for some time. Look at his face. Or rather, try to look at him without tilting your head.

He is leaning backwards, his head nestled against his fist, and his tired but unflinching eyes stare back at you. Or rather they stare into you, they burrow as deep as a corkscrew through the skull. His look confirms that there is nothing that can be done. His left hand steadies himself against the table. His face – and, therefore, the focus of the painting – is off-centre, and hence the immediate impression is that everything is slightly out of kilter. The world is worn down at the edges, as weather-beaten as his thin and haggard face. We have moved in so close that he need only whisper to be heard, though this is not necessary; there is a closeness between us that nudges beyond the limits of speech. We have been here for some time.

Get a better look. His body looms large – the canvas cannot contain him, and he threatens to spill over the sides. His heavy blue jacket appears stitched from some stormy ocean. It is buttoned close to his neck (the collar sags open, revealing a shock of white) and is almost indistinguishable in texture and material from both the cobalt blue mountains seen behind him, and, beyond them, the azure blue sky – each laps at the edges of the next, like waves crashing one after another at the edge of the shore. There is little attempt at depth: the background is blurred and empty of detail, a wash of swirling blues. The painter appears to suggest that his subject knows full well that blue is shorthand for a particular kind of melancholy, and knows too that he is already deep within it. His eyes affirm that this is the depth to which we test ourselves.

Though he seems to have been here in this same spot, in this same pose, for an eternity, the painting has been done in a hurry. The rapid, almost frenzied brush strokes and the minimal, hasty details (the ginger hair poking out beneath his pale flat cap, the rough yellow books, the spiky foxgloves on the red-speckled table cloth, the distance as flat as a stage set) tell us the artist was in a rush. He did not ponder it for days in some empty studio. He did not make preliminary sketches, trying out different angles and perspectives, nor did he work on a succession of drafts. No, he did it as fast as he could. He got the essentials of that gaze – those eyes – down while the expression was still burning in his vision. Nonetheless the figure must have sat for the painter for many hours, and indeed there is something unsettling about his stillness. It is a preternatural calm, an acceptance that there is nothing that can be done.

Step back from the painting and his eyes follow you. But nothing else moves. Nothing matters but the intensity of the gaze.

Where are we? Some bar or café, or a private picnic spot? What is out there, behind him, over the ridge? It is not important.

What time of day is it? Is that the glowing blue of mid-morning, or the simmering blue of early afternoon? Or is it instead the worn-blue of dusk, or the bristling blue of dawn? It is impossible to say.

Who is this man? We can cheat, of course, and look at the title, and see that he is Doctor Paul-Ferdinand Gachet. But he does not look like much of a doctor. His clothes are blank and anonymous, and so he could just as easily be a farmhand or a merchant, a fisherman or a landlord. It does not matter.

What matters is his expression. He is looking at you. He has tasted sadness, a full bottle, a draught, a flagon, a gallon, an ocean, and is drunk on it. That is not to say he understands, that he can comprehend it. But that he empathizes. He has been submerged, churned through its rain and spray, tangled in its nets.

The picture is, by the artist's definition, a success: it has that '*touch of the eternal*' that he was striving for. Van Gogh wrote to his sister that '*I should like to paint portraits which appear after a century to people living then as apparitions. By which I mean that I do not endeavour to achieve this through photographic resemblance, but by means of impassioned emotions*'. And that is exactly what we have here: an embodiment of that sadness that comes from dredging through the depths.

But where does this sadness come from? Did it grow slowly, like an acorn, in his heart; or was he pierced with it, and infected, at some particular moment in the past? For the artist, the only thing that was important was communicating what he called 'the heartbroken expression of our times'. But I am becoming obsessed. I cannot help but wonder what made the Doctor this way, how any of us might reach this point – what was it that made his gaze so sorrowful, his expression so heartbroken?

Who is this man?

As I said, it does not matter. But it mattered once. And so, if time is nothing but a trick, then it matters now. It matters to me.

# ANATOMY LESSON
## 1840

'Jump!'

Their voices ricocheted against the battlements. But Paul wasn't done yet. Even though his fingertips had been shredded down to sandpaper, even though his knees and elbows were painted red with scrapes – he'd bloody show them.

His hands reached out for the parapet, his feet scrabbling off every jutting brick and worn groove in the old stone wall as he pushed himself up higher. A few times his grip slipped, and once or twice his feet slid, leaving him wheedling at the air before he found another slim foothold or handhold and kept clambering on. The wind tussled his hair. Paul was twelve, and he understood one rule above all others – the worst thing you can do is look down.

Still, he could not climb high enough to escape the rowdy chant of the boys waiting at the bottom:

'Jump! Jump! Jump! Jump!'

But of course it was not like this at all.

You know that, though, don't you?

Yes, I think you do. I think you are colluding in this lie, pretending that together we can ignore the glaring problem with this account. You are probably urging me to get on with the story. You are happy to ignore a few small inconsistencies for the sake of the bigger picture. You are used to suspending your disbelief, to making yourself believe whatever the story tells you to believe.

But it is not so simple. As I said, this matters. It is a man's life. And his afterlife beside. The facts matter. Yet already I have run aground, and I have twisted something real into the most outrageous fiction.

So what am I getting so worked up about? This: there is no way on earth they would have shouted 'Jump!'

I know – it's a small thing, a trivial detail. But I'm stuck on it. Because if I cannot get even this far into his life without making it up, then surely I have already failed. I want the real man, the real sadness, and not something conjured from guesswork and speculation. But whatever I write now, you will know as well as I that these boys are saying only the words I am making them say.

The simple fact of the matter is that they would not have shouted anything in English at all. These were French boys, and so they shouted '*Saute!*', their accents thick and rough. It goes without saying that I am not supposed to draw your attention to this.

On the contrary, we are meant to take part in the ridiculous charade that even though we are in the city of Lille, in French Flanders, close to two hundred years ago, you and I are able to eavesdrop on a conversation and understand perfectly every word uttered in a foreign and archaic tongue. We are supposed to pretend that these words they never heard are the ones they really used.

So how should we proceed? Obviously I'm not going to write everything in French – I wouldn't be able to manage that in a million years. Besides, this is a reconstruction: it is bound to be truer to the spirit than the letter of his words. It is his life, yes, but only as filtered through my translation.

If we accept this is a rough translation, however, this only leads us into further problems. For instance, should I sprinkle the dialogue with a few '*Gadzooks*' and '*Good Heavens!*' and '*A thousand pardons, good Sir*' and a few references to crinolines, croquet, clackboxes and camera-obscuras to make it clear that all this happened long ago and things were different then? Or should I make them speak like us, to show that, underneath the unfamiliar customs and constricting fashions, people are always the same, no matter what year it may be? And while I'm at it, should I have the servants and rougher peasant boys use a bit of slang and contraction, as well as a sprinkle of mangled grammar, to make clear that great gulf between the classes in nineteenth-century France – or would cockneys in Lille be too much of a distraction, and stretch your credulity to breaking point?

In short, each little question leads to another, and each one seems to lead us further from his life and deeper into fiction.

So after all these qualifications and excuses, why bother?

Because there is no other choice. The story of any life – even your own – is cobbled together from faulty recollections and vague impressions. That thin line between memory and invention is one all of us have to walk each day, and we can no more quit fiddling with the past than we can choose to stop breathing.

Paul's fingers sought out the top, scuttling crablike higher and higher. He had to be almost there.

'Come on, slowcoach!' Henri called from the top. 'You can't give up now!'

Paul could feel his heart going haywire in his chest. His friend knew him well: if he could have given up right now without risking plummeting to his death, he would have done it. He was huffing and panting, and he only hoped the boys down below could not hear him wheezing.

'Get a move on,' Henri continued. 'You have got to see this!'

Paul gulped in as much air as he could and pushed himself higher, his hands reaching for the top. Instead his searching fingers found Henri. His best friend was leaning over the parapet, grinning at his struggle.

'Need a hand?' Henri laughed.

He grabbed hold of Paul's arm and helped haul him up, both of them grunting and heaving until the younger boy came tumbling over the top of the ramparts. Paul fell into a heap at his friend's feet, then sat clutching his sides.

'See? That wasn't so bad.'

Paul did not answer.

Henri was everything that Paul was not. Solid, heavy-set and strong, a ragged sack of parsnips and potatoes with a dark tan, and composed almost entirely of tightly-coiled springs. Paul, meanwhile, was scrawny and bookish and awkward, his hair a stark shade of ginger, his face sallow and most of the time scrunched into a bemused frown. Despite this – or more likely because of it – the two boys were best friends, blood brothers, comrades on countless Saturday afternoon adventures like this one.

'We should have brought a flag to put up,' Henri said. 'You know, to claim the territory.'

'I think it's probably best not to draw too much attention to ourselves,' Paul said.

'Right, yes, good point.'

Once his breath had slowed down, Paul felt able to open his eyes again and look around. The ramparts curved round to his right, and the streaks of birdshit and mess of stray twigs told him it had been a while since any guards had stood look-out up there. Over the edge of the parapets, Paul could see the sluggish green water of the moat, and beyond that the main track leading back towards the bustle of the city.

Henri went strutting round the corner to check out their spoils. Paul raised himself cautiously to his feet and looked out.

Down below he could make out a horse and cart rattling along the road toward the city, where late-afternoon sunlight was coating the rooftops in marmalade. Somewhere just out of sight on the fringes, nestled away behind the church tower just visible in the distance, was the house where Mama would at this moment be sitting in the garden, beneath her wide-brimmed parasol, one of her novels spread out upon her lap, while upstairs Mathilde was no doubt lecturing her dolls about their terrible manners and how they would have to be on their best behaviour if they expected to be invited to another grand ball, and the cat was trudging lazily from his sister's room to his, probably leaving pawprints on the Latin dictionary he had left open when he snuck out earlier, as the maids scurried to and fro below to make sure that everything was in order before Papa returned home. He grinned to himself. None of them knew he was here. Is there any pleasure greater than a pleasure stolen, an hour unexpectedly set free from others' expectations?

Henri came strutting back round the corner.

'Find any treasure?'

'Nothing but a few birds' nests. Think we should lob them down?'

'Why would we want to do that?'

'Spoilsport.'

'Oh, no, I mean, we could, you know, if that's what you think we should do, if you want.'

Henri laughed and instead came to stand side-by-side with

his friend, staring over the top of the battlements. They'd made it, even when the others had said they wouldn't dare, and now the whole world belonged to them. Every track snaking in or out of the city, every patchwork field swimming into the distance, every curve and crook of the river, and from up here they could see it all. They exchanged smiles. They were still at the age when it seemed the universe was made for them alone: many nights Paul and Henri would sit cross-legged at the eye of the telescope Papa gave him for Christmas, taking turns to focus on the moon and making up names for the creatures that lived upon its surface. The moon's monsters and beasts, its knights and scribes, and in the back of Paul's Latin grammar book they even invented a language that they imagined might describe the delicacies and the drinks, the rock flora and stone fauna, the sludgy grey lakes and black granite mountains there. They were twelve and there was nowhere they could not go.

Well, yes, I've begun with the interesting bits. There's no getting round it, unless you want to see baby Paul waddling round in nappies.

How young are we formed, anyway? When do we really start to become ourselves? I know some people argue that our lives are predicated on the quirks of our genes, that our destiny is inscribed in the code of our DNA. On the other hand, it is only when we are tested in the outside world that all the possibility bristling within us is whittled down and we really take shape. And that's why we can pass over all that happy-family crap – the timid eldest child spoilt by a besotted mother, the curious sneak stealing hours with his father's antiquarian books, the shy big brother getting his sister to play tricks on the maids and cook – and get straight to the important stuff.

We can assume that, at twelve, most of his days were given over to the everyday drudge of studying, schoolwork and daydreaming. So what makes each of us unique, what makes a life? The points at which our daydreams break.

Both of the boys noticed that the chanting had suddenly fallen silent, and turned to face each other.

'Do you reckon they've seen some guards?' Paul whispered.

'Don't be stupid, they would've given the signal. There's no way they'd just abandon us.'

'Then you think they're coming up too?'

Henri shrugged. 'Benoît and Theo? I doubt it. You know what they're like. Too cowardly by half!'

He was right, for their friends – or, more accurately, the children of Paul's father's friends, boys he had little choice but to muck in with, but who rarely did anything save moan and boast – soon appeared down below, on the other side of the moat. They had obviously abandoned their lookout at the back for a better sight of the main attraction: a gangly twelve-year-old trying to win a bet on whether or not he could fly.

Of course, the actual wording of the wager was not quite that outlandish. Neither Paul nor Henri was so dunderheaded as to think they might suddenly sprout wings and soar off into the clouds. But the other boys had mocked Paul mercilessly when he had lied that there was nothing in this world he was afraid of, and now he was honour-bound to prove them wrong. Pick anything you like, Henri had told them, stepping in to protect his friend, and we'll do it. Paul had stared on in worried disbelief. Choose the most hair-raising, goose-bump-brewing, spine-chilling thing you can think of, and we'll do it. We'll sit up all night in the haunted mill by the river, we'll have a staring-contest with a wolf, we'll go down to the taverns in the shadowy side of the city and arm-wrestle the old Bonapartists who only come out at night — Paul and me are not afraid of anything. Just you watch.

All right, they'd said. Scale the battlements and jump off the ramparts.

Ha. Henri had said back (while Paul blinked and blushed). Is that the best you can think of?

And now Paul knew why the boys below had stopped chanting. Maybe they were beginning to realize that he and Henri might actually go through with it.

'What now?' Paul asked nervously.

Henri pointed down. 'Race you to the bottom.'

Paul peered over. 'How deep do you think it is? The moat, I mean. And what about the crocodiles?'

'There aren't any crocodiles.'

'Sharks?'

'Listen, would you rather try to climb back down the wall? You'll slip off and break your neck. This is the only way. It'll be over in seconds.'

'But shouldn't we —'

'No,' Henri said. 'We shouldn't.'

'You think we should do it together?'

'Holding hands? Not on your life. No, you've got to go first.'

'Me? Why?'

'It's you they challenged.'

'Only after you gave them all those ridiculous choices.'

Henri shrugged. Paul knew his friend was right. There was nothing he could do. It was a question of honour, and he couldn't be the one letting them both down.

He stepped nervously up onto the outer parapet, his gut squirming and his head starting to spin. He hated himself for having made that stupid claim, hated Henri for goading them on. The wind began to tug at his shirt and he swallowed hard. His hands flew out, hovering in space as he tried to keep his balance.

'Wish me luck,' he said, and then he screwed his eyes shut to stop himself looking down.

'You don't need luck. It's a piece of cake,' Henri said. 'See you down below!'

Paul's mouth was too dry to reply. He knew if he waited his frantic brain would conjure up countless other excuses, that if he voiced his worries then he would be inviting fate to transform his doubts into fact, and so there was only one thing for it.

He took a deep breath, then flung himself off the top of the ramparts and into the air.

His arms jerked wildly and his heart did somersaults, and suddenly the whole world had come unanchored.

His first thought was that he was not actually falling. In that instant he knew what falcons felt, or turtles gliding through the deep: that moment before the dive when it seems possible that a single second, half a second, less, might somehow be suspended forever.

Or perhaps he didn't think that.

In fact, we have no way of knowing whether or not this is what he thought. He could just as easily have been thinking of the looks on the boys' faces below, or thinking of what he might have for supper later, or else thinking *Please Lord no! Please just make it all stop!* It is impossible to say.

I would love nothing more than to believe that all our thoughts exist beyond us, that they travel from our minds out into the ether, and that they drift invisible everywhere among us like radio waves that we might tune into at will. But it doesn't seem very likely. Besides, I have no psychic powers.

You know that. Yet how strange that in a story we so willingly accept that we can hear thoughts pouring out of every mind in sight, when we know how ridiculous this idea really is. And how strange that the thoughts we hear are rarely messy, confused, ungrammatical, woolly, illogical, repetitive – all the things that our everyday thoughts are really like.

Perhaps we do not want real life at all, but life as we think it ought to be. Life with all the peripheral ephemera – the cobwebs and cul-de-sacs, the background noise and toilet breaks, the petty accounting and moments of brain-frying boredom – edited out. We will not watch Paul squatting over the lavatory, nor overhear him thinking about his Latin declensions. I will follow only those twists and bumps in the road that seem to form the rough contours of that face, of that sad smile.

Not that it is really my choice. If I had my way, I would pause it here and keep him suspended mid-air forever. I do not want to let him fall. Far better to stay here, where life is all opportunity and adventure. Here, where death and disease and want are things that happen elsewhere, in other countries, in stories – or at the very least behind the scenes. Here, where there is something thrilling about every new morning. Here: where anything is still possible, and his horizons have not yet shrunk to fit a shrinking world.

Because in ten seconds his life will change, and he will come to realize for the first time how much we are at the mercy of these feeble bodies we lug around with us. Right now his body is something he does not have to think about: it is a kite, the vessel through which his soul soars, swoops, flies. It is the capricious giver and receiver of his whims. But in eight seconds he will begin to understand that it can be something else – a ragtag bundle of aches, a cage that multiplies pain, a prison. Remember the first time you realized you could not do anything you wanted? In five seconds he will learn that life is not effortless, nor easy, nor fair. In just three short seconds he will hit the water.

Two.

One.

The moat erupted as he came splashing in – a burst of spray that disguised the awkward way he broke the surface, the flail of his body as he fell. Neither the slack-jawed boys on the bank nor his best friend back on top of the ramparts saw what happened next.

Paul felt it before he could register what it was – the pain shooting up through his ankle as it absorbed the full force of the blow, so hard his teeth bit into his lip and drew blood, so sudden he saw only white as the agony exploded through his senses – his ankle twisting fiercely as his still-tumbling body struggled to stop sinking. Then he screamed.

 The ligaments ripping

   The bone fracturing

     The skin shredded

       The muscles torn

         The whole foot feeling as though it had been cracked in a vice.

He yelped and shrieked, made animal noises that were strangled by the ice-cold water. His eyes stung with tears. His whole body buckled in shock and it was all he could do to try and flap and thrash to push himself back up toward the surface.

He never saw the jutting rock his foot hit. He never went back.

So, is this where sadness begins?

Maybe. Think back to times you have experienced a migraine so strong light sears your eyes and you have to retreat to the throb of a dark room; think of times you have been hunched over a toilet bowl, heaving out your guts; think of being so drunk the room spins in crazy fairground circles; think of fever so high you start seeing things, of hospital stays if you have been forced to endure them, of the blinding pain of childbirth, of muscle spasms or unbearable toothache or concussion – when all you want is to be well, to be yourself again, to return to the world of the well where things are as they should be. Think back to that desperation, that yearning to be back to normal, that desire to be put out of your misery, and remember the thought that persists, more than any other: that this is not the real you, this is not your life, this is not how things ought to be.

Is this where sadness begins? Maybe not, but it is hard sometimes to escape the suspicion that our actions in child-hood ripple out across the years and echo in the adults we be-come.

Later, after dragging himself out and getting his friends to help him hobble home, Paul was thankful for one thing and one thing only: that the other boys had not heard his howls. He was grateful that the water stole them away and carried them as bubbles to the surface, where they burst and were instantly lost amid the indifferent air. For already, at twelve years old, he knew that pain was one thing, but pity was far worse.

# FALLING

People fall from grace (mimicking the Fall of Man, or so it is said: that time when Adam and Eve tasted the fruit from the Tree of Knowledge of Good and Evil and so condemned us all to be born into sin). We delight in the downfall of politicians, celebrities, and other public figures, revelling in how the mighty have fallen. Americans long ago decided to replace Autumn with Fall, to mirror the downpour of rust-coloured leaves once summer ends. Stock prices, temperatures, governments: all fall as often as the rain. We retreat, fall back, fall out, fall short, fall behind. Occasionally people and things fall traditionally, like Paul, at the mercy of gravity, but more commonly we cleave to idioms – and, most commonly of all, we fall in love.

And I fell in love with a picture. At least, I will call it a kind of love. If love is something that bothers you, that gnaws at you and won't leave you alone. If love is something a little obsessive and a little strange, something not quite bound to logic, something we cannot quite explain. If so, then it is a kind of love.

He bothered me. Like a car alarm that goes off outside your window at night, just as you reach the leg-slumping edge of sleep. He bothers me still. Like a thousand-piece jigsaw with nine-hundred and ninety-nine puzzle pieces set in place, and a tiny hole where the last smudge of colour should be.

And because he bothers me, I come back to him again and again. With every letter of rejection, every failed job interview, every relationship gone wrong, every silly falling out with a friend, every petty humiliation at work. The old man who knows how shitty life can be, who has been through the same, and worse besides. I have the postcard myself, on my desk now as I write. It is a talisman, yes, but also a living ghost.

I first saw him at a party. It was at a student house somewhere off Cowley Road, one of those ramshackle terraces that appear insignificant from a distance but seem to grow ever taller and more imposing the closer you get. I have no idea who lived there, and I cannot now recall how we happened to end up there that evening in October, though I do remember there were so many people crammed inside the house that my friends and I chose to spend most of the time in the garden, sitting on tatty deck-chairs that had clearly been salvaged from the local skip, passing round bottles of cheap white wine.

It must have been well past midnight when I went back inside. Since the downstairs bathroom had been taken over by a noisy couple, I was forced to make my way through the crowd packed elbow-to-elbow in the kitchen in search of another. I remember the living room was a wreck, with plant pots broken and the sofa upturned, though this did not seem to bother the dancers corkscrewing wildly round one another in the middle of the crusty carpet, and I had to fight my way past a group of people congregating on the stairs to get up to the first floor.

I tried the handle of the door at the end of the landing, and it opened. As soon as I poked my head inside, I saw it wasn't a bathroom. But I didn't turn around right away.

Most student bedrooms fall into one of two categories: either the occupant has left everything as they found it, so that the bare walls and generic design make the room resemble something from a low-rate hotel (as if to make it clear that they do not consider it their home, and to emphasize that they could disappear if they so wished with only a moment's notice), or else they have filled every available space with photos, prints, posters, wall-hangings, throws, knick-knacks, lava lamps and beanbags in an effort to stamp their personality on the room. The majority of my friends had done their best to plaster their walls with posters of their favourite bands, or else a montage of photos of their family and friends in a variety of drunken or 'hilarious' poses. Here and there you might find a picture of Che Guevara, or a black-and-white print of a jazz icon or dead movie star, but the closest thing you would get to art was a copy of Klimt's *The Kiss* with its dazzling shower of gold, or a Vettriano print showing well-dressed figures dancing on the seashore.

This room was different. For a start, there was not a single photo. Nothing to indicate that the occupant had a life outside that room. The walls were almost bare.

But there was a postcard beside the bed. It was on the bedside table, where a family photo ought to have been. It caught my eye because it was the only portrait in the room – the only human face. A man with a mournful expression. I had seen the picture before, but had only a vague idea of what it was.

But I knew that look. The second I saw it there, I recognized something in it. That dizzying feeling of being homesick for a place you've never been.

Have you ever been heartbroken? I hope, for your sake, that you haven't. But most of us have. Most of us know that kick in the guts, that feeling that the world has come unspun, and there's fuck all you can do about it.

I heard a sound on the landing, so I slipped out of the room as quickly as I could, feeling guilty for intruding. But I couldn't shake the picture from my brain. (Even now, twenty years later, I still can't.) Once I got downstairs I asked my friends about it. *Hey. Van Gogh painting, a man in a blue suit. Anyone know what I'm talking about? Anyone know what it's called?*

But they just shook their heads. Only one of my mates leaned over and said: 'A man walks into a pub and orders himself a beer. Then he notices the world's most famous painter sitting on the next barstool, and so of course he wants to buy him a drink. *Fancy a pint, Vincent?* the man asks. *No thanks*, replies Van Gogh. *I've got one ear.*'

In short, the party rumbled on. I forgot about the postcard. But not about the picture. It has stayed with me.

We all have one.

That song that speaks your heart for you. That knows its secret tongue. The one you turn to when your life is going to shit, to remind you who you are and who you might be.

That movie you love, the one where you can repeat every single dumb line. The one you watch when you're sick, or hungover, or just a little down-in-the-dumps.

That book that you dive into like a blue-lipped ocean at the frazzled edge of summer. The one you keep dog-eared and close, the pages smudged with thumbprints and folded corners. The one you give to all your friends as presents, that you sometimes disappear into.

That's what the picture is to me.

And that is why I have to know what it is that makes him look so sad. Because we all fall. But what is it that makes us fall apart?

# A STUDY OF HORSES
## 1841

Smoke – the kind of thick mist horses snort from fat nostrils on cold mornings – wheeled and tumbled across the rooftops. The old bell tower was ringing for Vespers, but the call was drowned out by the clamour of feet beating against the cobblestones as the shopkeepers and blacksmiths and stable-hands and everyone else who happened to be in the vicinity of Rue Sainte-Catherine fled the fire.

Everyone, that is, except for the boys, who, as boys tend to do, were running as fast as they could toward the possibility of danger. Though it should go without saying that Paul was not really running. He was hobbling, limping, dragging his bad foot alongside his good, trying not to slow Henri down.

Henri in turn was whining for them to get a move on, chomping at the bit to sprint to the scene of the fire, but Paul pretended he could not hear his sighs.

Consider this: before, Paul was simply ginger, a redhead, a carrot-top, a boy whose blush had spread all over his head. Now, they called him cripple too: a mangled, maimed, freckle-marked fool. In short, he was happy to still have a friend who hadn't deserted him, thinking him cursed.

'I heard that if a man dies in a fire his ghost will stay in the house for a hundred years and howl every time the landlord lights a candle,' Henri said, as they cantered along unevenly.

Paul laughed. 'If a man dies in a fire, then isn't it likely that his house will burn to the ground too?'

'I know that. Houses get rebuilt though, dullard.'

'Yes, and I suppose in the meantime the ghost just loiters around the building site, does it? Maybe even whispers some sage advice to the carpenters?'

'No one likes a know-it-all, Paul!'

They turned the corner and their conversation was cut short by the sight of it: the blaze spread across three buildings, the black and putrid fug of smoke pirouetting up towards the sky. They were short, stocky grey-bricks from the dog-end of the previous century, and fire churned and leapt across their rooftops. They could taste the charred embers from there, feel the hot flakes of ash falling like blistering raindrops on their heads. Paul stumbled to a stop and stood staring in disbelief.

It had been a hard year. His gangly, fidgety body had not had the chance for much fidgeting. He turned thirteen only a few days after the physician his father paid handsomely to bring good news brought only disappointment: he would probably limp for the rest of his life, though with luck in time it would barely be noticeable. He had been confined to his room for recovery, and during those long and restless weeks he had set aside his telescope and turned his attention to the problem in hand. He focused on the body, the psyche, the humours, the soul. He read the tomes from his father's library with the same kind of ravenous appetite other boys displayed at sport or at dinner. He copied the pictures from the anatomy books in his own loping hand, and with a box of pastels he brought to life the veins, the arteries, the tendons, the ligaments, the muscles. Soon, he knew the name of every bone, the temperaments and theories of the blood, and had even secretly dissected a mouse trapped by Cook. He had been awkward and shy before the accident, but now he was reserved in a different way: he understood that pain and misery spoke a language all its own, and he was becoming adept at recognising it in the gestures and expressions of those around him, in the men who came to plead with his father for work, in the crippled old soldiers begging in Lille, in the lame workhorses being led to the knacker's yard, and all of it reduced him to silence.

Henri took a few steps forward. Paul shuffled back as discreetly as he could.

'It's going to swallow everything,' Henri said, choking in awe. 'If it goes on like this there'll be nothing left.'

The whole street seemed to be twitching like flame. The air warped and buckled with the heat, while the building dead ahead was spitting out sparks and burning chunks of timber with the ferocious venom of some snarling dragon. Paul stayed where he was, rocking from his bad foot to his good foot and back again. Despite his lack of confidence, he had never been the kind of child who was good at keeping still: instead he was a restless twitcher, the type of boy who chewed his lips incessantly while reading, who couldn't see an animal without stopping whatever he might have been doing to pet it, who had five books open at a time — who was, in short, at the mercy of a constant stream of competing thoughts that never stopped until his head dented the pillow at the end of the day and he had started snoring.

The inferno hissed and thrummed, and Paul found it hurt his eyes to look directly at the twisting fire rising from the buildings in front of them.

'Get out of the bloody way!' A man with a peasant's cap and dirty breeches shoved past the boys and ran on down the street.

'Coward,' Henri muttered as he passed, and Paul laughed, less because he was amused than because he knew he was supposed to. In truth he was beginning to suspect that the fire might be better viewed from a safe distance.

'Bonapartists,' Henri said. 'Bound to be Bonapartists that started it. They're behind everything, my Father says. Everybody knows they're trouble.'

'Or horse thieves,' Paul said. 'Look where all the smoke is coming from. It's the stables – that's the one in the middle there.'

As if in answer, they heard a high-pitched whinny break the air.

'Pretty amateur horse thieves if they left the horses behind, dunderhead!' Henri scoffed.

Through the smoke another man with a blackened face come stumbling towards them. It was only when they saw his red eyes, the way his hands flinched and jerked frantically at his sides, and the sight of his mouth churning air as though chewing some invisible meal, that they realized that this might be more than just a brilliant spectacle. Paul watched in surprise as Henri approached him. He had never seen an adult male sobbing before – had never seen his father so much as laugh, let alone shed a tear – and was not quite sure whether they should help him or pretend they hadn't seen him so as to spare him the shame and embarrassment.

'What is it?' Henri asked. 'Is there someone left inside?'

The man simply moved his mouth up and down, flapping and gulping for breath. Despite his dirty and soot-stained coat, Henri grabbed hold of his shoulders and looked into his eyes.

'*Oui ou non?* Is there anybody in there?'

The man stared into the boy's eyes, then shook his head.

Henri let go and the man crumpled to the pavement.

'But... my horses...' he muttered with a ragged voice.

'Thank Heavens', Henri said, his face white. 'For a moment there I thought... well...'

'What?' Paul said to his friend. 'You thought what?'

'That it was something serious. That someone was trapped and... you know.'

'It is serious,' Paul said.

Henri snorted. 'Only if you don't fancy horse meat stew for supper.'

'But we can't leave them,' Paul said. Even though he had barely whispered it, more giving voice to his own doubts than building an argument, his friend looked at him as though he had recently fallen and broken his skull and not his ankle.

'Pull the other one,' Henri said.

'I mean it.'

'Don't be a dolt. No one's gonna give us a medal just for saving some old donkey.'

'So we just wait for them to burn?'

'They're only animals!' Henri was getting frustrated with his friend – it was one thing to slow him down, but quite another to argue with him so much.

'You're an animal too, dummy!' Paul shot back.

'And you're a lump of shit! Go to hell!'

'No, listen, Henri. Think about it: we live, we breathe, we eat. We're all animals.'

'What rot! Don't be a fool, Paul. You and I can speak, for a start. Or hadn't you noticed?'

'Animals bark at each other, they howl, they sing.'

'All right, then, if you're going to be contrary, I have a soul. Ha! Argue with that.'

'You don't think every living thing has a soul?'

'Of course not. They're just meat. They can't think or anything, and there's no way Saint Peter would ever let a stinking beast into Heaven. Everyone knows there aren't any fleas or skunks in Paradise.'

Paul shook his head. 'If there aren't any animals there, then how could it be paradise?'

The man with red eyes was still flopped in the middle of the cobblestone street, his hunched shoulders rocking to and fro. The fire was still raging across the buildings ahead of them, bridling and hissing at every window.

'Look,' Henri said, 'I know you're still irked about the jump, but there's no need to be like this. It wasn't my fault, you know.'

'It's not about the jump,' Paul said. He was blushing furiously, as he always did when he got riled up. 'You could just stand here and wait for them to die?'

'What's the other choice?'

'We could go and get them,' Paul said.

His friend exploded with laughter. 'Right, you're going to limp in there and neigh at the horses to follow you out before the building collapses!'

'That's right. That's exactly what I'm going to do!' Paul said. He hadn't thought of it before that second, but it seemed his friend's teasing had kindled some fire of his own.

He stared at the fire and took a deep breath.

'If you reckon horses can talk, why not call them out? That'd be faster than you hobbling after them!' Henri went on.

But Paul had stopped listening. He started a slow jog, lugging his bad foot along towards the burning buildings.

'Don't be such a dimwit! Come back!' Henri called, but he did not make a move to follow Paul. On the contrary, he started backing away, anxious not to be seen near the scene of the incident should anything go wrong.

Paul loped forward as fast as his leg would allow, not letting himself look back. He was getting better at ignoring the pain, at pushing through, and he upped his pace as he grew closer to the fire in the hope that momentum alone would be enough to stop him turning in panic and fleeing with his tail between his legs. The house to the left had already half-crumbled in on itself: the roof had folded inwards, and all that remained inside was a wiry skeleton of timber around which threads of fire coiled and danced. It must have started there, Paul thought, and only recently spread along to the stables. Or, at least, this was what he tried to force himself to believe.

The stables was a long squat building, with grey stone walls and a thatched roof now crackling and jeering with flame. Through the long windows he could see shadows flailing and spinning in a giddy waltz.

He gave the door a shove with his elbow and almost tumbled in. The bubbling heat made him pant and gasp, while the smoke clogged up his nose and wrung his eyes dry, and so he clamped his handkerchief to his mouth to keep from choking.

Inside all was echo: the skittish stomping of feet, the hooves clomping and banging against the doors as the unseen horses reeled and whirled and tugged against their ropes. Paul felt sick. He spun around – left, then right, then left again – so dizzy and befuddled by the tumbling reels of smoke that he found it impossible to work out what direction the commotion might be coming from.

It was darker than a crow's eye. He stumbled forward, trying to bat away the fumes and hoping beyond hope that his eyes might soon get used to it. If anyone else had been foolish enough to venture inside, it would have looked to them as though he was trying to doggy-paddle through an endless fog.

If Henri had offered to come with him, would Paul still

have gone in? Probably not. If his only friend hadn't poured scorn on the thought of his rescuing the horses, in his condition, would he have even considered it? It was unlikely. But Henri's mocking voice rang out in his ears as loud as the thumping and braying of the horses, and kept him stumbling on through the gloom.

You? You think you could do it? Really – *you*?

Yes, he chanted under his breath. Yes.

A fist of embers came crashing down to his left, and he staggered, dazed, away from it. The ceiling was dripping heat.

He raised his head and saw, above him, the rafters alive with wildly flitting serpents, hellish beasts made of flame and light. He had no doubt then that the fire was alive, that it was some distant sibling of his pain – that it too fed on suffering and misery, and that its appetite was just as furious and insatiable. He understood then what old men meant when they said they had seen devils. And then he caught sight of the horses.

Dead ahead, going beserk, three of them bashing into one another as they threw themselves against the partitions – one was spinning so frantically in mad and loping circles that he wondered whether it would knock him for six before he managed to get close to it.

Later, of course, in the retelling it would be six horses, then eight, then a good dozen, a whole school of unbroken stallions and haughty thoroughbreds – and then, just as quickly, none. He would repeat the story for Henri, for his family, for a handful of his father's friends, and then suddenly grow embarrassed by it, ashamed of his own reckless heroism. Unable to find the right words for the certainty that had possessed him, unable to make others understand why he had risked everything for a few workhorses – two out of three of which, it probably goes without saying, would never work again or be much good to anyone after the shock and trauma of that evening – he instead gave up mentioning it. So out of character, so unusual for the awkward and bookish redhead: it was almost as though in those moments he was someone else entirely, and this thought scared him so much he did not want to talk about it. Had it not been for the time he once mentioned it to his son, some fifty-odd years later while looking at a painting of horses on the shore, then it would to this day be forgotten.

But did it mean something to him? Yes. Sometimes it is the things we cannot put into words that have the strongest bearing on our lives. And so it is here that we see the hint of that famous look forming on his face, in the growing understanding that both our triumphs and heartbreaks are ours to bear alone – that people are a strange kind of animal whose primitive language cannot always touch upon the logic of our instincts.

He reached for the bolt and felt the burning metal singe his hand – as he went reeling back in pain, the horses spooked and rose up on their hind legs at him. Nonetheless he steadied himself and tried again, wrapping the handkerchief around his fingers before sliding the bolt across as quickly as he could manage. One gate. Then the second. Burning nuggets of ash came flicking against his back. Finally the third. And still they pitched up at him, their forelegs whirring violently, and in the pitch black ocean of their eyes he could see the flames behind him swirling.

'Stop!' He screamed out at them, coughing and spluttering in the smoke. 'I can't help you like this!' But the horses kept pulling away back into their stalls, banging into one another in their panic. And then he realized what he had to do. 'I'm sorry,' he whispered, his voice scratchy and rough, though he was not sure whether he was apologizing to the animals or to himself, to his family, to all those he had abandoned in his rush inside. He understood that it was not the words that mattered, but the tone, and if he could convince them he was calm then somehow he might soothe them enough to get them walking out.

'We're going on a little trot, all right? Just a little canter to the road, you see?'

They turned, blinking at him, snuffling and moving restlessly on the spot, so he reached out, running his fingers through sweat-slick manes and rubbing chins and muzzles with his burning palms until they were almost still. There were no bits, no bridles, no reins in reach and so he had to trust them. He rubbed his hands behind their ears, gently at first, then pushing more urgently, whispering all the while in a gibberish language of his own invention to settle them and drown out the raucous cackles of the fire above, around, beside, behind.

Then he plodded forward, still whispering to them, but not daring to look back. Miraculously, after a few steps he felt them at his side, trotting calmly as they followed one by one in his tracks. He felt jubilant, elated, heavy with relief, and yet all he wanted now was to close his eyes. Just for a second or two. His lips felt frazzled, like crisp bacon. He was in a furnace, churning out hell, but if he could just have a rest, just lie down for a minute and get his breath back, then everything would be all right.

His hands started to go slack, his ankle to give in on him, and he was just about to slump to his knees when he felt it: a heartbeat as loud as a martial drum, throbbing through the hides of the horses beside him, and he felt it with such force that he could not say whether it was theirs or his or all of them, joined together into a single pulse setting a guiding beat for their flight through the dark. He forced his streaming eyes open and lumbered on.

In later years he would wonder at that moment, wonder whether he had conjured it from among his most secret desires – to be a cloud-skimming bird, a fish flitting through the curves of the deep, a horse racing along wild mountain passes, to be anything but a boy cursed with a mangled ankle and a relentless shyness – or whether it had really happened. In his forties, reading Darwin's shocking new theories, he would remember it, and would spend much time considering what life might have been like if we were not the relatives of those solitary primates who live forlornly in the treetop world, but were instead descended from horses, a wild and primitive band of libertines, restless and nomadic and as quick as the wind.

He tried walking faster, but the door seemed to stay as far away as ever. A dull ringing came crawling into his ears, scuttling closer then further away again. The stables had turned into a fairground carousel, carrying him round in woozy circles.

He felt calm with the horses beside him, and he understood why, for the truth was he found animals easier than humans. They were less malicious and deceitful, far easier to trust and to forgive. He was hopeless with other people, but with these creatures it was different. He stole one more throat-shredding breath and tottered the last few ragged steps.

He came flying topsy-turvy out the door – as he led the horses into daylight he found he was crying hot, stinging tears, and the sound of the crowd outside burst like fireworks in his eardrums. He floundered and fell into the middle of the street.

The next thing he knew he was panting on his back on the

cobblestones, surrounded by onlookers. The faces spun madly around him. Where had they all come from? A group of men moved to help him, then froze to the spot as they saw the roof of the stables collapse in upon itself with a crash.

Paul rolled onto his side. Just in time, he thought. Then his eyes drew shut again and exhaustion claimed him.

The fire roared and whooped in triumph. The crowd were hypnotized by the blaze, frozen in wonder at the spectacle of such savage destruction – and so no one noticed when a chestnut mare dipped its neck to nuzzle the ginger boy's chin, and snort its red-hot breath against his cheeks.

# NEITHER HERE NOR NOT HERE

Shortly after my thirty-third birthday I travelled to Tokyo, partly because I had been asked to give a reading at a small literary festival there, but in truth more to escape a life at home that seemed to me increasingly unrecognisable – I was newly divorced, and stuck in a low-paying teaching job to make ends meet, while my second novel had recently been published to general indifference from readers and critics alike. It seemed at the time, for want of a better explanation, as though I was slowly turning translucent, and so I hoped the trip would help me shake off those dogged feelings of listlessness that followed me round my empty flat.

And yet, wandering that bustling and futuristic city, I felt that I was instead venturing further into the past. Restless thoughts followed me everywhere: in the Tsukiji Fish Market where in the early morning the desperate eyes of living, bucking fish laid tail-to-tail on beds of ice shone like the points of some desolate new constellation; at the Meiji Shrine, where prayers were sent out to the tolling of a bell and faded with its echo upon the air; in the green corners of Shinjuku Gyoen park, amid the ostentatious houses of Roppongi Hills, a bout of sumo between two gargantuan men with childlike faces, and amid the many bars whose names I cannot recall where I stopped for sashimi and sake and, yes, even during a one-time, reckless attempt at karaoke.

It was only at the end of the week that I managed to shake off something of my malaise – just in time to keep my appointment with a man named Rikuto Yin, a cataloguer for one of the more fashionable galleries in the Ginza district. I hoped that he might help me find out more about the painting that had come to mean so much to me, and so I felt buoyed by a sense of cautious optimism as I made my way to the Gendai Gallery on the Chuo Dori road, not far from the Imperial Palace.

Rikuto met me at the door (it was only later that I understood this was his way of making sure I did not come inside the gallery). He was tall, with a shaved head that suggested the perfect orb of some undiscovered planet, and an understated suit that I suspected cost more than my holiday.

'Mr Meeking?'

'Yes – well, Meekings, actually. Nice to meet you. You're Tony's friend?'

'He is... an acquaintance.' He narrowed his eyes. 'You are a writer?'

'That's right.'

He squinted down at my tufty brown coat and jeans. 'You do not look like a writer.'

'Ah. OK. Fair enough.'

He gestured down the street. 'Coffee?'

'Good plan,' I said. Rikuto nodded and started walking down the street, and from the outset I found it difficult to keep up with his brisk pace. 'Though actually, I don't really drink coffee.'

He raised an eyebrow. 'Are you sure you are a writer?'

'A cup of tea would be great, though.'

He led me into a café that seemed to double as the set for some minimalist space opera: everywhere I turned I saw sleek white antiseptic surfaces and girls with ruler-straight fringes and glittery spacesuits. We took the stairs up to the second floor, which was completely deserted, and settled at a table in the corner. In place of windows, the room had screens showing whirling spirals of light that made me feel cross-eyed if I looked directly at them (they reminded me of those old-school screensavers that risked hypnotizing anyone who stared at them too long). From an almost unfathomable menu I ordered a Cloud and Mist Tea.

Rikuto stirred his coffee for an inordinately long time with a tiny silver spoon before speaking.

'I read your *Book of Crows*.'

'Oh. Well, thank you. Did you enjoy it?'

'I do not usually read historical fiction.'

'Ah. I see.'

'I find it usually wants to do one of two things. Either it shows how strange the past was, how different lives were then. In that case, it raises the question of whether we can ever truly understand the lives of people from different times. Or else it tells us that nothing changes: that no matter the odd costumes and the strange beliefs, deep down people are always the same. We see always the same joys, the same fears, the same passions, and it is only the scenery that changes. In that case, it suggests there is nothing new, only the same experiences repeated again and again with the tiniest of variations.'

'So, you didn't like it?'

'It is not a question of like. I do not care to spend too long in the past.'

'But you work in a gallery,' I said. 'You are surrounded by history every day.'

'That is not how we see it.'

'Really?'

'History is not of interest to us. You must understand, we do not deal in representational art. We trade in works that of-fer an individual communication between the subject and the viewer, one that is different each time. The viewer brings his or her experience to the work. No history, no faces, no context. Only the painting and the person.'

'I see,' I said. 'Very modern.'

'In a sense, yes. We are more interested in the present moment than the past.'

'And the future?'

He spread his hands before him. 'We are a commercial enterprise. As in all businesses, we pride ourselves on being ahead of the curve. We are trained to discern where current tastes are heading, what might be popular in six months time, or six years from now. Which pieces will see their value increase, which artists will soon fall from fashion. Not only do we predict, but also we seek to define. It is a privilege and honour to nudge the future into shape. But that is – how do you say it? By the by. I was told you had some questions about a particular piece. For another book?'

'Yes, well, I think so.' I answered. 'I'm not sure.'

And so I told him about my growing obsession with Doctor Gachet and his melancholy look. I admitted that for some reason or another I could not forget that picture – the image had got stuck in my brain, a tiny marble rolling round the inside of my skull. So much seemed to hinge on the painting, on the old man with the sad smile, though I could not say how or why.

I am not sure I did a particularly good job of making sense of everything (not least because little of it seemed clear to me), but Rikuto nodded solemnly as I spoke.

'You want to see it?'

'Oh, I'd kill to take a look at it. To come face to face with him, that would be amazing. To be able to follow the curve of the brush strokes, to see the colours up close... but I know that's not going to happen.'

'It is gone.'

'I know. I've read about it all. I know it got sold to Ryoei Saito for a record price –'

'The most expensive painting ever sold.'

'Exactly. And I know it hasn't been seen since he died in 1996. It just disappeared. Twenty years ago now, and no one seems to know where it's gone or who owns it now. Or if they do know, they're not saying. The whole thing is a mystery. I know it's impossible to see it, but I'd just like to know where it is. If it even still exists, I mean.'

'So that your book can have an ending?'

'No, because it's important. I don't understand how something that famous, something that historic, can just vanish into thin air.'

He shrugged, as though it was something that happens every day.

'I am afraid it is gone.'

'So you think he wasn't bluffing? That he actually had it cremated with him when he died?'

'Ryoei Saito? No, I suspect that was a joke. He was most probably just trying to ruffle some feathers. When he made those remarks he was under arrest for bribery and corruption. That was his way of spitting in the face of his accusers. No, if he had actually wanted to do it, he would have done it publicly, with international simulcasts to news channels around the world so that everyone could watch the 75-million-dollar painting go up in flames. Now, I would have liked to have seen that. That would have been art.' For the first time since I met him, he smiled.

'So, if it's not been destroyed, where do you think it is now? Paris, London, New York? Or somewhere nearby?'

He shrugged. 'It is locked up somewhere. But I do not think it is here in Japan. It must have been sold, to appease Saito's creditors. Perhaps more than once. Zürich is the best guess I have heard. It is probably in a subterranean bank vault there, still in its foam-padded crate.'

'Why would anyone buy it and not look at it?'

'As a commodity, of course. That is why it is unlikely to be in the big cities you speak of. It would garner attention, not least from the tax authorities. There were rumours last year that it had been bought by some oil-rich Sheikh in Qatar or Dubai, but I do not believe that. They would have bragged about it by now, or shown it off to someone. No, I am certain that no one will see it for a very long time.'

'Why not? People often loan important paintings to exhibitions, or they leave bequests in their wills.'

'That used to be the case when such loans or bequests carried with them huge tax incentives. But that is no longer true, particularly in America and much of Europe. No, it will remain invisible. It is better as a mystery, as a legend.'

'Because that increases its value.'

'Exactly.'

'So you're saying, basically, it could be anywhere. It's a ghost.'

Rikuto finished his coffee. The stars on the screens beside us burst silver, regrouped, exploded into waves of light.

'You will find the art world is full of ghosts.'

'Ghosts sell,' I said.

'Not always.'

'This one did.'

He smiled – this time it was a wolflike grin, all teeth. 'So perhaps you must choose which ghost you are trying to catch.'

I did not like the turn the conversation was taking. I sipped my tea – in contrast to my expectations, it was strangely bland and almost tasteless – and then cleared my throat.

'Well, I can't catch anything if all that's left are copies.'

'All ghosts are copies,' he said. 'They are pale facsimiles of the original. Think of your English ghosts, with their see-through bodies and rattling chains.'

'OK,' I said.

I was not entirely sure where he was going with this (and, in truth, I remain to this day uncertain as to what exactly he meant when he referred to English ghosts – all I could think of were those phantoms and poltergeists depicted in the pencil illustrations that accompany some Victorian novels – and also how they might be different from Japanese ghosts).

I waited for a couple of minutes for him to explain, but it dawned on me after a while that this was all he wished to say.

He soon checked his watch and made his excuses, explaining that he had to return to the gallery to help prepare for a private viewing that evening. After a long and protracted battle for the bill, I thanked him for giving up his time, and we bowed to each other in goodbye.

'I am sorry I have not been able to be more help,' he said as we parted at the door.

I waved away his apology, and made my way out into the afternoon. Already, the neon signs above the shops and on the lips of skyscrapers were flickering into hazy light, and it seemed I walked for a long time without covering any distance. Each street seemed to mirror the last: the phone shop, the newsagent with its sprawl of Manga comics, the ramen-ya, the wacky clothes shop, the karaoke bar, all appeared and re-appeared in some mathematical sequence whose randomness was itself chillingly predictable. I stopped at one of the computer outlets and watched the faces on the display screens form and reform from sprawling pixels until my own head began to throb.

Turning back to the street, I found I could not look at anything or anyone without them seeming dull and unreal in comparison. It was as though I was seeing the world in inadequate resolution, the regular human faces in the city unable to compare with their digitized and animated counterparts. I rubbed my eyes so much they began to feel blurry, so I stopped at a small shop to drink some Pokari Sweat and then retraced my steps. As I walked back towards my hotel I kept my eyes trained firmly on my feet and on the pavement ahead.

Near the hotel, however, I looked up at last and spotted a sushi bar with a blue neon fish on its roof, and, after staring at it for a while, I went inside, thinking some food (and a few bottles of cold Asahi) might help clear my head. But instead I found I could barely eat, at least not sushi, since I could not forget the moving fish with the shining eyes at the ice market, and so I settled for pickles and beer. Even when I returned to my room to pack my suitcase, I found that in the right position I could see the blue light from the corner of my window: the tip of the fin glowing as the sunlight dissolved around it, the first few ridges of its long back curving down toward the tail. It was time to go.

By the time I got back down to the street to hail a taxi it was early evening and the city was swimming with traffic. As I loaded in my bags, I saw the blue fish opposite bucking its tail again and, as I watched, it winked. I climbed in the cab and asked for the airport.

# STILL LIFE
## 1845

Ambroise tilted his head and hummed, quietly at first but then growing progressively louder, as though attempting to impersonate the loping drone of a bumblebee. After a minute he lifted the paper closer to his face, and tried tilting his head the other way. He licked his lips, then used the fingers of his free hand to dab down the unruly edges of his beard. At last he set the paper flat in front of him, then reached for the table, over the two dark mugs of *chocolat chaud* that sat between them, and took from the little box one of his cigars. He lit it with a flourish, then leaned forward and stared hard while plumes of yellow smoke spooled from the corner of his mouth into the ill-lit study.

Paul took a cautious sip of his drink, and placed it down again equally carefully. 'So?' he asked, wondering why the older man had been silent so long. 'What do you think?'

'Hmm...' Ambroise furrowed his brow and squinted down at the ink drawing. 'Well...'

'Yes?'

He took a series of tugs on his cigar and turned to his young charge.

'Honestly?'

'Please, tell me the truth.'

'It is truly terrible,' he said.

'Oh.'

'I mean, honestly, Paul. What were you thinking? It's lazy, derivative, and insipid.'

'I see.'

Paul's freckled face turned the colour of sunset, as it always did when he was nervous, or angry, or overjoyed – he got through blushes the way other boys got through handkerchiefs. He reached for his sketch, but the gentleman with the fine cocoa suit and even finer cocoa grinned and moved it quickly from his grasp.

'Not so fast. You asked for my appraisal, remember?'

Paul wished he had never taken it from his sketchbook. Perhaps, he thought to himself, the fire had left his brain decrepit, turned to jelly and marrow by the heat and smoke. After all, what else could have possessed him to show his amateur doodles to a real painter, to Ambroise Detrez, a student of one of the finest art academies in all France? If his ankle had not ached so badly, he would have kicked himself.

'Now look,' Ambroise said, tapping his fingers upon the picture. 'The left side, over here, is cluttered with people, while the right is almost empty. Save for this turret, of course. Or is it some kind of garrison? At any rate, this leaves the composition frightfully asymmetrical. The disharmony is enough to make one feel quite befuddled.'

'I understand,' Paul said. 'I'm a rotten artist. Now please hand it back.'

Ambroise grinned a steely grin. 'I'm not finished.'

Paul gritted his teeth: he could not think of any reply that would fall into the acceptable category of being respectful to one's elders, and so he said nothing.

'So we have angry crowds around a tower and some old stone walls. Can I presume you were aiming to represent the Storming of the Bastille?'

'Yes, I thought –'

'Dear me. You do realize the whole picture is flat? No

depth at all. I mean, where are we supposed to be seeing the action from? Are we part of the crowd at the front or watching the action from afar?'

'I was hoping that the perspective might allow –'

'And here: this waning moon in the upper corner tells me it is evening, and the man at the front of the gang is holding a flaming torch, but despite all this no shadow is cast! Why ever not?'

'Well, I wished to suggest –'

'Also, if you're going to imitate better artists so shamelessly, you might at least try to get them right. The impassioned faces in the crowd here are straight from Delacroix's *Liberty Leading the People*, except your faces are squashed and dog-like. If you aren't going to pay attention to detail, then better not to bother at all. This woman near the garrison, for instance, has two left hands. See, both her thumbs are on the same side. That's shoddy work, my boy. And the castle here, the turret and the battlements, they are all borrowed from Jacques-Louis David. You've been copying *The Intervention of the Sabine Women*, haven't you?'

'Perhaps I was a little eager in following my inspiration,' Paul shuffled his weight from his bad ankle to his good.

'Quite. Now in the corner, the crying woman clutching a child to her chest. Too sloppy and sentimental by far. And why is she so much bigger than everyone else?'

'She's important. You see, I wanted her to be symbolic of –'

'But worst of all is the indecision.' Ambroise shook his head. 'Make up your mind. What is the viewer expected to learn from all of this? Where is the lesson? To be frank, your subject deserves much better.'

'I know,' Paul said.

Ambroise set down the paper and chewed on the end of his cigar. 'I understand the impulse, of course I do. Everyone worth their salt knows that history is the only thing worth painting. But you cannot start with the fireworks. First you must learn how to strike a match.'

Paul nodded. Like all art-lovers, he was well aware of the fashions, knew exactly what the Academy favoured: lessons from the past. He too had marvelled at the giant canvases that were all the rage. He had gone to Paris with his father and had stood among the crowds before the huge panoramas of heart-breaking scenes from recent history. This was TV before TV: period drama and action movie and documentary rolled into one. And, like everyone else, he was fixated: he stood before *The Raft of the Medusa* and felt himself being pulled by the turgid waves and  sway of the painting. He felt seasick staring at the figures clutching onto their raft in that tumultuous ocean. He went to galleries to spark his imagination into life.

But this was not what he had intended for his own picture. He could not explain it to Ambroise, but the truth was that he was not interested in being faithful to the past. In fact, he could not care less about what the history books said had really happened. He was interested only in what-might-have-been.

Yes, at seventeen he was already the time-traveller he would become in his strange afterlife. It seems like a rich vein for irony, doesn't it, and yet I am not making this up. He imagined getting to the horses earlier, and being rewarded for his bravery. He returned to the battlements again and again and this time did not jump. He did not want to recreate history. He wanted to rewrite it. He wanted to be there at the Bastille when things could still have gone another way. Before the guillotine and the cracks in the paving stones that puddled with blood, before the little Emperor and his grand plans, before the men of his grandfather's generation were left lying in their thousands on the Russian steppes, before everything collapsed and went back to how it had always been. He wanted to conjure up an age when anything had been possible. He knew that time was lost – or, worse, had never been anything more than a story old men told to one another to make the nights seem shorter – but that only made him want it even more.

Shall I labour the point? Yes, why not: he wanted to escape into a canvas.

That could be the moral of this story: in the end each of us gets what we always wished for, and that is our tragedy.

But that would be trite and simplistic.

Tragedy is conjured by hindsight. Sadness is so often a by-product of comparison, or of the tricks of nostalgia – that lazy glossing over, the sloughing off of perspective that reworks even the worst of times until they have acquired a warm and hazy glow. But Paul was not yet sad: he was a daydreamer, a shy and hopeless hoper, a broken utopian. And so he did not just look back. He was a teenager, after all, and so like all teenagers he yearned for a future that might belong to him alone, counting down until the day when he might somehow remake the whole broken world.

The biggest problem was progress. He did not believe in it – though he could no more admit this to Ambroise, nor to Henri and his other friends, nor to his stern father or distant mother, than he could admit he did not believe the sky was really blue. The very idea was unthinkable, for what else was history but the slow march forward to something better? And yet it did not make sense to him. Nothing got better.

The older he grew the more he felt as though he had been born a little out of time – born into an age of promises broken, of hope turned to disappointment. Whenever he studied the books on his country's recent history, whenever he saw the crippled veterans in the rougher side of town, whenever the peasants came begging to his father, he felt as though history had failed them all.

Haven't you sensed this sometimes too? That time has not set you down where it should have.

Think how different your life might have been if you had only been born a few years earlier, or just a little later, or in another city, or in another house, with another mother or father? Who might that other person have been, that shadow-you who could have claimed a different life – the life that was perhaps meant for you, but that remained a few steps out of sync with your own.

But now, once again, I am falling out of step. This is his life, not yours – though perhaps I have that wrong too. It used to belong to him. Long ago. Now it is a ghost you are swallowing in tiny pieces, one that would live inside you, as all ghosts do.

Please, take another bite.

'Let me ask you this, have you ever seen a daguerreotype?' Ambroise said, shaking Paul from his wandering thoughts.

He thought about it for a moment. 'Those grey plates with a foggy image burned onto them? Of course.'

'Excellent – so you know what we are up against.' Ambroise rose to his feet. 'Now listen. Those colourless reflections will never be art. They may capture and hold a moment in time, but it is one divested of meaning. The great men you are trying to emulate – Delacroix, Ingres, Delaroche, Gericault – they are not churning out representations of the past, they are working towards something greater. Their pictures show a few key details picked out and magnified, to illustrate something more important. They are moral lessons, yes, but more than that: they are a way of awakening an emotion that has been slumbering deep in the soul of the viewer. None of that can be done without the artist's guiding hand, without his singular vision.'

'It sounds like you are asking me to play God.'

'Oh, my dear boy – you are nowhere near ready for that!'

Ambroise shook his head and laughed his wolf-like laugh. Paul shuffled his feet, waiting for the continuation of the lesson. Ambroise was one of those teachers who took no greater pleasure than in proving his pupil wrong.

'But your tenet, though blasphemous, is accurate: to bring forth meaning from chaos, yes, that is what we must strive for. The formal details – perspective, character, spacing, light and depth – will come with study and practice. But there is more to it than that.'

'So… then how should I begin?' Paul said, his voice sounding small and childlike.

'You find something that can stir in you some sense you had forgotten,' Ambroise said, as though it was perfectly obvious.

Paul hung his head. His ankle was pulsing, and he did not want to admit that the older man had lost him. He was not interested in some grand metaphysic, nor in epiphanies or sublime moments of wonder, nor in schooling anyone – he wanted only to make a picture good enough that he could sink into it. But he was too embarrassed to say any of that to a renowned painter (the only real-life artist, in fact, that he had ever met).

Ambroise ran a hand through his thinning hair and then dabbed at the corners of his beard.

'I'm sorry, but what kind of thing do you mean?'

'Don't worry yourself so. You'll know when you see it.'

'Oh,' Paul said, the noise he made like that of a punctured bicycle wheel quickly deflating.

The maid knocked, then entered the room, lighting the lamps one by one as dusk approached. Ambroise set the sketch back down upon the desk. Paul watched as he smoothed down its corners.

Why spend so much time on Ambroise Detrez?

Because he was the one who, starting only a few days later, taught Paul how to paint in watercolour. Without this, Paul would have sunk. When everything else is broken, he will come to live for those swirls of dreaming light.

And maybe that is where that sad look comes from: the old man in the painting understands that he has given away his life to something beyond his control. Or perhaps it is far simpler, and his sorrow is rooted in the understanding that though he loves painting more than anything else he will never be quite good enough. That he will always be second-rate, an also-ran, a failure at the thing he longs for. That his life, in some sense, has been wasted.

But enough foreshadowing. For Paul the future has not happened yet. Right now, he still believes in all hope he will be the next Chardin or Delacroix.

Ambroise Detrez will go on to become a noted professor at the Valenciennes Academy of Art. But his paintings will largely be forgotten, his dry and studied Romanticism swept away by the burst of freedom and colour unleashed by the Impressionists. And perhaps Paul would have gone that way too, had it not been for the epidemic, or the war. But see – I cannot stop myself. No more jumping ahead, I promise.

Alright, just once more. Because only one of Ambroise's paintings still interests the world today. And certainly not for its style – formal, fastidious, with all the shadow and gloom of a Rembrandt but none of its life or character. No, it is interesting only because of its subject. It is a portrait, of course, of one Paul Gachet.

In Ambroise's painting, Paul's hair is beginning to recede, its colour already less magical red than sun-dusted brown. He looks pale and drawn: a thin, horse-like face that tapers into a chin of truly epic proportions. His moustache is thin and waxed to a sharp point. He was twenty-two when he sat for it, but he looks as though he might be closer to forty. His eyes are heavy and serious, his lips pursed. He wears a solemn brown coat too large for his narrow and weedy shoulders. In this portrait, he looks like someone who has stiffened into shape, the kind of man who hides his shyness behind his learning. The kind of man who cannot quite tell the difference between the shadow and the shade.

'What's this?'

Paul rose to his feet and scrabbled over – Ambroise had picked up another sheet of paper, one that had lain half-buried beneath the others, and was holding it up to the lamplight.

'It's nothing,' he stuttered, but it was too late.

'I believe I will be the judge of that.'

'It's just another sketch,' Paul said by way of apology. 'A hurried doodle, just something I copied from a book. It's not important.'

Ambroise turned to him and smiled. In his hand he brandished a charcoal sketch of a human arm dissected to reveal the ribbons of tissue beneath.

'Ah, but there's something here,' Ambroise said, and tapped the paper.

The arm stretched across the page, and as the eye followed it from left to right, more and more was stripped away to reveal the workings beneath. Though the surgeon's cut ran along the wrist and palm, the fingers were still dressed in skin and nails, as if these were the tips of some silken glove waiting to be tugged off. Further down, the flaps of flesh were pulled back to show the coils of muscle, the stringy reams of sinew, the tendons pulled taut. The lines were crisp and exact. The arm seemed to be reaching out for something, ready to grab and grasp.

'This is what I mean!' Ambroise said. 'Now why did you copy this?'

'Why?'

'Yes. What was it about this image that stirred you?'

'I don't know,' Paul said.

'It is fascinating. But is it the macabre spectre of Death? Or an indication towards the resurrection of all souls? Is it a depiction of the frailty of human life? Or a tribute to the grand possibilities of science?'

'I told you, I don't know. I just saw it and copied it. That's all.'

And it was true. Paul had no idea why he had painstakingly reproduced the dissected arm from the illustration in his father's book. No idea why he had spent a couple of hours following each curve, each arch, each anatomical contour until he had it right. No idea at all, except that something about it had stuck in his mind long after he had closed the page and set the book down – though what that something was, he could not quite put into words.

# A SUIT OF BONES

One of my History professors used to keep a skeleton in her office. By that time it was a tatty old thing, the teeth crusty and yellow and the bones in good need of a scrub, and it hung feebly from its stand in the corner of the room, grinning madly at the overflowing stacks of manuscripts and first editions piled haphazardly on the carpet. According to campus legend, it was either the last remains of a seventeenth-century criminal that medical students had dissected in lessons long ago, or a beloved relative that Professor Buckridge could not bear to part with.

At any rate, its function was obvious. It was a prop. It allowed her to play up to the role of eccentric old don, and it was clearly a part she relished (it was not until I stood in front of a blackboard myself that I realized how much of teaching involves amateur dramatics). The unusual distraction also allowed her to spot the wandering eyes of students not paying enough attention to her words, and so to catch them out with impossible questions (something else she clearly took much pleasure in). But most importantly, it served to illustrate the theories with which she would bludgeon impressionable young minds.

'History,' she would say as she ran her fingers over the pale cranium, 'is a tale of death. It starts with death and ends with death. All we have left are the bones. It's our job to dress them up.'

She would proceed to regale us with an almost insurmountable list of examples (how the assassination of Archduke Franz Ferdinand in 1914 led to 16 million soldiers dying in the trenches of the First World War; how Elizabeth I's childless death led to Civil War and the King of England being forced to rest his head upon a chopping block; how the murder and framing of Franciszek Honiok by the Nazis to justify the invasion of Poland led, through many twists and turns, to the suicide in the Führerbunker in April 1945; and countless others that I do not have space to recount here) until all of us were well and truly under her spell.

It didn't matter that her theory was easy to disprove (what about the convoluted international treaties that made the Great War almost inevitable, we argued back. And who is to say that a war ends with the dead on the battlefield – what about all those left behind, what about the social upheaval that followed? The more forthright students among us would argue with her until we were blue in the face. What about the militarization of the Rhineland, or the annexation of Austria? And so on, and so on). In fact, that was the point. As I progressed from eager first-year to wary graduate under her supervision, I learned she did not even believe it herself (she would not have got very far as a distinguished academic were her research really so reliant on generalizations, or her conclusions quite so glib and full of holes). Her little speech was intended to provoke, to antagonise, to kindle debate: to get us all arguing about what history meant.

But lately I have been thinking there may be some truth in it. Take this story. It seems to me to hang between two deaths. The first one of the most famous in history (if, by some extraordinary chance, you were unaware that Van Gogh killed himself soon after painting Doctor Gachet, then I can only apologize for the spoiler). The second the death of the painting, the way it has disappeared and become a ghost. And though it sounds ridiculous, I wondered if Professor Buck-ridge could have been right, if there might be some strange chain of links and coincidences leading from one to the other.

'Do you still have it? The skeleton, I mean?'

We were sitting in her study, on a warm Sunday in late spring not long after I had returned from Japan. It was more than ten years since I had last sat on that lumpy settee as an undergraduate, defending some hurriedly cobbled-together essay about the underlying causes of the Peasant's Revolt, and the effect of returning there made me feel as though I had travelled through time. The room was the same as I remembered, though it seemed smaller somehow. It was that familiar mix of the rarefied and dowdy that is peculiar to Oxford: great swirls of crimson and yellow paisley on the wallpaper that was beginning to peel at the corners, a chipped teapot and a collection of mismatched mugs, a framed drawing of a medieval woodcut, dusty shelves for books with cracked spines, and that poky window through which the crisp green lawn below was just about visible – the only thing missing, in fact, were the bones.

'Oh yes. It's away at the cleaners at the moment. I used to do it myself, you know, with a toothbrush, but I don't have the energy any more. It took an age. I considered getting rid of it, but the students wouldn't be happy. I suppose these days you would call it part of my "personal brand". *She's that mad old woman with the skeleton* – that's how they remember me. And that's certainly better than what they say about some of my esteemed colleagues, let me tell you! Now, do help yourself to sugar.'

She set the little tea tray down on the coffee table between us and, after pouring from the polka-dot teapot into both mugs, she settled herself down into her armchair, her arms folded and legs crossed, as if waiting once more to hear some poorly-supported thesis on the social ramifications of the Black Death. I could not help but notice how old she looked: her short bob was threaded with frost, and she seemed to stoop even when she sat, her milky green eyes squinting at me through her bifocals. As ever, she was dressed more for hiking than teaching, with laced-up walking boots, loose trousers and a worn fleece over a heavy checked shirt.

'Thank you, again, for the invitation,' I said. 'It was most kind of you.'

In fact, it had been something of a shock to hear from my old teacher again after all this time.

It was Professor Buckridge – *Clarissa, please* – who had contacted me after I started writing about the history of China. Her email, in fact, turned out to be a list of historical inaccuracies in my novel. After that, she would occasionally send me links to academic articles about the Qing Dynasty, all in a futile attempt to get me to mend my ways and turn from novelist to historian. From then on, Professor Buckridge and I stayed in contact, emailing each other sporadically, and when I found I would be passing through the city again for a friend's wedding, I decided to take her up on her always-open offer and pop over for a cup of tea and a chat.

'Nonsense. It was good of you to come. It's always a pleasure to see an old student again. Sometimes I forget there is another world beyond the campus, and it's nice to be reminded. I've read your second book now too, by the way.'

'Oh. What did you think of it?'

'I appreciated your efforts in not letting the facts get in the way of a good story.'

I was not sure whether this was a compliment or an insult, but Professor Buckridge smiled pleasantly enough as she sipped her tea, and so I decided not to ask.

'Thank you,' I said, and stared out of the window to see two students setting up for a game of croquet on the quad. How strange, I thought, that things go on here as though it is another century altogether, as though time is held at bay by some collective act of disbelief.

'Are you working on anything now?' She went on. 'Something historical again, I hope.'

'That's all I know how to do,' I joked. 'Actually, I'm working on a book about Doctor Gachet.'

'Hmm, that rings a bell,' she said. 'But you'll have to prompt me.'

'Most expensive painting ever sold.'

'Yes, of course. The man in the Van Gogh. Not quite my period, you understand, the modern world.'

She said it with a smile, and I laughed, but I think this is probably true for many of us who are drawn to history. I have rarely felt at home in the present, and I think perhaps Professor Buckridge felt the same.

'Yes, yes,' she went on. 'I can see it now. Blue suit, Kitchener moustache. Grumpy old fellow. But goodness me, why him?'

'It's... Well, I can't get it out of my head. The sadness in him. I want to find out where it came from?'

'Ah.'

Then she placed her mug on a coaster and pressed her palms together in front of her face. She said nothing for some time, and I gradually came to remember this tactic of hers being deployed in tutorials, when she would remain silent for so long one of her students would feel compelled to make some risky counter-argument or come up with some hasty new theory in an attempt to fill the unnerving quiet. At last, however, she spoke.

'I see.' She drummed her fingers together. 'Something of a mystery then.'

'In a way. I thought perhaps you could help me, actually, if it's not too much to ask. Only I don't have my Bod card anymore, so I don't have access to the libraries here...'

'So this is why you came,' she smiled. 'Yes, of course, you can use my privileges. I can sign you down as a junior researcher quite easily, if that's all you need. Happy to help.'

The students down below had staked the hoops and started their game, bashing away at the coloured balls as friends gathered around them, lazing on the grass. A girl with grungy hair seemed to have conjured up a bottle of wine. I could see one of the porters hurrying towards them, no doubt to give them all a thoroughly good ticking off. Some things never change.

'What about you?' I asked. 'What are you working on at the moment?'

She rubbed her eyes and then pushed her glasses back up. 'I am trying to write a history of medieval medical practices.'

'Ha! Sounds upbeat.'

She nodded. 'You know what they say about academics. Publish or perish. As soon as we stop we disappear.'

I motioned to her desk, where a facsimile of a page from an old manuscript showed a man having his skull drilled into by a tall physician. His tongue was lolling madly. 'Looks pretty gruesome. Be careful it doesn't give you nightmares.'

She glanced over. 'Come on now, you are trying to trick me. Surely you must know about trepanation?'

I shook my head.

'Really? It was a remarkably popular practice, from the ancient Greeks all the way through to the Renaissance. A hole is bored into the skull, and this was believed to be the best way to let out many illnesses.'

'It sounds almost like an exorcism.'

'There you go with your flights of fancy. No, it was nothing so spectacular.'

'It was common?'

'Remarkably so. Medieval physicians prescribed this treatment for epilepsy and fits, as well as for migraines and seizures. Many of them also used it as a cure for lethargy, ennui and melancholy. Some even turned to it to relieve the symptoms of grief.'

We sat quietly for some time, the dregs in our mugs untouched. The old computer on the desk was humming away. I looked more closely at my mug, and noticed that it commemorated some obscure academic conference held the year after my birth. I was thinking about her words, and that it is not only diseases and afflictions that might become trapped within our skulls, waiting to be released. Other things get caught in there too. Memories, regrets, longings, obsessions. There is no mistaking the nest they make in that little padded cell.

I tried to pull myself back to the present, and focused on the window. The students below, having received the customary telling-off, were playing now in a much more restrained fashion (by which I mean the wine was kept hidden under jackets, and only snuck out for surreptitious sips).

'Well, it sounds suitably barbaric,' I said at last. 'I think you're just drawn to the macabre.'

'Now there you go again,' she said. 'Just like an undergraduate: always jumping to conclusions. Not barbaric at all. The success rate of the procedure was remarkably high. Safer to bore a hole in your skull than to have your appendix out, or even have a tooth removed. No, when you think about it, it makes a great deal of sense.'

    I did not reply.

# A RATIONAL MAGIC
## 1853

At times it seems inevitable, Paul wrote, that with each diurnal gyration the motion of our celestial sphere must slow by some imperceptible degree, much akin to an old grandfather clock that if left unwound will after a few days lose a minute, and then more, until time itself comes to stop. In the same way it is hard not to think that one day our restless perambulations across the heavens must, too, decline in speed until this planet of ours comes to rest, anchored amid the stars. Or at least this is the conviction of the melancholy mind, for the melancholic experiences this slowness in his very blood. The melancholic is one whose mind has slowed, and he finds that the very act of moving is like struggling through some thick and obscure fog, that all the agility and ease of the morning has sunk into twilight's languor.

Paul, too, felt like everything had slowed down. At first he assumed this was because he had given over so much time to his studies – after several awkward years he had failed to complete his degree, and so, in a last-ditch attempt to get through his medical training, he had transferred from the prestigious University of Paris to the Montpellier School of Medicine – but now after three months of work experience at the Salpêtrière asylum for women, he was beginning to wonder if he had become infected with melancholia by proximity.

'Monsieur Gachet?' The woman's voice startled him. 'The famous doctor is here. And he has asked for you.'

His eyes darted up to take in the prim young woman standing in the doorway. She was one of the Catholic nursing order that provided daily care and sustenance for the patients and, like most of her order, she was somewhat suspicious about the doctors and students milling constantly around the grounds.

'For me? Doctor Duchenne? Well... yes... I, well, of course... I mean, yes... Tell him it would be an honour... No, I mean, if you would kindly communicate the... erm, well, if I might impose on you to pass on the message that I should be, well –'

'Monsieur, he is waiting outside.'

'Oh! Yes, of course.'

It did not happen often that the famous doctor appeared, least of all asked for an assistant. Most days, Paul was merely cataloguing, or traipsing behind the local physicians on their daily rounds, then making copious notes that might, he hoped, somehow aid his dissertation. So he leapt quickly to his feet, and in the process banged his leg against the crooked desk they had given him (in a stock room in the Salpêtrière's far western corner) and sent his papers flapping away from him, his inkpot upturned and everything sprawling to the floor.

The nurse cleared her throat awkwardly, then looked down at her shoes as Paul swallowed a curse and came hobbling round the desk to pick up his scribblings and dab at the pool of black ink dripping over the edge.

Was there something ironic about a young man – no, let's be fair, he was the wrong side of twenty-five to be called young in the nineteenth-century – who could not talk to women ending up serving his apprenticeship in an all-female asylum?

Yes, it was official: he was a mess with women. A gibbering, stuttering mess. He was either so tongue-tied it was as though he had a gobstober lodged in his throat – blushing, hiccupping, blinking furiously if a beautiful lady should even glance in his direction – or else he went the other way, and disguised his shyness with haughtiness. Though not yet qualified as a doctor, he had mastered the doctor's art of being dismissive, the art of the raised eyebrow and disdainful glance, because that was the only way he could get through a conversation with a member of the opposite sex without his head exploding. It goes without saying that he regretted acting like this immediately afterwards and went over these conversations in a state of morbid embarrassment, yet at the same time he felt trapped. He had never been one of those people who was comfortable with the world around him. It fascinated him, yes, but only from a safe distance.

He wanted to check his moustache and his collar before seeing the famous doctor, but since mirrors were strictly banned within the asylum he had to make do with a quick rub-down with lip-wetted fingers – only to notice that the great physician was watching him. Doctor Duchenne was waiting in the doorway, his sullen and owl-like eyes squinting at Paul with wry amusement.

'East wing this morning, Gachet,' he said, by way of greeting.

'Very good, Doctor,' Paul replied. But Doctor Duchenne had already started striding down the winding corridor, and so Paul had to run from his room to catch up. The venerable Guillaume-Benjamin-Amand Duchenne de Boulogne wore a black necktie and black frock coat, above which bobbed his head, a great bald globe that seemed to be fitted for a man at least several feet taller – indeed, it seemed to wobble upon the frail support of his fine neck, and more than one of the nursing order was heard to observe that the appearance of such a large head on such a body was as a watermelon balanced upon a scarecrow. Paul, meanwhile, was as sallow and wiry as half the inmates, and had yet to shake off his limp, which was why he was struggling to keep up at the great man's side.

Resisting a permanent appointment in Paris, the father of French neurology chose instead to wander freely, making consultations across the city. Today he had returned to his favourite haunt. The sound of their brisk footfall clanged and echoed through the old stone cloister.

'This racket is atrocious, truly atrocious,' Duchenne said, his voice too ringing off the cold stone and bouncing down the corridor ahead of them.

'Sir?'

'Haven't you ever been to the opera, Gachet? Heard a libretto that resounded through your senses and moved you to tears?'

'Yes Doctor, of course.'

'And then perhaps one evening you were at a salon and heard that same musical phrase hashed out by an amateur hand upon a drawing-room piano or harpsichord, and it awakened in you those exact same emotions, and before you knew it your eyes were wet once more?'

They turned a sharp corner and strode on past the outdoor courtyard and towards the cells. Paul nodded vigorously.

'You think music – no, sound itself – stimulates some corner of the brain, activates some portion of memory? Of course, of course! Astounding.'

Duchenne smiled gruffly. 'Quite so. The neural pathways are conductors, and yet it is not by electricity alone that they may be stimulated. So think then what this infernal noise must be doing to the patients! It must sound like thunder to them, or like the clod of pounding horses, the terror of flight, of alarm and emergency. Imagine the effect upon their already-strained nerves.'

'Perhaps, if I might be so bold,' Paul said, 'We could suggest investing in shoes with rubber soles? Or advocate the wearing of slippers within the grounds?'

Duchenne glanced sideways at his companion. 'A most commendable idea. And yet I cannot help thinking it was part of the original design of this place. Perhaps the idea was to rouse the devils within them and so somehow cast them out, as when Our Lord healed the man from Gadara by sending his demons out into a herd of swine.'

'Was that why the old doctors used to keep these women in chains? Because they feared them possessed?'

'Yes, I believe it was. Why else the bloodletting, if not to purge some deep-rooted evil? And if that failed, to keep them locked alone with only the rats for company – it speaks of some terror of infection, of contagion, does it not?'

'I quite agree, Doctor. From my humble experience, I believe –'

'And yet,' Duchenne continued, even though his pace was slowing as they reached the first line of cells, 'every falsehood contains a kernel of truth. Perhaps possession is as good a metaphor as any for what some of them suffer. The damaged pathways between brain and muscle that leave many of them deformed and wracked with pain – these must seem to them like forces beyond their control. Yet if we can stimulate these same neural pathways... perhaps, Gachet, perhaps we might convince them otherwise. Now, who have we here?'

Duchenne had stopped at the first cell of the block and squinted into the little peephole.

Inside was a young woman in her early twenties, her arms and legs streaked with scars where she had hacked away at her flesh with a meat knife. Here and there were swollen purple gashes and bulging stitches, and in those few patches of her forearms unmarked by larger wounds there were many red marks from where in frustration she had scratched her ragged nails frantically across her skin.

'Nothing for me here, I'm afraid,' Duchenne said, shaking his head.

He looked across at Paul and saw his quizzical expression. 'One for your thesis, though. Melancholy, that's your specialisation, is it not? I have no doubt that one day we will find the part of the brain responsible for such self-destructive impulses and so eliminate them, but for now we must constrain ourselves to muscles, and to those we might help.'

'Of course, Doctor.'

They kept on down the corridor, peering in to different cells as they passed. The grey stone was cold and bare, and the walls cleaved as close together as a throat constricting.

Paul found the scale dizzying. He had thought through medicine he might make a difference in one or two lives, and that would be enough. He was desperate to believe that the world could be changed not only by grand wars and revolutions but also by small acts of kindness. But the size of the asylum was almost beyond his comprehension: approximately 900 women with various mental illnesses that had been deemed incurable, 120 women classified as 'insane but under ongoing treatment', and 250 with different forms of epilepsy or seizure disorders. The vast numbers were almost impossible to grasp – it felt as though he and the other doctors were nothing more than paper ships floating on the scummy slick of an endless sea of human misery. The thought made him feel sick.

Duchenne came to a halt at the end of the corridor, and looked into another cell.

'Aha!' He said. 'This is more like it.'

One of the prim sisters with a bunch of rusty keys on a chain came scurrying to meet the doctor at the door. From afar Paul could hear the rowdy squawks of the river birds: whenever the Seine overflowed, water came rushing into the cells and ended up sloshing around the inmates' ankles.

'This is Mademoiselle Élodie, Doctor,' the nurse intoned. 'She has not eaten in two days.'

'Now, we can't have that,' Duchenne replied, and gestured toward the lock. 'Gachet, if you wouldn't mind,' he went on as the nurse hurried to open the door.

'Doctor?'

'Ready the equipment, would you?'

'Very good, Doctor.'

The door swung open. Inside was a woman who looked to be in her mid-to-late forties, though Paul knew well enough by now that time did not work the same inside the asylum as it did in the world beyond. Her hair was white, but this was true for a vast majority of the patients, and while one side of her face sagged and drooped, the other half was twisted into something almost resembling a grin. She was sitting on the cold stone floor, no doubt because her calf muscles were wasted away, the flesh shrivelled and the sinew swollen and matted. Her eyes stared up at them wildly as they entered the cell, and a mewling sound emerged from her mouth.

'Please,' she slurred.

'Paralytic,' Duchenne said, 'but not discernibly spastic. History of seizure or epilepsy?'

The nursing sister shook her head. 'But she is stuck like that, Doctor. It is an awful trouble to get her to her ablutions.'

'As I suspected. Now pray help her into position, sister. Gachet, how are the preparations coming along?'

'Nearly there, Doctor,' Paul said.

He had opened the medical bag and taken out the strange contraption kept within. A machine of Duchenne's own invention, the nurses referred to it as a box of portable lightning: it appeared to be a long black case with a copper cylinder running along the top and two rubber wires extruding from the sides. Paul opened one of the drawers at the back and checked the circuit, then set the capacitor to the lowest voltage: the machine juddered to life and began emitting a distinctly feline thrum.

'Excellent. Now raise her up please.'

While the machine whirred in the corner, Paul and the nurse lugged Mademoiselle Élodie up to a standing position, one of her arms slung over each of their shoulders. She slumped forward, like a drunk at the end of a bad night, and would have crumpled to the ground had they not held on tight. She whimpered when she saw Duchenne pick up the two electrodes and move towards her.

'Come now, you will barely feel it,' Duchenne assured her.

But nonetheless her upper body continued to tremble as the doctor drew nearer with the wire tips, though her legs remained as still as ever. Paul could understand her panic, for he had never seen such a thing before he met the famous physician, and even now was still amazed that a simple electric current could mimic so artfully the messages sent from the brain – could set off the involuntary flexing and straining of each individual muscle – could, in short, transform any man into a marionette being tweaked and pulled against his will.

As Duchenne pressed the electrodes to her withered legs, she made bird noises, little oh, oh, ohs, and Paul felt her flinch and jump with each touch.

Each muscle in turn was tested from the foot up to the

knee: flexor hallucis longus, flexor digitorum longus, extensor digitorum longus, tibilias posterior, tibialis anterior, fibularis brevis, fibularis longus, soleus, plantaris, popliteus, gastrocnemius, and each muscle in turn strained and contracted, though the movement of those twisted at the back of the calf was a feeble echo of the others.

'What is your diagnosis, Gachet?' Duchenne asked as he knelt at the woman's legs.

'Wasting of the gastrocnemius muscles. Localised atrophy of the lower muscles that aid movement, probably further worsened by disuse.' He looked up, caught the woman's wild eyes. 'She must be suffering terribly.'

'I concur. This is progressive atrophic paralysis, and looks to have destroyed the muscles of locomotion in the lower limbs. I would warrant this is another case of neuralgia, for there is no evidence of trauma.'

'Very good, Doctor,' Paul spoke up nervously. 'But she is clearly in much pain.'

'Agreed. Now let us try the face.'

The woman was breathing short, panicky breaths punctuated with bursts of snot and nervous swallowing, and instinctively she tried to tug her head away as the doctor raised the electrodes.

'Now this,' Duchenne said, 'is the universal language given to us by Our Lord. The emotions are always written on the face, and so can be comprehended by any man of any nation upon the earth. Even with this palsy in the left side of her face, the terror etched upon the rest is plain to see.'

He set the electrodes to her cheeks and Paul watched, fascinated despite his concern for the patient, as the electrical stimulation triggered the movement of the muscles on both sides. Slowly her face was hardened into a ferocious smile, caught halfway between laughter and snarl.

'There, you see, despite the paralysis the muscles respond to electrification. The localized stimuli is enough to bring them back to life. What does that suggest, Gachet?'

'That there is hope for recovery?' Paul ventured hopefully.

'Ridiculous! Paralysis is irreversible. You ought to know that by now. Do pay attention! No, no, it tells us something about that subtle language between the body and brain. The connection has been broken, and so the message from the neural pathways is unable to reach the nerves. And yet the muscle itself is still fluent in the language, can still remember how to respond to its call. Is that not remarkable?'

'It is indeed remarkable that she is smiling.'

'Ah, but she is not smiling. Look closer. Have you ever been at a ball and seen some handsome woman smiling at you and wondered whether she was simply being polite, or whether the smile was a genuine proof of affection?'

'I must confess I do not usually spend much time –'

'The trick, as we can see here, is in the eyes,' Duchenne went on. 'The true smile is involuntary, since it is sparked by pure emotion, and so can be seen in the muscles that bunch up around the eyes. The false smile involves only the mouth. Muscles do not lie, Gachet. They cannot cheat us. It was Our Creator's will that we should understand this immutable language of the heart. By sight alone we understand, we empathise.'

Paul wanted to say that giving a series of electrical shocks to a clearly petrified paralysed woman did not seem much like empathising, but he knew better than to argue back.

'Yes, the smile is everything,' he continued, 'From the clues in the face, the twitches and tics, you can read a whole life. There, we have it.'

Duchenne removed the electrodes and Mademoiselle Él-odie collapsed back into the arms of Paul and the nurse. They set her gently upon the wooden bed in the corner, her pant-ing and heavy sobs filling the silence. Duchenne switched off the electricity and began packing his contraption back into the medical bag.

'Thank you, nurse, please lock the door behind us,' he said as he made for the corridor. 'A little less leisurely, please, Ga-chet.'

'Must we leave her right away, Doctor?' Paul said.

'Yes, we must write it up. Then we compare it to our case histories. Once that is done we look for a similar case, to see if the symptoms present in the same way. That ought to keep us busy for some time.'

The woman was sobbing – a broken, animal sound that made the hairs on Paul's neck prickle and stand on end.

'But... can we not offer some palliative?'

'She will get all the care she needs from the nurses, as well as much spiritual sustenance.' He turned to the woman, lying curled-up and shaking on the bed. 'My advice is to find com-fort in prayer. Thank you for your time.'

With that, he swept out of the room, and Paul had no choice but to limp after him. As he left, he heard the wom-an call something out to them – but in her slurred, phlegm-choked voice he could not tell what it was.

He had some trouble catching up with Duchenne as the doctor marched back down the narrow hallway.

'But, Doctor, she is in pain.'

'They are all in pain, Gachet, that is why we are here.'

'We can't just leave her, Doctor.'

Duchenne sighed. 'Do you know how many thousands of

women this institution houses? How many are abandoned by their families, how many wander the streets, how many new turn up each year? Think of the bigger picture. We are wasting our time if we spend it only on her.'

'I'm not suggesting some miracle cure, but surely if we stayed with her, if we experimented with some medicinal palliative, we might –'

'You must not lose focus, Gachet. Why, if you continue to think like this, it will be another four years or more before your dissertation is finished! Do not be feeble-minded. We must choose the human race over one individual. If we can work out the pathology, if we can isolate the cause, the pathogenesis, then we might help a thousand or more in the years to come.'

'So we give up on one life for the possibility of saving others – maybe, if we are lucky, at some indefinite point in the distant future? With all my heart I am in favour of the grand project, but we have a duty of care to our patient. We cannot just forget Mademoiselle Élodie!'

'If you are so fixated on comfort and platitude, perhaps you should consider joining the nursing order instead of studying medicine. Decide where you stand.'

That stung him to silence. But he did not turn back. He did not stop walking.

The two of them – the renowned physician with his miracle medical bag and the awkward and self-conscious student – paced on down the corridors, past a line of cells containing various epileptics whose complaints were of no interest. Paul had to restrain himself from biting his nails as they walked. The sense that they were doing little more than categorizing the misery and pain of these poor women made him sick with worry, but what was worse was his growing sense of humankind as others saw it, of a whole mass of people reduced to nothing more than numbers – a faceless and unknowable blur, a catalogue of suffering to be filed away and kept out of sight – and this scared him, for he could discern in that feeling a shutting-off of empathy, a shrugging-away of common care and responsibility.

Maybe that is where his melancholy took root: in wondering whether, despite the best intentions in the world, the difference one life might make is infinitesimal, is statistically irrelevant, and that history will go the way it wishes, regardless.

'I know what I believe,' Paul said. 'You may think me ridiculous, but I cannot trade one life for a hundred, no matter the cause. If we choose to neglect just one patient, then what is the point?'

Duchenne shook his head. 'Do not worry, I am sure you will soon outgrow such childish sentiments.'

Paul was just about to argue back when Duchenne swung open the heavy wooden door at the end of the corridor and strode out of the cloisters, into a courtyard. Paul followed, the sudden burst of sunlight forcing his face to scrunch into a scowl as he squinted ahead.

'See, it is as I told you!' Duchenne remarked with much mirth. 'There is no escaping it – your whole heart is written in the expression upon your face!'

# A VISIT FROM THE MONEY GOD
## 1990

The moonlight was reflected through a thousand panes of glass: broken up, refracted, reconstructed and reworked as something sharper than mere moonlight. Turned into something that sparks, that stings, that spikes the city's drinks, and up here, on the forty-fourth floor, shards of it reached across the polished floor and antique chairs, across the bright blue vases and the spray of orchids, and one barbed tip almost touched the tips of the shiny shoes of the men in Gucci suits, standing in perfect silence. Moonlight too had dipped into the bottles of sake, and the swan-necked pot of swirling tea, but the mood was sombre: the Master was gone. Two of the men had moved closer to the window that stared out over Tokyo. From high above they watched the sleek black Cadillac snake through the streets, away from the tower. They knew where it was heading, and both burned with an unspoken jealousy that they had not been invited along.

Another car crawled behind, carrying a retinue of assistants. In the Cadillac, Ryoei Saito sat with his eyes closed, as though sight was something he no longer wished to waste on the ordinary world. His white hair was slicked back in waves across his head, and his skin was sallow, scrunched, made of paper – just like his fortune.

The call had come in only ten minutes before on the private line: 'It is here.'

Saito had been waiting for this. In the car behind, his assistants babbled and gossiped, but Saito was pensive and oblivious to the sound of the traffic, the whirring and honking music of the city. He was going for a meeting with a god.

This was not unusual. After all, another god was sitting beside him at that very moment. Go on, look a little closer: in the hazy corner of your vision, there's something you might have missed on first glance. That's right. There on the plush leather seat. That tiny, gnarled old man with an egg-shaped head. That's Fukurokuju, the God of Wealth. One of Saito's allies. Yes, Saito had met them all (and had made crooked deals with half of them). There were gods everywhere in those days, their calling cards littering the phoneboxes, their grubby fingers in every pie.

'You are not invited,' he said to Fukurokuju.

Fukurokuju only grinned.

But Saito still had his eyes closed tight, so he did not see.

Everyone knows that there are seven Lucky Gods. Saito had met the God of Fishing Folk first, when he took over his father's business just before the Emperor led the country into war. The God of the Kitchen also fed the fire in his belly through those dark times, and kept his profit margins brimming. Later, he was tutored by the God of Warriors, who helped him turn the Daishowa Paper Manufacturing Company into a billion-dollar corporation. Things were good. Though the God of Contentment had evaded him at every twist in the path, one morning he managed to catch the God of Longevity between his fat palms, and he squeezed that little god until it promised to keep him ticking over for a few more years, so that he might make it to eighty.

That left just two. Wealth and Knowledge.

Fukurokuju rubbed his hands together and chuckled. He was at home in the Cadillac. You see, Fukurokuju the Wealth God was also known as the Money God: the Big Kahuna. Saito knew him intimately. He knew Fukurokuju was not a god of cold logic but a capricious god of luck and black magic. The Money God makes illusions. His enchantments were everywhere in those tall offices in the financial district, whose work depended on the conjuring of numbers from nothing, and his servants were those City Boys who he helped turn negatives into positives by sheer force of the imagination. Safeguarding reserves, slipping and darting between currencies, balancing rates, modifying assets, pricing shares, fixing interest, moving stock: even the most innocuous of financial transactions has a touch of alchemy about it. That is where the Money God does his stuff. (It is no surprise that the Money God is also responsible for virility – according to those same City Boys he makes dicks hard as steel and coaxes life back into stinking corpses.) In short, the Money God was like a brother to him: Saito both loved him fiercely and was at the same time permanently exasperated by his wiles and deceits. He knew his tricks.

'We should do this more often,' Fukurokuju said.

'Do what?' Saito whispered, his eyes still closed.

The little god mimed taking out a stethoscope and holding it to the old businessman's chest. 'Prove that you are still alive.'

Saito ignored him.

Gods are notoriously fickle. The God of Longevity tricked him, and the Money God will abandon him – by the time he dies, in 1996, Saito will be a frail figure under house arrest, convicted of bribery and corruption and given a suspended sentence, while his company, Daishowa Paper, will have amassed a debt of close to 400 million Yen. By then the painting will be lost among squabbling creditors and heirs, its exact location known only to a handful of people in the world, none of whom seem keen to spill the beans. The Seven Lucky Gods, it must be assumed, like nothing more than laughing at us.

It did not take long for the entourage to reach Kobayashi Gallery on the Ginza. Though the gallery was officially closed, the guards moved away from the door to let Saito slip inside, then locked it once he had passed. The manager was waiting in the atrium, his assistant holding a silver tray.

'Champagne, sir?'

Saito shook his head, a gruff movement that sent the assistant scurrying away.

Saito strode through the building to the gallery's back entrance. Then he waited. The manager reappeared behind him, followed by a servant carrying a chair. The chair was set down, as quietly and carefully as possible, but Saito ignored it. He stared at the door. If a fly had landed on one of his bushy white eyebrows, he would not have blinked.

It was another twenty minutes before the door was thrown open and he got a glimpse of the truck. The guards carried in the foam-padded wooden crate that had only an hour before touched down from Manhattan. Then Kobayashi appeared.

It was Kobayashi who had gone to the auction at Christie's, where he had fought against a telephone bidder in Zurich who had helped drive the final price up to 75 million dollars, plus a ten percent buyer's commission, making *Portrait of Doctor Gachet* the most expensive painting ever bought. It was Kobayashi who had claimed the prize for his master. And so it was Kobayashi who got his face plastered across the papers, next to the sneering and envious comment pieces that suggested the Japanese upstart had shelled out far too much for a work that was not even one of Van Gogh's best. It was Kobayashi whose fingers flinched when the Money God twitched the strings.

Kobayashi pried opened the crate. He then directed two

of the assistants to put on their gloves and lift out the canvas. They carried Doctor Gachet to a small alcove at the back of the gallery, where they climbed up the stepladder awaiting them and hung it on the wall. Their work done, the assistants slipped discreetly away. Kobayashi closed the door behind them, leaving Saito alone at last with his purchase.

What happened then?

This is what happened: two hours passed.

Then the door opened. Saito emerged, his face as blank and inscrutable as ever. The painting was placed in a white cotton bag that was then sealed in a cloth-covered plywood box. This was returned to the truck and driven to a warehouse where it would be kept in a well-guarded, climate-controlled treasure room (the location of this warehouse is unknown – the painting disappeared from public view as soon as Saito was done with it). Saito returned to his Cadillac and signalled to the driver to go.

His legs and back were beginning to ache after having stood still for so long. But it was worth it. It was his. A moment in time, suspended. One of the peaks of human achievement, and he was the only one allowed to gaze upon it, to unlock its mysteries: like a jealous lover, he found the pleasure was magnified by knowing that now no one else would see it except by his grace. He had earned it, he had claimed it: it was his alone.

'What did she say?' Fukurokuju asked.

Saito did not bother to respond.

'Silent type, isn't she?' The Money God carried on, enjoying teasing the old man.

For he knew that the Goddess of Beauty and Knowledge never speaks. The last of the Seven Lucky Gods was the most elusive: she was the only goddess among a bachelor's den of old men, and so she held herself apart. She was slippery, hard to catch, and harder still to define. You do not see her, though sometimes you sense her presence, feel something brushing against your back as she passes close by, catch a hint of her perfume long after she has left a room.

But the Goddess of Beauty and Knowledge was also a riddle. For how exactly are the two intertwined? Saito could not unravel it.

'Don't worry.' Fukurokuju grinned. 'I have her number.'

Of course he did. The Money God could reach anyone he wanted with a click of his fingers.

Does money really matter that much?

Let's get real. It matters. Maybe that's not what you want to hear. This is a novel, after all. It would be nice to pretend that love is the only thing that counts in the end, or that history is the engine of our fates. But money has the power to trump both of those. Anyone who says money doesn't matter is either lying or has enough not to lie awake each night worrying about it.

How much is enough? Enough is not having to choose between the heating and the food bill. Enough is not having to hear your children tell you they're hungry and not having anything to give them. Enough is not driving yourself crazy wondering how on earth you're going to pay the rent this month. Enough is being certain, half-certain, or even just hopeful, that your incoming may one day catch up with your debts. Enough is thinking that you might be in control of your own life.

Money is like art. They are woven from the same fabric. Both are symbols, both are intangible and dependent upon the power of the imagination, and both promise to deliver us from ourselves.

'Perhaps,' Saito said. 'But she is not like you.'

'True,' Fukurokuju replied. 'But you are.'

Things had turned out exactly as Fukurokuju had wanted: the painting remade as an asset, locked away in a vault so that, like all mysteries, its allure would grow and its value would not be allowed to diminish. Fukurokuju rubbed his sweaty palms together happily.

'Shall we go to the penthouse?' Fukurokuju asked. 'Or the private club?'

'No,' Saito said. 'Back to work.'

The driver nodded and indicated right as he overtook. He was used to the old man talking to himself. When you are that rich you can do whatever you like.

The city rushed by as the black Cadillac weaved through the streets. Saito sat in silence, trying to keep the image blazing in his mind's eye for as long as he could. He would not see it again. He had no need. It was there, inside him, and to repeat the viewing would only diminish the experience.

He stared out of the window. He knew he was alone, but also knew he had no one better to talk to than them. Who else but a god would understand? Who else could know what it was like to be able to detonate mountains on a whim, to swallow cities and in a blink break men's lives, to lord over history and yet also stand apart from it?

Outside, the salary-men were now spilling from the offices. The low-slung lanterns had been lit at the night markets, and the night was crammed with taxis racing towards their destinations. Saito could see a swirl of blue reflected in the mirrored windows of a skyscraper: broken moonlight, and the fragments of a face. They would be there soon.

But they were not returning to his office, to the orchids and the sake and the well-dressed yes-men. Instead, they turned left at the traffic lights and were on a rickety country road: the neons fizzled out and the night was suddenly nothing but cloud and stars. Saito blinked, and then pressed his face against the window to see the giant and ragged shadow of Mount Fuji floating over the little sleepy town like a bird might hover above its prey. Time had gone reeling backwards: it was that balmy evening in early August 1945 once again and they went bumping slowly round the bends, past a horse and cart, and past the uniformed watchmen standing guard on the street corners, and on towards the big house near the mountain, where, at this hour, everyone should have been in bed.

The car stopped outside. Before he knew it, Saito had his hands on the ornate brass rings and was nudging the gate open and slipping inside. He wandered through the dark courtyard, pausing for a moment under the peach blossom trees, then made his way under the eaves and into the house. There was no one there to greet him, which was odd. When had they last let protocol slip like this? The reception room was empty save for the ceremonial seats and the small shrine for their illustrious ancestors. When he looked down he saw he was wearing his uniform. It was 1945 and he was young again. He moved on quickly, remembering the urgency of his visit. He strode down the hall, no longer his lumbering self, but a young man again, someone more expert at the fine art of the unexpected entrance. He checked the buttons on his uniform as he walked: the proud and prodigal son returning home, but he was worried and anxious, though he knew there was nothing worse than showing it.

As he walked past the servants' quarters he caught the sound of muffled sobbing, and then a few hushed voices repeating the fragments they had overheard about the unspeakable thing. They knew. It was that balmy evening in early August 1945 once again and everyone knew.

He began to walk faster, appalled that even at such a late hour the house was in such disarray. The maids moving between the rooms were stumbling as if drunk. As he passed the business room, one of his father's associates reeled past him, not even stopping to bow or give the traditional greeting, his face pale and sweaty and fixed into a terrible blank mask.

Saito paused, watching the man rush out, trying to recall his name. He realized with a jolt that all he could hear were hurried footsteps and the hiss of urgent whispers: the air raid sirens had stopped. Was that good or bad? He could not say.

When he started down the hall again he could feel his chest throbbing, and he understood why he had come back home: not to do his filial duty by checking that they were all safe, but because now he did not know where else to turn.

He reached the door to his father's study and took a deep breath. Then he stepped forward. The paper screens trembled as he passed.

His father was standing at his desk, facing away from the door. The wireless had been switched off. There was no need for it now. Everyone knew what was happening. The lightning, the shock, the fires, the flames, the smoke, the skin dripping from bone like hot wax from a burning candle. The drawers of the desk were locked. He knew, from childhood curiosity, that this was where his father kept his treasures: the ivory netsuke, the little monk and the bear and the giant carp, the sitting Buddha, and the little book of ink-brush pictures of places he had never been. Special things are not meant for everyday eyes, his father had told him.

You keep that which is precious to you hidden from the world. Saito remembered the feel of that giant carp in his hands, the weight of it jiggling in his palm, the way the ivory scales rubbed against his skin. You have a whole world inside you, and sometimes all you need is a key.

'Father,' he said.

He saw his father raise his head, as if slowly awaking from some terrible nightmare.

*It has happened again*, he wanted to say. *They have dropped the bomb*.

Or, *What should we do? Tell me, please?*

Or, simply, *Nagasaki*.

But he could not find the words.

'Father.'

His father turned around, and gave his son a weary smile, as if to say, he understood.

And there it was.

Yes, that was where he had seen that look before.

# SKIN DEEP
## 1863

'This!' The bearded man spat out the words, as though the taste of them was rotten. 'This is not art!'

'Calm yourself,' a rotund man with a bulging waistcoat said. 'That is precisely the reaction they are seeking to elicit. You are playing into their hands. Just ignore it and you will have thwarted their childish desire for notoriety.'

'But that is the worst of it,' the bearded man went on, gesturing at the painting in front of them. 'That a child might wander in and see such perversion – or, worse yet, a lady!'

'Come, you will work yourself into a fit. It will be closed down within the week, mark my words.'

The bearded man shook his head vigorously, like a dog bothered by a particularly troublesome flea. 'That a man might make a mockery of all that is right and good and proper and be allowed to get away with it. It beggars belief!'

'Well said, well said.' A third man, tall and hunched and wearing a silk cravat, had joined them, and the three of them stood side-by-side, expressions of disgust etched upon their faces.

But not a single one of them moved.

In fact, Paul thought, the three men themselves were as rigid and inert as a canvas on the wall, while the painting before them blazed with life. He was watching them from the opposite end of the gallery, leaning on his walking cane, and listening intently to their conversation while pretending to look at a blurry landscape nearby. Had his professional experience attending to the bizarre and banal afflictions of the city's middle class not inured him to ridiculous utterances, he might have brimmed over with laughter. Instead, he merely raised an eyebrow as he heard one of the men suggest that the picture ought to be burned.

Today was a treat. On those days when his afternoon schedule was free from appointments, he would often leave his practice in the heart of Paris and stroll down along the banks of the Seine. He enjoyed time spent on his own. The cholera had not only left him pallid and with a lingering touch of yellow around his eyes, but had also made him hair-raisingly frank and dismissive of social mores in the way that only those who have drawn close to the edge and returned can be. It should go without saying that none of this had done much to help him raise his social standing. Still a bachelor in his mid-thirties, he scared away many potential companions by being over-earnest about his passions (for painting, for socialism, and, more lately, for the benefits of homeopathy) and unwittingly offended others with his brutal honesty. In short, he had learned to take comfort in his own company, and only occasionally did he lapse over into talking to himself.

For three days now he had made his way down to the Palais de l'Industrie and lingered outside the entrance to the controversial exhibition of the artists the Academy refused to show, but only today had he ventured in. The delay was not down to any doubt or uncertainty, however, but because he wanted for a while to savour the anticipation of what he might find inside.

He could wait no longer, and so he walked across the great hall and sidled up next to the three men stood staring at the large oil painting. *Le Déjeuner Sur L'herbe*, he read. By Édouard Manet. It showed a clearing in the woods. Between the trees can be seen the edge of a river, and a woman bathing. In the foreground, a picnic: bread, fruit, discarded clothes. Two fashionable dandies are lolling on the grass in their heavy black jackets and black neckties and black hats and carefully-trimmed black beards. They are deep in conversation – perhaps picking apart the latest works by Flaubert and George Sand, or perhaps discussing the finer points of the strategy of the Union Libérale in the recent elections under Napoleon III, or maybe just recounting a mildly amusing anecdote from a soirée the previous evening. Whatever the two gentlemen are talking about, it is of little interest to their companion. For there, sitting beside them, is a naked woman. Her milky-white skin is almost glowing amid the shade of the trees. She is not listening to the men. Instead she stares out of the canvas. Her eyes meet the viewer's. Her gaze is a challenge: look back or turn away. A knowing smile plays about her lips.

'*C'est magnifique!*' Paul said.

The three men turned round to stare at him in shock, and he was sure he heard the rotund man snort.

'Perhaps the good gentleman's valet forgot to remind him to wear his spectacles this morning,' the bearded man said, and the others snickered.

'Oh, surely you would not deny me the same pleasure as you have received from admiring this fine work?' Paul replied.

'We are certainly not admiring it!' The rotund man shot back. 'It is an abomination.'

'Forgive me, friends,' Paul said with a smile. 'Only you have been standing here so long, I must have mistaken your abhorrence for appreciation.'

'If you must know, we were trying to work out its function,' the bearded man said. 'Obviously, it is meant to shock. But there must be a moral, a lesson in it somewhere, and I'll be damned if I don't stand here until I find it!'

'What if there's no lesson?' Paul said.

The three men looked at one another and chuckled.

'You may not have noticed,' said the bearded man. 'But it claims to be a work of art. Perhaps you did not see the sign over the door as you came in – the Salon of the Refused. That is the point of this exhibition, to attempt to prove that the paintings refused by the Academy are as good as any accepted. However, this is evidently a failure. For if a painting has no lesson, then it cannot be considered art. You can surely see the problem.'

'I would venture that perhaps the problem is the point.'

The bearded man sighed, as though he was talking to the slowest of class dunces.

'Let me tell you how it works. Historical pictures educate and elucidate, teaching us both about our age and ages past. Portraits allow us to bear witness to our great leaders in all their noble splendour, and also give us intimations of our mortality. Even landscapes and still lives demonstrate the Glory of He who created all. Yet this painting seems to have only one purpose: to offend the morals of good and honest men.'

'You may be right,' Paul said, still smiling. 'But what if its purpose was simply to capture an instant of pleasure and joy? That seems to me as lofty an aim as any. It reminds me of those rare moments when we feel most fully alive, when nothing else matters.'

Again they did not bother to hide their guffaws.

'It is in bad taste. One would have to be a pervert to find pleasure in such things.'

'Besides, it is clearly incomplete. None of the figures has a shadow, and the bathing woman is out of all proportion. I could do better myself.'

'I quite agree. You can see the brush strokes! It is half-finished.'

'Aren't we all?' Paul said, but the men were not smiling anymore.

'Titillation for commoners. It is not meant for the educated eye.'

Paul felt his own laughter come bubbling up like bad champagne. Finally he could take no more and started giggling.

'Good sir, perhaps you would do me the honour of explaining what exactly is the purpose of *your* life?'

He found himself laughing so much his cane started stuttering against the marble floor.

Yet instead of debating with him, the rotund man and his bearded companion simply looked at each other in consternation before quickly walking away, muttering veiled comments about his sanity as they went.

After all, everyone knew that the point of life was Progress with a capital P, with perhaps a little side order of Good Works thrown in for good measure. The gradual fulfilment of the Lord's plan for the Earth. Or, from the perspective of the people below stairs in the big houses, or filling the factories – the people too busy to bother with art – the point of life was a sharper one: cling on as long as possible.

Paul felt giddy. Now he had the picture to himself, and he fancied he might lose an hour within its spell. It was only then that he realized that the tall man in the cravat had held back, and now moved to his side.

'Listen,' he said, his voice a whisper amid the echoing gallery. 'Do you really believe that? That it is not meant to better us? That art could have no purpose at all?'

'Oh, of course it has a purpose,' Paul replied. 'But why

should it have to teach us something? This is no classroom, and we are not students. Why need it be such a terrible thing to provoke? To shake us from this malaise?'

The man with the pince-nez scrunched up his face. 'I confess I am not sure whether you are right or they. But I can say this: it is impossible to stop looking at it.'

'Yes, quite. There is nothing else like it.'

It was raw, he thought, staring at the brush strokes the artist had made no attempt to hide. Like a raw wound. It made him recall the cholera epidemic that had broken out a couple of years before. It was shortly after he had completed his dissertation at the asylum, and, filled with the bluster and vim of the newly-anointed, he had let two other graduates of the Medical College persuade him to volunteer with them to help those afflicted in the poorest of the Paris slums. Both men were dead within the year, and Paul too had been struck, his stomach turned to burning liquid, his skin to paper, his lips to sores, his dreams to swarms. Somehow, he had survived, and limped away a living corpse. It was only in the last few months that he had felt himself once more. But what he was reminded of now was that heady realization: that the sickness struck the beggars and the servants and the chimneysweeps just the same as it struck the merchants and the landlords and the aristocrats – that it did not discriminate, and neither did the afflicted, for all writhed and cursed and spat and shat themselves the same, with no thought to their social standing or the world beyond their sickbed. The painting did the same: it cut through the rules of polite society like a scalpel blade.

'What I wouldn't give to be there too,' the man in the cravat muttered.

Paul knew exactly what he meant. It was deliciously care-free, a reminder that sometimes we are able to strip away the petty anxieties of daily life and forget who we are supposed to be. But if we are often happiest when we forget ourselves, and our own peculiar worries and problems, then what happens later, when we remember?

We come crashing down to earth. Paul knew this, and I know it too. It has happened to me more times than I care to remember. Maybe, then, this is where sadness is born: in the understanding of the limits of your life. Sadness, by my reckoning, is a product of comparison: of coming to realize that you are not fated to be like the people you see in paintings, in books, in movies, on TV, in your favourite songs, or even in the photos posted on Facebook or Instagram. That moments of bliss and satisfaction may be all around you, but somehow they remain just beyond your grasp. Take Paul. He was in his mid-thirties now, the only bachelor amid his peers and contemporaries. A solitary doctor with few close friends and a habit of saying the wrong thing at the wrong time. A man with a failing leg and a failed artistic ambition. All sentiment and daydreams, and nothing to pin them to. He had, as far as he could remember, never been invited to a picnic, much less a wistful and freewheeling one like that in Manet's glorious painting before him.

Paul could not help but compare it to his own paintings, the overwrought watercolours he worked on in his spare hours between appointments. He suddenly understood his problem – not just with his artworks, but with his medical practice too, with his limited social circle, and most of all with the women he dreamed of courting but who, up close, seemed to recoil from his unrestrained intensity – he wanted everything to be perfect, right down to the tiniest detail, and so he could not stop himself from going too far. That was how his paintings ended up so overworked, his acquaintances so overwhelmed.

Take that very morning: a dark-haired woman had come to his practice to ask his professional opinion about her father's dropsy, and he had frightened her off with his earnest account of the horrors of purges. He could not control his enthusiasms. So he turned instead to the other world where he might better master the outcomes of his passion: he spent hours at his easel, touching and retouching the watercolours. He enjoyed the process, there was no doubt about that – he could lose hours mixing paints, finding that perfect eggshell-innards pink he needed for the dawn-touched clouds, studying the contours of the landscape as though it was the most intimate curves of a lover's body – but nonetheless always ended up disappointed.

It did not matter if it was the view of the Seine from his rented rooms in the city or the empty fields on one of his trips back to his family in the countryside around Lille. It was always the same: he wanted to replicate the view exactly as it was, to package up a memory and store it away. Sometimes he could get that melancholy sensation of shimmering sunset, or evoke the smell of summer grass, but that was as far as it went. It was never close enough. He could not quite do proportion, could not hint at how the confluence of space and time lent each moment a depth all its own. He craved real life, but it always ended up slipping from his grasp.

The painting in front of him was not like that at all.

Paul rubbed his eyes. The naked woman was still smiling that knowing smile.

He stepped back, the better to take it all in. The picture bristled with energy, the daylight exploding upon the woman's skin.

'Hold out your hands,' he said to the man in the cravat.

Or at least this is what he thought he said, for he felt

strangely giddy, as though the interrogatory gaze of the woman in the painting had quite unbuttoned his brain.

'I beg your pardon?'

'Like you did when you were a child. Fingers threaded together and held down at your waist. I just need a quick bunk up. There, now hold tight.'

He raised his boot into the man's cupped hands.

'Now steady on!'

'I won't be a minute,' Paul said, and he put his hand on the man's shoulder to steady himself. The other visitors to the gallery were beginning to turn and stare.

Then he launched himself up, his hand clutching tight as he pushed above the heads of the crowd. His walking stick came clattering to the ground.

He wobbled awkwardly in the air, like an ice-skater with neither ice nor skates but only impulse to keep him in motion – and then he released his grasp of the shocked man in the cravat, and leaned forward to grab the painting's heavy gilt frame.

The man holding him up swayed uncertainly as gasps burst out from all around, but Paul ignored them and pressed his face forward. Finally he was close enough, and he opened his mouth and ran his tongue across the rough and mottled canvas.

I know what you will say here: this last bit never happened. I have conflated the real with the imaginary, his actions with his dreams, his life with a fiction.

Guilty as charged.

And yet, memory is a fickle thing, a swirling mess, concocted as much from regret and desire as from history and fact. Perhaps this is where sadness comes from then – in the possibility that one might so easily lose the way amid those twisting paths.

So ask yourself this: it is always the things that really happened that you remember, or is it sometimes the things you wished had happened?

He stirred from his daydream and looked around. Nothing had changed. The man in the cravat had walked away, and the gallery was as busy as ever. He took one last look, in the hope that the image might be branded upon his eyeballs, then turned away, the acrid taste of paint still burning on his tongue.

# LIMBO
## 1941-1990

What exactly is he staring at?

Sometimes he looks into your eyes, but other times he gives the impression of looking straight through you, as though his mind is elsewhere.

Visitors wandered by below him. Perhaps he saw time as trees do, for years must seem to them to pass in mere seconds, and so maybe he hardly noticed the changes in the costumes of the strangers who looked up at him – from grey overcoats and frayed uniforms to spick suits, from sunshine-bright miniskirts to flared trousers, from shoulder pads to artfully-ripped jeans. We must assume he was happier here than at Lola Kramarsky's apartment with his owners, for surely paintings long to be seen, in much the same way that food must be eaten or else it will go rotten and songs must be played or else they will fade from memory. This was his second home: the Metropolitan Museum of Art, a giant building on Fifth Avenue, New York. It was here that he was first displayed in America, after he escaped from war-torn Europe in 1938, and it was here that he was last seen by the general public in 1990, just before the Kramarsky's sold the painting and it disappeared into limbo somewhere in Japan. In the half-century in-between, he spent most of his time here, with a starring role in half a dozen summer 'blockbuster' exhibitions, and from the 1980s onwards he remained on indefinite loan to the museum.

So, what exactly is he looking at?

Perhaps, for a while, he stared right back. He had always been a people-watcher, had always been fascinated by the quirks and eccentricities of the men and women around him. From the inmates in the asylum to his bourgeois patients in Paris, he often felt as though he was witness to a vast human zoo, and he was saddened and amused in equal measure by what he saw. But after a while it was clear he had seen all he needed to see. His expression says this: there is nothing left that would surprise me. And so now instead he is lost in thought.

Perhaps you find all this talk of 'him' a little strange. It is after all decidedly not a man – it is a heavy wooden frame, holding a rectangular canvas, on which has been smeared heavy daubs of paint (mostly blue). And yet that is not what anyone who looks at it sees. It is something more.

By the end of his life, Gachet had become a staunch socialist. He was a passionate devotee of Darwin, a fierce believer in the republic, and a dismissive critic of any ideology that might clip the wings of the imagination. Do not get me wrong – he still believed in some vital spark that animated a life, that inspired the heart to wonders (he was, after all, the most eccentric and unorthodox of cardiologists), but he had little time for the church, or talk of the afterlife. *Heaven?* He would say. *No, my wife lives on in here, not there*, he would continue, his clenched hand held to his chest.

In short, he believed that what remains, after we are gone, is that indelible mark we leave upon the world. So perhaps it is not so strange to call the painting 'him'. It is the only part of him that is left.

It is no surprise that in the Met he looked so exhausted: the world outside the canvas is stumbling always from crisis to crisis, and all he can do is watch. He is forever sixty-one and overcome with grief, and that sadness is multiplied by every visitor whose eye he catches as they wander past beneath his frame – for he knows how each story must end.

When I was a child, every time I picked my nose or practiced going cross-eyed, my grandmother would say: 'Be careful; if the wind changes, you'll be stuck like that forever.' But I think there are worse fates than to be frozen. The more I researched the painting, the more I began to dream about time coming to a stop. Often in those minutes between climbing into bed and falling asleep, when the tired brain corkscrews back upon itself and thoughts snag and get stuck, I found myself imagining a moment suspended in time. If you could pick just one, which moment would you choose to last forever?

The world around changes, but he does not. Are we still talking about art? Because this is also the work that death performs: it freezes people in time. The rest of us grow up, grow older, grow old, but those who are gone stay the same age, as though suspended in ice. Now he has all the time in the world.

But we don't have time, not really. It has us. Doctor Gachet is stranded in the past, while those of us who remain are trapped in the present. Yet certain pictures, and certain songs, can unpick the threads and free us, briefly, from its constraints. Maybe that is why art has always been viewed with such suspicion and fear.

To take one example, Sunni Islamic law traditionally forbade the creation of images of men and women. To create a picture in which you might look into the eyes and see the soul of a person is the worst kind of blasphemy, since it usurps the role of the supreme creator. Furthermore, such images are dangerous, and may encourage idolatry. When we see pictures of people, we empathize. We leave our own lives behind – for a moment – and lose ourselves in other lives. We remember things that never happened to us. We recall places we have never been. We taste the wild and bitter taste of other dreams. Those early Muslim scholars were right: it is dangerous.

In that half-century, on and off, during which the *Portrait of Doctor Gachet* hung in the Metropolitan Museum of Art, tens of thousands of eyes must have met his. It is not unreasonable to imagine that he was looking right back.

# THE PRINCIPLE OF ATTRACTION
## 1867

He was not really there.

The swan-necked goblet in his hand was an illusion. The red curtains drawn back to let the summer in, and the well-dressed guests milling past the grand piano, all were fake. The waddling banker in last year's shrunken suit who was picking his brain about troublesome symptoms, and the serving girls slipping in and out of the sitting room bearing trays, had all become phantoms. Everything was out of place, everything was out of focus – except her.

The woman in the pea-green dress.

She was on the other side of the room, staring at a still life hanging on the wall. Paul recognized her straight away as a fellow time-traveller. Someone else out of place in a world of kitsch and progress. Someone else who scrunched up her nose at the dull paintings dotted around the drawing room, at the bland attempts at good taste, and whose mismatched crinoline and ribbons told that she did not give a fig for what others thought. She was dark-haired, with an uneven look to her face, a nose more potato than flesh, teeth too big for her mouth, and a mocking slyness to her lopsided smile – features that suggested she had been forged from elements far more earthy and mercurial than more conventional humans were made from. She was a walking Delacroix, he thought, a canvas come alive.

'So you are saying it is something like magnetism?' the banker said.

'Sorry?' Paul replied, trying to remember what they had been talking about before he got so distracted. 'I beg your pardon.'

'You were talking of the new medicine?

'Oh yes, the principle of attraction,' Paul said. 'It is really quite simple. Like cures like.' He grinned, showing his yellowing teeth – a side-effect of the pipe he smoked throughout his consultations.

'I am not sure I follow,' the banker said, his brows knitted into stormy waves.

'Well, the body is a miraculous thing. The best approach to a suffering patient is not to cut him open in some barbaric surgery but instead to inspire the vital forces of the body to action. We can do this with a tiny amount of a remedy, diluted many times over, that causes the same symptoms as the illness. For example, for a man like yourself who suffers from hay fever, we might give a tiny amount of pollen, because that which sickens a man may also cure him. In this way the body will be stimulated to heal itself.'

It was all a question of distillation. Love, Paul thought, is something life dilutes, until it is almost lost amid the everyday. He thought it might have disappeared by now – he had noticed that his family no longer asked him about his prospects, that they had at last recognized him as a lost cause – and yet that small trace became suddenly discernable when inflamed by the senses.

What can we say about Paul in his early forties: is it that he's gullible, or eccentric, or simply that he takes a certain pleasure in going against the grain and cherry-picking those beliefs most likely to shock and offend?

'Fascinating,' the banker replied. 'But it sounds implausible. Why aren't all the best doctors using it?'

The woman in the pea-green dress was twirling a stray reel of her dark hair around her finger as she studied another of the paintings on the wall.

'Let me tell you a secret,' Paul said, leaning in close. 'Most doctors are cretins.'

'Excuse me?'

'Imbeciles, dotes, morons. They learn by rote and repeat like parrots.'

'Surely you are not being serious?'

'Without a doubt. I used to be the same myself. But I have seen the new medicine in action and there is no doubting it. Do you recall the cholera outbreak in '54?'

'Vividly. Whole districts were as good as out of bounds.'

'Well, I was a volunteer surgeon then. Now, the regular hospitals were full of the usual treatments – blood-letting, purgatives, and so on. Most of the patients who went in never came out again. But those in the new clinics? More than half were saved. Myself included. Yes, I had cholera, and I survived, through nothing more than drinking water that contained a miniscule amount of mercury. What better proof is there than experience?'

'So you really believe most traditional doctors to be incapable?'

'Quite so. But it does not matter too much.'

'Why ever not?'

'Because most patients are fools too,' Paul said.

'You go too far,' the banker huffed.

'Not at all. I am being rather restrained. Take your problem. You do not need a doctor, man, only a modicum of common sense. Hay fever is simple to avoid. Stay away from fields. Ban all bouquets of fresh flowers from your house. Keep your windows closed. A child could cure it.'

The affronted banker set down his drink and waddled off, his face red and his lips pursed. Paul grinned, for he got an inordinate amount of pleasure from upsetting expectations. That was the only reason he still attended such formal gatherings. He would rather have been in a cramped and dimly-lit bar with Pissaro, arguing about recent exhibitions or about the quality of light, but his painter friends were all out of town for the summer. Therefore the best he could hope for was to provoke polite society for an hour or so, just as a bored cat might toy with a mouse for a while.

He could now turn his full attention to the woman in the pea-green dress. She had now moved on to the landscape of hills and meadows above the fireplace, and was pulling such a grimace that she might have been sipping vinegar.

Paul smiled to himself – he hated that landscape too. Flat, lifeless and with no sense of light or joy. The kind of picture, he thought, bought by someone with no interest in painting beyond how the colours might go with the curtains. He watched as the woman in the pea-green dress tilted her head, her nose scrunched up as she assessed it from another angle. Paul was so absorbed that he did not even notice the serving girl topping up his goblet as she passed.

But of course, he was not really there.

I am not repeating myself. I do not mean that he was not paying attention, that he no longer occupied the present moment – that his mind was already racing ahead, frantically conjuring up a future for the two of them – though that was of course true.

I mean it literally now. He was not there. And neither was she.

In fact, I have no idea how Paul-Ferdinand Gachet first met Blanche Elisabeth Castets. It could have been during a walk in the park or a stroll by the Seine – she drops her handkerchief and he gallantly bends down to retrieve it for her. It could have been during a Salon or exhibition, the two of them drawn to the same corner. It could have been at his private practice, with their eyes meeting as he checked her racing pulse. All I know is that it was the summer of 1867, and that they would be married within twelve months. The soirée may never have happened. But does that make it any less true?

Think before you answer. History is not some river through which we can drag our cup and retrieve a mugful of the past. There is no such thing as the past, only a story we make up to try and explain how we could possibly have ended up here. There is no certainty, no proof, no way of ever knowing for sure. We need just enough facts to hang a theory on. It is as though from a few tattered threads we must recreate a coat – without knowing if it was not actually a hat, or a blanket, or a fishing net.

In other words, this chapter is my sock; you may prefer to think it was a necktie. We may both be wrong. But the truth is that they met, and they fell in love, and this deeper truth is the one that counts, so let us return to the story, for even as we speak, the present is slipping from our grasp.

He looked around and found himself alone. He would not get another chance. He finished his wine in two hurried gulps and set the glass down on the table nearby, then instantly regretted it, for he realized that now he would not know what to do with his empty hands. As a last-ditch solution, he thrust them into his pockets, and started to make his way across the room.

It had been a long time since he had felt this nervous, and he tried to fix his face to bear the inevitable rejection with good grace.

He drew up beside her, but she was so engrossed in the landscape on the wall that she did not notice. He took a deep breath.

'It is truly abysmal,' he said.

The lady turned to stare at him in shock. This was so far beyond the rules of polite conversation that she half suspected the hosts would suddenly appear and throw this rude man with the finickity moustache out into the street. She looked around to see if anyone had overheard, but there was no one nearby. There had been no formal introduction, no one to vouch for him, and no chaperone to keep check upon their conversation. She felt, not unreasonably, as though her whole dignity had been affronted.

'I beg your pardon!'

'The painting. You were thinking the same thing, were you not? A terrible waste of paint. I pity the tree that had to die to make the frame to hold this horrible thing.'

Her face flushed red, as though her private thoughts had been intruded upon. Was he calling into question her standing?

'Sir, you have insulted me! I have never...'

'Oh, I wouldn't say never,' he cut in before she could finish. 'After all, there are worse paintings out there. It is the sheer mediocrity of this one that is offensive though, is it not? That it dares pretend the senses might be stirred by something so easy, so banal, so trite.'

She tried to stay angry, but seeing the smile upon his face, she could not help but smile too.

'I admit I do agree, sir, but I think you are forgetting etiquette.'

'Quite right,' he said. 'It has none of that either. It is a truly ill-mannered painting. The trees are shapeless and the sun there is lumpen and wan. It has the effect of making one wish to never venture into the countryside again, which is quite an impressive achievement.'

She laughed, a little too loud – her rabbit teeth on show – then rushed to cover her mouth.

'In truth, I agree. Indeed, it belongs on a bonfire... but this is quite improper. We have not been introduced.'

'Then please allow me to tell you everything you need to know,' Paul said. 'I am nearly forty, as you can see from these bothersome grey hairs, and no doubt past my prime. I am becoming quite scatterbrained, while my eyes find it harder and harder to see by dark. I am unmarried and I cannot say I blame the female race for having so far avoided me, for I have a narrow range of interests and have been told I talk far too much upon subjects that have no place in polite society.'

At first her mouth hung open in consternation and surprise, but before long her eyes were sparking with light.

'Well then, let me be fair. I am an eldest daughter forced to smile gaily when her sisters were married off ahead of her. I have been told my deportment is unladylike and my laugh distinctly equine. I spend a great deal of time alone, and among a single lady these days, that is apparently much cause for suspicion.'

Her lips drew up into one of those sly smiles that made him want to attempt a cartwheel on the plush carpet. She was challenging him.

'That is nothing, my lady. I limp terribly and am consequently as slow as an old turtle.'

'I have been assured by my sisters that I snore.'

'I once had cholera.'

'I suffer from colds all summer long.'

'My closest friends are painters, which for many marks me

out as a madman.'

'All my closest friends live in books.'

'I find the city tedious.'

'I hate needlework and horses and dresses.'

'I am an unreformed daydreamer.'

'No more so than I!'

With that, both of them burst into laughter. A serving girl wandering by with a tray of canapés glanced across at them, yet neither the middle-aged doctor nor the lady in the green dress cared about how they must have looked.

'It is officially a draw,' he said. 'There is no bettering you.'

'Then, a truce?'

She stretched out her gloved hand, and he shook it.

'A truce.'

'We are clearly equally poor specimens,' Paul said.

'Or else, we are equally exceptional,' Blanche replied.

That was all it took. They joked for a time about how terrible the paintings were, making hushed comments about the poor taste of their hosts, and then he offered his arm and escorted her into the garden.

The sun was beginning to set, and as the moths and midges began to gather they talked – awkwardly, at first, in that stilted stop-and-start fashion that often holds sway when every tentative word is measured against the possibility of misunderstanding, but then in growing excitement as they discovered all the passions they held in common. They talked of their shared love of those radical new painters of light and emotion, of his passing acquaintance with Monet and Renoir, and of how both felt out of place in fierce and fashionable Paris, until their words were almost rushing over one another's.

'Look!' she said, breaking off the conversation as they reached the flower beds at the furthest borders of the garden.

'Foxgloves. My favourite.'

And there they were. A bloom of pink-tinged finger-tip tubas, being bothered by bees. Flowers the swirling colour of an inner ear, thrumming in the sunset.

'Hmm, late coming into bloom this year,' he said. 'In a painting, you know, they symbolize wishes.'

'Really? Ha. Wishes that come true, or wishes that are not answered?'

'Oh, I think all wishes come true,' he said. 'But not always when it is convenient for us.'

She snorted, then caught his eye. After that they walked in silence.

Once they had completed their lap of the grounds they found that, back at the house, the first guests were beginning to say their farewells.

'Have you visited the *Exposition Universelle*?' Paul asked.

'I have not yet had the opportunity. I have read much in the papers about the Japanese prints there.'

'Perhaps we should see for ourselves what all the fuss is about?' he said.

'Perhaps,' she said.

But they both knew it meant something else.

Paul escorted her back to the drawing room, where they found Blanche's chaperone was red-faced and fuming at being given the slip. There was nothing for it but grovelling apology and assurances of best behaviour, which for once Paul managed to get through without bursting into fits of giggles.

'Was the garden party to your liking?' he asked, as the serving boy brought her coat.

'I do not recall another where I spoke to so few people.'

'I will take that as the best of compliments.'

She smiled, and turned to go. The chaperone was already

lurking outside the front door. Then she paused, mid-step.

'I do not usually enjoy these soirées.'

'No,' he said. 'Usually I cannot stand them. But tonight...'

He did not need to finish the sentence. She smiled her uneven smile as she walked away. It was all, he thought, a question of perspective.

And as she walked away the lights faded out – or at least they may as well have. We do not need to see more. After all, we know the logic of love stories, the well-worn rules of romantic comedies. We know what this scene means and so we know how the story must conclude: they will meet again at galleries and exhibits. He will shyly ask for her hand. They will marry, then move to a cottage in the countryside (in the picturesque village of Auvers-sur-Oise, to be exact). They will have a little girl and a little boy. One of each. They will grow old. So really there is nothing more to be said than the obvious:

*The end.*

Or better yet:

*And then they lived happily ever after.*

I would love to end their story here, when both were brimming over with hope and anticipation, when everything was still possible and they had no doubt in their minds that, after waiting so long, something wonderful really was just around the corner for both of them.

If we could freeze our lives, preserve one moment forever, then for them it would be now. That halfway point, between longing and knowing, that sets butterflies whirring in the stomach. I want nothing more than to give him this: to let them have their happily ever after.

Except you and I both know that life doesn't actually work like that.

# OLIVES, EGGCUPS, AND THE AMSTERDAM OFFICE OF YOUTH ALIYAH

## 1938

It was a Thursday. More precisely, it was the day the painting changed hands. The day Lola Kramarsky became the portrait's longest and most devoted owner. She was not yet orphan, not yet widow, not yet refugee, and so it did not yet mean refuge. But it would.

While her husband (Siegfried Kramarsky, the well-known German banker) made the deal, Lola was here. In this ramshackle building on the outskirts of Amsterdam, up on the second floor in an old schoolhouse until recently abandoned, heading towards the old dorms with a bucket of water in one hand and a wet rag in the other. One of the boys had vomited on the stairs, and she was the only volunteer free this late, so it fell to her to deal with it.

The sound of her footsteps rang out against the stone floor, and each step flung up flurries of dust. The children shouldn't have been here yet, not before it was all ready. But it was not like they could turn them away or send them back. Cobwebs were slung from every corner. A hundred years before, this house had been an orphanage, and Lola found herself wondering whether something of that same sense of uncertainty and doubt had hung around, trapped in the cracks that ran down the walls.

Following the smell, she found the spill easily enough, and it was not long before she was crouched down beside the lumpy yellow puddle of vomit. She started by mopping up the bigger bits, the half-digested mess of cabbage and the globs of grit floating in mucous, then once she had herded the larger chunks to one side she set about dabbing away the goo. Finally, she unstoppered the disinfectant and dug out the wiry brush. She tucked a stray ringlet of hair back behind her ear and bent her head to the floor, pressing down to draw the scrubbing brush in scratchy circles across the filthy stairs. The irony of it all was not lost on her. Her own pristine house was bustling with cooks and maids, and here she was running her knees ragged on a floor that reeked to high heaven. The stink of fear. Her chauffeur had taken the car to the border to pick up a handful of kids who had slipped through that night, for they were coming now in waves, and each week brought more, each teen adding to that ragtag army of stragglers whose slim hopes had been whittled down to this.

Lola bucked and pushed the scrubbing brush but the crust would not budge.

Perhaps I owe Lola a better introduction than this, knee-deep in a pool of vomit. After all, she was the painting's most faithful owner, holding onto it for close to fifty years, before it was finally sold to Ryoei Saito and disappeared.

So here we go: meet Lola Kramarsky. Born in Hamburg, lost her father in the First World War, and about to lose her mother in the Second. She had a quiet intensity to her features, a stern and striking brow, with dark curly hair and even darker eyes. She had worked as a tutor to the meek children of wealthy German families before her marriage, but now her husband's banking success had pulled her up in the world. And yet on the day she became Doctor Gachet's most faithful custodian, she had swapped a house of fine art and antiques for a crumbling wreck full of unscrubbed refugees. A gang of gangly children who would soon be smuggled off to Palestine. I'm not going to speculate on why she was volunteering here, for where there are good causes there will always be well-to-do women with too much money and time, but I would like to think that anyone who loved that heartbroken painting must have had a strong sense of empathy.

From the corner of her eye she could see into the old dorm. It had been transformed into a makeshift classroom where twenty odd-bodied boys – the gangly and the gawky, the squat and the scrawny, the moon-faced and the moon-eyed – were standing to attention and trying not to fidget as Mr Limstein rattled on about the trip.

She caught the flurried movement of one of the smaller boys nervously raising his hand.

'Sir, I heard they have lizards there bigger than a dachshund.'

'I will take questions at the end, Schwartz, and we shall cover flora and fauna in Hebrew later during language practice in the garden. But suffice it to say: no, that is not the case. Now, back to the rules for travel outside the house...'

Lola could feel, up through her aching arms, that thrum of quiet anxiety that ran like a current through the building. Mention of the garden reminded her that she or one of the other volunteers would have to pick out the weeds, cut back the tangled and overgrown flowerbeds, and unthread the rusty spoils of what might once have been some kind of hunting trap from the hedgerows.

The class finished with Mr Limstein reciting the *Shehecheyanu* blessing, and as she heard the familiar cadence of the Hebrew coming from the hushed room, Lola drew still and whispered along beneath her breath: *Blessed are you, Lord our God, who has given us life, and sustained us, and brought us safely to this place*. Then before she knew it they were lolloping out in pairs and small groups, and she huffed up onto her knees to flap them away from the wet patches.

'Slow it down please, boys, or you'll break your necks,' she chided, and they bowed their heads meekly and slowed to a shuffle.

Most of them were hushed and disinclined to talk, though she was not sure whether this was because so far from home their accents now tasted sour on their tongues, or because they had so much brimming over in their minds that their mouths had become clogged up. But the last few were boisterous enough, chasing each other from the dorm and jesting about hunting genies in the desert – in fact, they ran so fast that the taller of them, turning to make some quick joke about camels, collided with a younger boy on his own, and with a stagger and a yelp both of them went tumbling to the floor in a tangle of limbs.

Lola sighed and turned back to her bucket. It was hard to begrudge them a little mischief, and it was better they let that nervous and frantic energy run wild here, in the safety of the house, than let it curdle or spill out in other ways. She heard the taller boy mumble a hasty *sorry* before pulling himself up and jogging away to catch up with his friends, but when she looked again she saw the younger boy still on the floor. He was sitting where he had fallen, his knapsack on his lap. She rose to her feet.

'Scrape your knee, dear?' She asked, approaching the boy.

He looked to be about twelve, a child with features too large for his face, with a ski-jump nose and mountainous eyebrows and hair as tufty as her scrubbing brush, a boy as yet untouched by the fickle god of growth-spurts, wearing a shirt and jacket a size too big.

He did not seem to hear her. Up close she noticed his fingers were clinging to the knapsack as though it was the edge of a cliff. She knew what it contained without having to look. They were all the same: a couple of vests, a handkerchief or two, pants and socks, a hastily-knitted pullover or jumper, and, among the better-off, perhaps a picture of the parents they would likely not see again. She could never quite decide whether these were the lucky ones, those with good luck charms from their past lives to help them cross over, or whether those who arrived with nothing were in fact better off, since they would have nothing holding them back.

'It takes a while to get used to everything, doesn't it? But you'll get the hang of it. Remember, everyone's in the same boat.'

He looked up at her then, and she recognized that familiar look that told her he was doing everything in his power to keep his lip from wobbling.

'It's broken, miss.'

'Your leg?' she said, torn between panic and disbelief.

'No, no,' He shook his head, then gestured at his bag.

He seemed to be giving her permission, and so Lola leaned across and peered inside his open knapsack. She could see, rattling about the bottom, three jagged splinters of broken china. It had obviously smashed in the fall, and come apart into the sharp edges of some unsolvable puzzle.

'What was it?' she asked.

'My eggcup,' he said.

She nodded. She knew there was nothing that could be said. It didn't matter that it was about the most useless thing he could have taken with him to Palestine, nor that no one else would have one either. She knew none of that was important.

He looked up at her, his eyes smudging with tears. His

front teeth were biting down frantically on his lower lip. She looked left and right – she did not want to give the others reason to tease him – then placed her hand on his shoulder.

'It would have broken on the ship. Better here, now.'

He gulped. 'Only it's –'

'I know,' she said, to quiet his squeaking voice before anyone heard. She did not want him picked on. Not for this.

And it was true. She did know. She understood that last thread tying you to your home. At that moment, her own house was a muddle of bags. She had to shrink her whole life down to the size of a suitcase. Would have to trade her tongue for one that was neither mother nor daughter nor distant cousin twice removed, but some stranger with strange mumbles. She knew.

She and her husband will flee from Amsterdam to Portugal the following year, then cross the Atlantic aboard the ocean liner *Rex*, waiting at Montreal until they are finally granted the visas that will allow them to make their new home in New York. Lola's mother will stay behind with cousins and aunts unwilling to risk everything in running away, and so in a few months will be deported from the Netherlands, and taken to the concentration camp at Bergen-Belsen.

But Lola Kramarsky and her husband will not go to America alone. For, travelling ahead of them, rolled up and packed tight in a cargo crate, will be Doctor Gachet.

How did he get there? That very afternoon, while Lola was scrubbing sick from the floor, her husband bought the painting – through an intermediary – from the Nazis, who were selling off much of their collection of 'degenerate' art. Doctor Gachet would help them make their way to the new world. Far lighter than gold, far quicker to fold, far less conspicuous at customs, and so far easier to exchange for a new life. He had become collateral – the best kind of currency to ensure the refugees safe passage from that godforsaken continent. The painting was an escape plan, an investment in the future. There was something about it that granted them the tiniest pinch of hope.

'Are you coming?' he asked, sniffing back the phlegm in his throat.

'No,' she said. 'Someone has to stay back and wait for the others, and make sure everyone gets through all right.'

She did not mention that she had other plans, that like him she too shuddered at the idea of the desert, that she too would have been far too scared to forsake civilization to try and build some fragile new country in a hot and unforgiving land.

'Can't I stay here with you? I could help.'

'No,' she said. The ship would leave in two weeks, and all the kids had to be on it.

He sniffed, but did not argue back. They both knew why. The eyes at the door. The turn of the handle in the night. The song broken glass sings

'I'll be terrible at farming. No one ever picks me for outdoor games. I get sunburned if I stay out too long.'

'There's more to it than that, you'll see. They just call it a farm because everyone lives off the land.'

'And I hate olives.'

'You'll feel differently when you get to taste the fresh ones straight from the vine.'

'They taste sour. Like they've gone bad.'

'You won't only eat olives.'

'Oranges give me tummy ache.'

'Don't be silly now, it's not just olives and oranges,' she said. 'There'll be meatballs and stew and chopped liver and all the things you love. And you'll be able to play outside all day long, without having to worry about anything.'

Not like here, she wanted to add, but decided it was probably best not to remind him.

'But –'

'It's our land,' she said, cutting him off. 'It's our home. It's in our blood. It's where your forefathers lived, and where we have always promised to return. You must do this for your family, to fulfil that promise.'

His wrinkled his nose, but said nothing. He seemed to have run out of excuses, so instead turned to fiddling with his sleeve. Lola, meanwhile, had lost patience with him. Moaning was a luxury they could not afford to indulge.

'That's quite enough. You've had your cry,' she said, rising to her feet. 'Now pull yourself together and be a man about it.'

His mouth fell open, making him look just like a comic-book character whose speech bubble has yet to be filled, his face as pink as if she'd slapped it.

'Anyway,' she went on. 'Far better to be the first there than to be a Johnny-come-lately.'

The boy's eyes darted up and a flicker of recognition tugged at his eyebrows. Yes, that was it. Finally, she had found a language he understood. He knotted the knapsack tight and rose to his feet. Then he hurried off down the corridor without looking back.

Lola returned to her bucket.

But it wasn't quite right – no matter how hard she scrubbed, she could never get that spick sheen her servants managed back at home. She didn't know how they managed it. And deep down, she didn't quite know how this gang of gawky teenagers would cope once transported to some arid and sand-battered commune in Palestine either. It sometimes seemed as daft as setting up a colony on the moon. But she understood the alternative, and so there was nothing else to be done.

Doctor Gachet's expression says as much: there is nothing else that can be done. Perhaps that is why Lola clung on to him.

Despite their plans, Siegfried and Lola will not look for a buyer when they arrive in the US. Instead they will hold tight to the painting. It was a souvenir of their crossing. Lola would not sell – not when her husband died, not when her finances began ebbing away – not ever. It stayed with her until the end, and only after she could no longer see it did her children allow Christie's to sell it to Ryoei Saito in 1990 for a world-record price.

Why would she not let it go? The answer is simple enough. Because it haunted her as it has haunted others. Because when she saw him hanging there on the wall of her New York apart-ment – or when she loaned him out to the Met and went to check on him there – her heart got snagged on the past. For the simple truth was that she recognized that sad look on his face: the look of a man who knew what it meant to have to leave so much behind.

Lola tossed the brush into the bucket and rose from her achy knees. The stairs were as good as they were going to be. She didn't know when the next accident might happen, nor when there'd be another emergency to attend to. But it was usually better not knowing.

# JE SUIS UNE BANANE
## 1869

He came prancing into the room with a ripe banana balanced upon his head. He had chosen that particular custard-yellow specimen as it had the same slight sag and droop as his own moustache. He did a strut and a turn at the end of their double-bed, his nose wrinkled in concentration, his hands held out penguin-like to stop him wobbling and sending it toppling off.

Then his hands shot up above his head and he executed a deft and graceful pirouette, imagining himself a hero of the vaudeville, before slapping his heels together upon the floorboards.

Finally, Blanche looked up from her book and laughed – an ungainly, yak-yak-yak of a laugh, distinctly unladylike, and as relentless and ear-piercing as the rattle of a machine gun – then raised her hands to cover her rabbit-teeth.

He removed the banana with a flourish, and took a bow.

'Dear me,' she said. 'What ever has gotten into you this morning?'

He shrugged. He could not find a way to say that he had done it all to see her smile.

'You know, you're really rather silly,' she said, and reached out her hand. He moved to the side of the bed and took it, rubbing her knuckles with her thumb. The round arc of her brimming belly pushed against the covers, and he ran his other hand against its outline.

In the past, he might have considered suggesting some

electrical remedy for a grown man who chose to walk around with a banana nestled upon his perfectly-combed hair. He might even have sneered, or talked quite seriously of marbles lost and dignity forsaken. But he no longer cared. Funny thing, love, he thought. Slakes away the sense of irony that fills the empty places in lonelier hearts, and makes you wide-eyed and childlike and hungry for the world again. He could no longer remember how to look at things askance, for she somehow brought it all to him headlong.

'Silly? Yes, perhaps. Maybe I should refer myself to a specialist?' he said, still rubbing her knuckles.

'Oh, I'm sure that won't be necessary,' she said. 'In fact, I have a far better prescription. Stay here with me today.'

He let her hand fall and shook his head with a smile.

'Blanche,' he said, as though her name itself were some kind of magic spell, the start of a powerful incantation known only to the two of them.

She looked up then, at her silly husband, at his wonky grin as he tried his hardest to be serious.

'Come on now, here I am like an inflated balloon, stuck in bed on *doctor's orders* –'

'You need to conserve your strength, the third trimester is –'

She cut him off with a stern look, as though to emphasize how much she suffered for being married to a fussy physician.

'If I'm not allowed any fun, then I really don't think its fair that you get to go out gallivanting!'

'I can assure you that the term "gallivanting" cannot be applied when one is hard at work –'

'Poppycock. There ought to be some kind of punishment for you too! In sickness and in health, remember?'

'Well, yes, but...' he trailed off.

She could tell he was considering it. He had been the kind of studious child who had never missed a day of school, never played truant, but now he was giving serious thought to abandoning his rounds in favour of spending the day lolling beside his new wife in their new cottage.

There were days when in the middle of examining some patient – poking about in ears, peering down throats, or angling his stethoscope against clammy chests – he felt like bursting into giddy laughter. I can't believe they don't know, he thought to himself. I can't believe they can't see that I am playing a part, that they have been tricked into thinking I'm dutiful old Doctor Gachet. And it was true, for these days he felt he was only really himself with her, and everything else was somehow fake.

Nonetheless, he could not do it. There was a voice of duty that he could not shake free from, a spectre of the guilt that would hang over him if he let his own desires trump his professional responsibilities.

'I'm sorry,' he sighed. 'I know it is interminable, but it cannot be helped. What if I stayed here at home and a patient's condition became critical? What if, without treatment, Monsieur Lagrete fell prey to another seizure, or without her medicine Madame Etta were to suffer from a relapse? I could not have it on my conscience.'

'But you cannot be responsible for everyone.'

'Perhaps,' he said, but already he was thinking of the day ahead. 'But if not, then why bother?'

'Do not fall into one of your moods,' she said. 'You do good work, you make a difference. Isn't that why you became a doctor in the first place?'

He shook his head. 'Oh no, I became a doctor because I was not talented enough to be an artist.'

She picked up her book. 'Silliness again. I shan't listen to it.'

He bent down and kissed her forehead. 'I will be back for supper.'

'Very well,' she said. 'But I believe I shall be quite entitled to sulk a little.'

Then she took the bookmark from its place between the pages and started to read.

Blanche, you may have noticed, is a problem.

We have facts about Gachet. There are fixed points in his life we can track. We know a lot about where he went and who he met and what he did – to say nothing of what he looked like.

But Blanche is an enigma. There is a Blanche-shaped hole in history. She is a shadow, a vague outline, a muted voice.

There are no contemporary accounts of her, save a couple of brief mentions of her marriage to Doctor Paul-Ferdinand Gachet in 1870. There are no letters from her, nor any letters to her. There is nothing in her own hand. Stranger still, there are no paintings or pictures of her – though maybe Paul thought that at last he had found something that no work of art could compete with.

So I have no choice but to reconstruct her from a few meagre details. She had a few books, so I have made her an avid reader, a devourer of novels. Her house was covered in paintings, and so I have decided it must have been that love of the Impressionists that first bound the two of them together. And so on, and so on. Do I feel bad about this? Yes, of course. How would you like to have your whole life second-guessed based only on a quick glance at your bookshelves? Unfortunately, I have little choice – it is either that or write her out of his history. And I would not dare do that.

I know her only because I know what Paul felt about her. This is not the real Blanche, then, but a Blanche reconstructed from his feelings and memories. We can see her only as reflected in his gaze.

But then maybe that's what love is: a reflection of something we have always felt. As much as it is a feeling, an energy, love is also a way of seeing. A way of looking at the world. And maybe that is where sadness starts, when the still water is broken by storm, the ripples start to spread across the surface, and the reflection is twisted out of shape.

Or perhaps the truth is that all love contains within it the certainty of sadness. Because even the best love stories – those that escape separation, betrayal, divorce, bitterness – have an ending. If life does not succeed at tearing a couple apart, then death will take up the job instead. Heartbreak is a seed buried deep inside love, and the longer it must wait, the more it will bud, blossom, and grow. There is no love without despair.

Paul began to move toward the door, but something would not let him go quite yet. It must be a force with similar properties to magnetism, he thought. A homing signal of sorts set in motion by the subtle laws of attraction. But he knew what she would say if he tried to tell her that: more silliness. And perhaps that was for the best. Best not to try to dissect love to see how it worked, best not to try to pull it apart into theories or propositions – better just to let its currents pull him along in its drift.

Blanche glanced up from her page. 'Change of heart?'

'Yes, I forgot my banana!'

She tutted under her breath, but he could see she was trying hard not to smile.

That was a lie, however. He was not really going back for the banana. He wanted one last look. Not at her, directly, though it was true that sometimes she caught him staring at her, after which both of them, even after a year of marriage, would blush and look away. But this was not what he had in mind.

No, what he really wanted was to catch a glimpse of the two of them together in the mirror at her dresser. He could not explain it, but there was nothing he liked more than seeing the two of them framed together and staring back at him. It stirred the same feeling in him that was awoken when he stared at his favourite paintings. When he saw her beside him, everything made sense.

He took the banana, and walked out backwards, to keep the sight of their reflection floating on his retina just a little longer.

Then he trotted down the stairs towards the front door, and with each step months flew by and his future took shape: the baby that would soon appear and play between their feet, her blissful happiness at motherhood and his at seeing her so happy, the garden in their new cottage full of strutting chickens and tall pagodas and the foxgloves he planned to plant for her, and beyond that the whole world dissolving into light.

Yes, I have pressed fast-forward. All biographers do it – after all, it would be impossible to reproduce even a single day with any fidelity. To attempt to faithfully recreate every half-formed thought that skittered across his mind as he lay in bed in the morning, between waking and dressing for the day ahead, would take each page of this book and more. Besides, time hates happiness. It tumbles, races onwards, desperate to return us to something more like our natural states. But when you are lonely, or lost, or hopeless, the hours stretch and warp out of shape, until each dull beat of the clock takes weeks. For once, Paul felt his life rushing by. The days melted together.

Of course, our story does not end there. But let them bask for a while in the warmth of the sun, for it is inevitable that in the end they must learn that sunlight only makes shadows possible.

# CAN A SMILE BE A POLITICAL ACT?

We live in an age of memes. Where every second Facebook post is a picture of a cat, or a sunset with a pithy soundbite telling us to be ourselves, or that when you smile the world smiles with you. We live in an age of inspirational quotes, where we should always be the best we can be. We live in an age of validation, with Instagram feeds clogged with laboriously-filtered selfies, pics of exotic holidays, wild parties, elaborate meals, and classy cocktails, all in collusion to preserve the carefully-curated fiction that our lives are much more exciting than they sometimes seem.

In the twentieth century, we moved death from our cities. We hid it, covered it up. Slaughterhouses, public executions in the town square, long wakes where the body would lie exposed in an open casket. We made death private, taboo. Fit only for films, for art, for catharsis. In the twenty-first century, we seem to be doing the same with sadness. Depression may be on the rise, but there is more pressure than ever to hide it away, to disguise it. To play a role, to pretend. No one likes a complainer, a moaner, a whinger. You're supposed to think positive, to share pictures showing your triumphs and joys, to write witty little self-deprecating posts celebrating your tribe and your mates. Or else you're a killjoy, a buzzkill, an Eeyore pissing on everyone else's fireworks. Worse still, you're a bad friend. And since so many people seem to think that sadness is infectious, there's every chance you could soon be shunned. Better to suck it up and pretend that everything is fine, great, fantastic, and you're having the time of your life.

So now, more than ever, a face of sadness seems important. Someone who doesn't ask you to *get over it* or lecture you that *it could be worse*. No, someone who seems to understand. Who makes no attempt to hide his pain. This smile is an act of protest.

Can a smile really be a political act? Of course:

- It can be revolt. Far stronger than sticking up your middle finger or telling the world to go fuck itself, is the act of smiling even when everything is falling apart.
- It can be a disguise: think of all those people who smile when they are nervous, afraid, backed into a corner.
- It can be a door: a way in, or a way out.
- It can be an act of solidarity.
- It can be an act of war against everything that tries to keep you down.
- It can be an act of compassion, no matter with strangers or those closest to you.

Can a smile sometimes be a political act?

- No.
- It is *always* a political act.

# ELEPHANT SOUP AND NIGHT BALLOONS
## January 1871

After the boy died he decided to treat himself to supper.

He had not eaten for twenty-four hours, and the choice was clear: give up now and sink into grief, or keep going. He kept going.

While the scrawny body was wrapped in the last reels of an old curtain, Paul picked his way across the hotel-suite, through the sea of sickly figures sprawled across the floorboards and propped up along the walls, treading carefully to avoid crushing fingers or toes beneath his mud-shod boots. He limped up the creaking stairs to the hotel's attic where his own camp-bed was set up in the furthest corner, and retrieved his tatty hat and coat, as well as the letter he had written the night before.

On his way out he paused in the lobby to peer over the night porter's shoulder as he totted up the dwindling list of supplies against the growing number of patients in twin columns in the guestbook. Paul could not stop himself from correcting one or two of the calculations. Then he reached into his coat pocket to retrieve his pipe. He set the gnarled end in his mouth: it had a metallic taste, like water from a rusty vat, though he could not say if this was from the pipe or his own cracked lips. He chewed upon the end until he could pick up a trace of something older. There was no longer any tobacco in the city – hadn't been since the first month of the siege, and anyway, the tobacco factory had long since been taken over to make munitions – but the simple act of sucking upon the empty pipe calmed him, tricked his senses into believing, if only for a second, that things were still as they used to be.

From somewhere above him the low hum of hushed voices that filled the hotel-turned-hospital at all hours was broken by a rasping scream, the kind of noise an animal caught in a trap might make, a sound of unbroken panic. Paul slipped the pipe back into his pocket, pulled on his hat and ventured out into the evening.

The early evening was so cold his breath turned to ice while still on his tongue. He strode down the steps and towards the square. The fountain there was frozen over, a pool of splintered starlight and cracked galaxies. Sitting at its edge was a young man, his heavy coat flecked with frost.

'Doctor Travere,' Paul called out, and only upon opening his mouth did he discover how hoarse his voice sounded. 'Join me for dinner.'

'Doctor Gachet,' the young man said. He stumbled to his feet, and stood glumly to attention. He had deep bags beneath his eyes, and a patchy show of downy hair upon his cheeks. His hands, Gachet noticed, were fidgeting in his pockets, as though, try as he might, he could not still them.

'It is really most kind of you, but I fear I could not eat a thing,' he stuttered.

'It was not a request, my friend. It was an order. Come, I am going to the Café Provençal, but we better hurry if we want to be done with dessert by the time the shells start raining down.'

The young man raised his red eyes to the sky and sucked in his breath. He made no effort to move, and so Paul took him by the shoulder and began to steer him down the street.

'We have a busy day tomorrow, and we will need the sustenance. It may be a week before you get a good meal again.'

'A good meal? We've more chance of growing wings and flying away from this godforsaken city,' Doctor Travere said, though there was no trace of laughter on his face.

'Ha! That's the spirit,' Paul said.

The last of late-afternoon light had slipped behind the rooftops, and they knew the shells must come soon. The streets in the second arrondissement were deserted, and it seemed to Paul as though they were walking through a well-crafted set for some elaborate theatrical performance where all the actors had been called away at the last minute. The frost on the windows of the houses and the distant flicker of gaslight made everything sepia. Everyone in Paris was inside, trying to stay warm or else hiding out the night.

The two doctors passed a wall that had shaken off bricks like a wet dog might shake off the rain. They picked their way over the rubble, past tiny puddles of dust and soot, and rounded the corner.

The next street had taken a direct hit. One of the houses had been sucked into a whirlpool of dust and bricks, leaving nothing but a couple of stone stumps. Another had lost its roof, front wall, one of the side walls and a good chunk of the floor, though most of the staircase stretched out of the debris, desperately trying to escape the ruins. Despite the sprawling mess of rubble, quite a few of the damaged houses had only lost a few walls or had the roof blown in, and the two doctors kept going without paying any of them much mind, for it was all second-nature to them now.

Lying prone in a boarded-up doorway halfway down the street was an old man. Paul moved instinctively towards him. The old man was curled on his side, the fringes of his coat torn and dark. His ear was gnarled and bloody, as though rats had been chewing away at the only scraps they could find.

'You really think there's room for another patient at the hotel?' Doctor Travere asked.

'Oh, I shouldn't think he'd make a very good guest,' Paul said, squatting down beside the body. 'Rigor mortis has already set in.'

'May the Lord have mercy upon him. Cause?'

Paul shrugged. 'Oh, the usual.'

Paul rolled the body onto its back. The old man was crooked and chicken-limbed, his features bloated and almost blue.

'Then what the devil are you doing?'

Paul had started peeling the frayed woollen gloves from the corpse's stiff and black-tipped fingers. One got caught on a black and ragged fingernail, but a firm tug soon freed it. Paul rose to his feet, waving his prize: a crusty pair of soot-stained gloves.

'We'll be glad of these at the front.'

Doctor Travere stared at him in disbelief, his mouth set open in the shape of a question.

'Come on, no time to dawdle,' Paul said as he started striding on down the street, the fingers of the gloves flapping from the top of his pocket in the breeze. 'Have you done field surgery with frostbitten fingers, with your hands shaking from the cold? No? Me neither, and I hope not to start soon. You know as well as I that the smallest of details might tip the balance. So keep your eye out.'

The main windows of the Café Provençal were papered over, but that did not stop them wandering in and commandeering the table farthest from the door. Both men angled their chairs towards the hearth before settling down. The owner hurried over, for despite his stinking clothes and untamed beard, Paul was still recognisable as a gentleman. He called for wine – the city's cellars, at least, had not yet run dry – and for some time neither man spoke. Instead they stared at the fire, at the shadows leaping and warring behind the grate.

The owner soon returned, flicking persistently at the few greasy strands of hair with which he sought to cover his threadbare head.

'I am most delighted to report that we have received a fresh delivery from the Jardin des Plantes. Our chef will be proud to serve you an elephant consommé for your entrée.'

'I have been to that zoo,' Paul said. 'Pray, tell me: which elephant?'

The owner smiled an unctuous smile, while Doctor Travere raised his eyebrows.

'Well, sir, I believe it is Castor, the younger of the two brothers.'

'Ah, of course,' Paul turned to the younger man and smiled. 'I believe it is poor manners to let such a great beast grace one's table without first understanding its genealogy.'

He was trying hard to rouse his companion from his stupor, but Doctor Travere's worried face did not show any light.

'It does not put you off? Those proud and noble creatures?'

Paul rubbed his unshaven chin. 'You know, at the start of the war I might have said yes. But these days I find it most prudent to take the long view. The whole zoo is already slaughtered, and to let those animals go to waste would be senseless. At least this way they are doing their bit. It is the same with the gloves. When we return tomorrow, they may prove the difference between saving a soldier's life and a surgeon's shivering fingers missing the mark. This is why I ask you to eat something. We cannot help them if we ourselves are not in good health. It is all connected –'

'Excuse me, good sirs,' the flustered owner cut in. 'But if I may also suggest the kangaroo stew, and perhaps some begonias from the botanical gardens to finish?'

'Yes, yes, excellent, thank you,' Paul said, and the owner bowed and scurried away.

Again the two men fell to silence. Presently they heard the sound of drunken chanting from the street outside. It was a posse of students marching by, and Paul turned to watch through the holes in the windows as they passed. He smiled at how easy it was to trick the brain, to fool a person into thinking they were safe simply because they were part of a crowd. Then he felt a sudden surge of envy, a wish to give away his private worries and join in their defiant roar. He thought of flocks of birds reeling through the autumn sky, all bound by that same common thread, held in formation by a certainty born of pure instinct. The analogy would make a good monograph, if he ever found his way back to his writing desk. He could picture it, the hard wooden desk and the easel facing the window, and beyond it Blanche lolling by the flowers in the garden, their baby daughter bouncing upon her knees. He felt that catch – the hook of the heart suddenly snagged – and desperately tried to turn his mind to other thoughts. It was his own fault, after all. He'd volunteered, against her wishes. He'd asked for this.

The soup arrived, and Paul set to it with vigour. He could not recall when he had last eaten. Though the meat was tough and stuck easily between his teeth, and the liquid itself was somewhat briny, he found it was not too difficult to convince himself that it was a most delicious mutton soup. As ever, imagination was all. In fact, he wolfed it down so ravenously, his spoon a whirr as it dipped and dipped again to his bowl, that his beard was soon damp.

Doctor Travere, meanwhile, barely touched his save to stir his spoon listlessly through the broth, as though he sought to read something in the ripples upon its surface.

'It is as though it is a kind of fever dream, a hallucination,' he said at last, his eyes still on his soup. 'For when I am here, I cannot believe the battlefield can actually be real, and yet when I am there I can hardly remember that I once had any other life but one of mud and stitches and gunpowder.'

Paul set down his spoon and reached for his wine. After draining his cup he peered into the carafe, then called for a new one.

'For me, the problem is the opposite,' he said, at last.

Doctor Travere looked up. 'How so?'

'Well, let me explain. Back in my old life, my closest friends were artists.'

Doctor Travere leaned forwards in his chair, frowning at the older man. It was an unspoken rule among the military men not to mention life back home until the fighting was over, because to do so might tempt fate. But Paul had never cared for such superstitions.

'Not the old-fashioned type, you understand, pottering away on some dull portrait of a king or duke. But the new kind: the painters of real life, who show things how they really are, warts and all.'

'I follow the papers. At least, I used to. I have heard something of the controversies.'

'Good, good. Now, I paint myself, but I am strictly an amateur. The thing my friends always tell me is to forget the past and the future, and focus only on the present moment. To look at the world with an unflinching gaze, that is the key. To experience life as it is right now, without turning away. But I could never quite manage it.'

Doctor Travere gave a sad smile.

'And it is quite the same here,' Paul went on. 'I feel that I live only in the past or in the future, but never the present. While I am at the front, I am thinking of the city. While I am in the city, I am worrying about the front. I try my best to remember those happy times in my house in the country, to imagine my baby daughter's smiling face – I missed her first birthday to be here, can you believe it? – all so that I have something to fix my mind upon. The present on its own is sometimes too much to bear.'

Doctor Travere nodded solemnly, and they filled their glasses in silence.

The bowls were cleared, and the kangaroo stew arrived.

'Hold on to your plate,' Paul said with a grin. 'You wouldn't want it hopping off!'

Travere merely raised an eyebrow in response. Paul was becoming aware that his young companion viewed him with the peculiar mixture of mild embarrassment and unspoken re-spect more common to the relations between fathers and sons, and this made him feel suddenly old. He thought of his baby daughter, Marguerite, then quickly chased away that thought with another drink.

After draining his cup, Paul attacked the main course with gusto, while Travere stared at his wine.

'Do you think it will end soon?' he said at last.

'No,' Paul replied, his mouth half full of stew. 'Even when it finishes, it will follow us home. Wars do not end until they are forgotten.'

'The siege, then?'

'Ah, well, I suspect that will end within a month.'

'You are still optimistic then?' Travere stared hard into his companion's eyes, his voice suddenly charged with emotion.

Paul sighed. 'No, you misunderstand me. We will surrender. It is inevitable now. The Prussians will take the city. It is but a matter of weeks.'

'Lower your voice, I beg you,' Travere hissed, leaning so hard across the table that he almost upset the plates. 'Someone will overhear, and we will be lynched.'

Paul set down his fork and made a show of looking around him – at the well-to-do married couple on the table to their left, at the group of middle-aged men in top hats and mourning suits to their right – and raised his hands, as if to ask where this outraged mob might appear from.

'Everyone knows this. We cannot go on as we are. Come, there is no shame in honesty. It is a simple question of mathematics. You are a doctor – how long can a wound fester until it is infected? How long might a man bleed until his veins are dry? The zoo is empty, and you must have heard the men joke that the rats are now more afraid of chefs than they are of cats.'

Travere did not answer, but instead reached down and began, tentatively, to eat.

They worked on their stew in silence. The wind hissed in through the paper covering the broken windows, and the fire in the hearth cackled and spat. This is the truth of a siege, Paul thought: it is a toss up which will happen first, the people turn against themselves or die of starvation. Either way, the end result is the same. He shovelled in another mouthful. From somewhere outside, church bells struck the hour, and the diners at the next table set down their cutlery mid-mouthful and hurried from the restaurant. The two doctors slurped up the rest of their meal without even glancing up.

And really, what more is there to say?

It was a minor war, after all, and honestly, haven't we all had it up to here with people droning on about war?

As far as history is concerned, the Franco-Prussian War was little more than a few short skirmishes, a pissing contest, barely enough to even register in the great book of human misery. The siege lasted only a couple of months, and the revolutionary commune that followed – a mismatch of half-baked ideologies, along with a bit of priest-bashing, all under the loose banner of socialism – was shorter still. So why dredge it all up now?

Every age has its own glut of war. We are not sick of it; worse, we are apathetic. We have seen it all before. War is old news.

In that decade alone there will be twenty more wars. The population of the earth at the time Paul-Ferdinand Gachet dined on elephant was around 1.3 billion. Within fifty years, more than 70 million will have been killed by war or else will be living with its lingering effects. Yet this is still small change.

How many wars have there been in the whole of human history? How many have died? The calculations are impossible, and serve only to suggest that our species must be half in love with the possibility of its own annihilation.

Aren't wars all the same? So why study history at all? It is evident that we do not learn from it. We make the same mistakes, again and again and again.

No, that is not quite right: we get better at it. We perfect the art of the impersonal slaughter. Whether flint-daggers, or bows and arrows, or broadswords, or bayonets, or muskets, or machine guns, or mustard gas, or missiles, or gas chambers, or atom bombs, or WMD – it is only a matter of degree. The essentials remain: the churned mud. The screams. The scrum of bodies. The froth and foam of bloody puddles. The writhing limbs. The blood-gurgled curses. The same unbelievable words delivered to the same unbelieving faces back home.

Aren't you bored of war yet? In the end, it is only numbers. In the battle of Buzenval the following day, there will be close to 4,000 French casualties. How many does Paul save? How many maimed men does he stitch up? How many bones does he hack through with his rusty surgeon's saw? How many dying men's hands does he hold? Enough to earn him a medal when it is all over. Enough to stop him sleeping another whole night through.

But why should we care? We have our own wars, and most of the time we cannot summon much interest in them. As far as suffering and slaughter goes, there is a simple truth: we have heard it all before.

The plates were cleared, and the red-faced owner carried out the final course himself. Paul made a good show of tackling the dessert, plucking off the pink and yellow petals and stuffing them one after another into his mouth, then chewing – and chewing, and chewing some more – until he could attempt to swallow the unpleasant and sticky mulch sticking to his tongue.

Despite Travere's protests, Paul paid the bill and the two men made their way back to the street, both shaky with wine and heavy with the first meal either had touched since dawn. The cold stung their cheeks, and in the distance they could hear the crack of cannon fire battering the city gates. Frost was blossoming upon the paving stones, and the night had an uncertain quality to it, as though the darkness and everything it held might be easily unravelled. Paul missed the sound of owls, the nocturnal music of snuffling foxes and impassioned cats, and longed for anything that might fill those ominous moments when the besieged city fell briefly silent.

'Care for an after-dinner stroll?' Paul asked.

'Thank you, but I am afraid I am poor company,' Travere replied.

'Nonsense. If you keep those thoughts rattling round your head they will go as sour as corked wine. They'll turn your brain to vinegar, if you are not careful!'

Paul said it all with a smile, but Travere merely nodded his head curtly.

'I must prepare my kit bag for the morning. My tools...' His voice drifted off.

It was Paul's turn to nod. They bowed clumsily to each other – both with an awkward sense of too much shared – and then Travere started back towards their makeshift barracks.

Paul took his pipe from his pocket and set it once more between his lips. Then he sucked hard as he watched the younger man disappear into the night, and for a moment he had the sense that he was watching his own past retreat from his reach. He set the pipe back in his pocket and turned, following the wall east, away from the hotel.

Even though he stayed close to the city's stone perimeter, he passed a number of houses that had recently been wrecked by shells. He saw blown-out windows baring jagged teeth of broken glass and walls that had great gaping wounds in their centre; he saw roofs that had been ripped open to let the sky in, and houses that had fallen in upon themselves like badly-arranged dominoes, and one or two wooden structures that had been gutted by the ensuing fires. Nonetheless, most were still inhabited, with sheets and broom-threaded blankets arranged to keep out the cold. A few badly-damaged houses had been abandoned, and as he passed them he caught sight of strange treasure and junk – the glint of a belt buckle, a corner of curtain, a charred chair leg, a bright silver Sunday-service spoon, a few bars from a toddler's cot, springs from some new-fangled brass bed, and a single charred shoe with its tongue dangling out as if trying to speak.

Once he reached the glass factory, he made his way through the unlocked door and out to the courtyard. A pale, whippet-faced man was sewing a patch onto the stained blue canvas of a hot air balloon, while a boy was throwing handfuls of seed into a pigeon coop.

'Good evening.' Paul called out, doffing his hat. 'Monsieur Rallat, Monsieur Apere. How goes it?'

'Evening, doctor,' the man replied, biting off the end of a piece of thread. 'Can't complain.'

'Am I too late for the last post?' Paul asked.

'Afraid so. There'll be nothing going till morning, now, what with the shells and all. Plus the boys can't manage the navigation in the dark, you see. Dim lot, but the best we can get in these circumstances. Had two last week set down in enemy territory by mistake, though both managed to escape, believe it or not!'

'That's fine. I'm in no hurry. Any shot down this week?'

'None, I'm proud to say. Plenty of wear and tear, though.'

'Ah. Well, that's true for all of us,' Paul said.

He took the letter from his coat pocket, as well as a coin for the cost, and handed both to the boy feeding the pigeons. He had spent the previous evening hunched over a candle, drafting and redrafting his message to Blanche. He had written ten pages, pouring out every detail of the siege, every image from the battlefield that had got lodged in his insomniac brain, every creeping fear and every urgent longing – and then, sated, he had thrown it in the fire and started afresh. His final letter read: *Kiss our daughter for me. In my heart, I am already home.*

'Anything arrive for Paul Gachet?'

The man with the sewing-kit shook his head. 'Afraid not. Half them pigeons never find their way back, you see. I'll warrant there's a good dozen in some Prussian cooking pot right now. They're dozy birds, but it's better than nothing.'

Paul thanked the men, and made his way back through the streets. As he walked he thought of all the messages the balloons carried up into the heavens to escape the besieged city – they seemed to him akin to prayers being urged ever upwards, hopeless and unanswered and serving only to clog up the clouds.

Back at the hotel he paused in the lobby to chat with the night porter as two volunteers lugged the latest corpse down the stairs. Then he lumbered upstairs and poked his head round the door of the main suite. For a while he watched as an old doctor tried to revive a middle-aged woman, before climbing up to the attic.

At the top he hung his coat over a chair and collapsed onto his cot. All the candles had been guttered and the other men curled on the camp-beds dotted across the loft were already snoring.

He lay for a long time in the darkness, his thoughts flitting back and forth, until at last it came: and in a second all the voices in the hotel fell to a hush as they heard it. That long, high whine of shells slipping through the sky. For a second all was hiss, and then they hit.

The thump of them sent shudders running through his bed, and he heard them burst like the ack-ack-ack of fireworks. He let himself breathe out – they had obviously landed far from here.

There was a minute of peace, while the Prussian troops reloaded, and then they started lobbing them up over the city walls once more. He heard their shrill whistle and braced him-self. The second volley landed closer still – so close the bangs made his ears pop, so close the floor shook when they came walloping down – and a seasick groan echoed through the hotel. Paul stared up at the sloping attic roof, as if he might somehow read the fate of his small corner of the city in the tremors that spread across the ceiling.

The other volunteers camped out in the attic were wide awake now. Soon, worried voices were murmuring away, though in the chaos Paul could not be sure whether they were uttering prayers for safety or the most elaborate curses. He could hear a woman on the floor below sobbing hysterically through the thunder.

As the third round came, he felt as if he was in the hull of a schooner being tossed around by feverish waves crashing against them. The whole building seemed to lurch wildly, and horrified shrieks erupted all around. The impact lifted him three or four inches from his bed, and knocked the wind out of him. Paul tried his best to summon Blanche, since it calmed him to think of her asleep, her night untroubled by shells or cannon-fire or nightmares.

Then another moment of calm. Outside, he could hear a dog barking. He could picture the poor animal running round and round in circles as the stars came unhinged and started plummeting down around it.

Finally he could bear no more and pulled himself up from bed. There was no point lying around in wait for it.

'Calm down, get some sleep,' the man in the next cot said at the sound of footfall on the floorboards. 'It will all still be here in the morning.'

'The morning will not come without someone to welcome it,' Paul replied, and, slinging on his coat and picking up his stethoscope, he made his way down towards the screams.

# VANITAS

The next time I was able to visit the campus was close to two months later, deep into the summer run of weddings and engagement parties, and close enough to the end of Trinity term that even on that short stroll through the quad I passed scores of students lolling on the grass and on the benches under the shade of crook-backed oaks, worrying the ends of pens between their teeth, or pressing the smudge of their fingers against the screen of shiny iPads, smoking or doodling or playing with their phones as the hours counted down towards their Finals.

The number of people around made it all the more surprising to find, outside the door to the old west tower, a dead pigeon in the middle of the pathway. Its slate-grey eyes were staring up and its feathers were pulled tight across its chest as if to shield it from something unseen. I wondered if I should call the porter, or just leave it to nature; the cats that did this would surely be back to claim their prize. It reminded me of those preserved sharks and dead sheep displayed by Damien Hirst: the uncanny stillness of it, the look of expectancy in its eyes.

Sam Taylor-Wood's short film, *Still Life*, was first shown in 2001, around the same time I first saw the painting of Doctor Gachet. It is a little less than 4 minutes long. In it a bowl of fruit (a couple of apples, a pear, peaches, nectarines, a few fat red grapes) slowly decomposes. At the beginning a fuzzy prickle of mould creeps across the fruit. By the final minute, the individual fruits are no longer distinguishable; they have melted into each other and there is nothing left except a sea of mould and decay. Tiny insects whirr and pick around its blurry fringes. Finally it turns black, with snowy white peaks, and folds in upon itself. Of all contemporary art, it is perhaps the most classical, since it nods back to the Dutch and Flemish still lives of the 16th century, which occasionally focused on rotting fruit. The *Vanitas* style of painting used this symbolism to draw attention to the transience of our hopes and achievements, and to remind us of the utter emptiness of the physical world. Everything you hold dear, these images seem to say, will be slowly stripped away until all that is left is the taste of decay. For these paintings do leave a sickening taste in your mouth, the kind that sits rancid on your tongue and sours your taste buds for hours. They are unsettling. They unsettle us. I stepped carefully over what was left of the pigeon carcass, and made my way inside.

At the top of the old spiral stairs I turned left, as ever, and made my way to Professor Burkridge's rooms, where the kettle had just boiled. It was comforting to see her dressed, as ever, for a blistery night upon some distant heath, and it heightened the illusion that she had no sense of what might lie beyond the campus gates, and so had prepared herself for the worst the vicious elements might bring. I settled on the sofa and, after accepting a mug of tea, told her about the pigeon and the paintings. She sat back in her armchair and pressed the tips of her fingers together beneath her chin.

'What amazes me,' she said once I had fallen silent, 'is that anything survives at all. I mean, consider the odds.'

'Are you talking about in history or in real life?' I asked, smiling.

She did not smile back, and I remembered she had never been the kind of teacher who brooked any joking about her subject, perhaps through some fear that if one did not take history seriously then it would close itself up and refuse to reveal its secrets.

'If you can find a clear distinction between the two I should be glad to hear it.'

I considered giving it a go – history is life as seen from a safe distance, say, or history is life with the gaps and grey areas filled in with guesswork – but I knew these would only provoke either disdain or debate, and so I decided against it.

'No, no, I'm sorry. Please go on.'

'Thank you. But to clarify, I was talking about art. After you mentioned you were going to write about the painting, I did a little research myself. Since it is not my field I started with the basics, the facts in the papers as it were.'

'The price.'

'Quite. The most expensive painting ever sold, allowing for inflation and so on. And, straight away, it didn't seem quite right. That more money had been paid for *Doctor Gachet* than for any other painting. It's a classic example of a misleading statistic.'

'What do you mean?' I asked.

'Well, it's like that old chestnut about the First World War. You must have heard it. In 1915, the British soldiers were made to wear steel helmets for the first time. As soon as that happened, the number of head injuries rose dramatically.'

'Yes, I've heard that one. Head injuries went up, but only because deaths by head wound went down. The helmets saved lives.'

'Exactly. And all this business about your painting being one of the most valuable in the world is the same. It hinges on a common misunderstanding. The painting is only so expensive because so little else is available. Now one reason for this is that the most valuable works of art – the *Mona Lisa*, say, or *Guernica*, *the Scream*, *the Birth of Venus*, *the Night Watch* – are owned by museums that would never dream of selling them. Others will never come on the market because they've been hidden away by private collectors. But the truth is that the great majority of masterpieces simply don't exist any more. It is truly staggering how much has been lost.'

I set my mug down on one of the coasters, carefully sliding it away from a manuscript set open on the coffee table. I turned to the window. The quad was still crowded with students.

'So basically you're saying its price is over-inflated not because of its own merit but because there's no real competition?'

'Essentially, yes. Think about it. The Colossus of Rhodes and the gods of the Parthenon are now legends to us. Most of the Bayeux Tapestry is gone. The great works that changed the world and inspired the Renaissance, by Giotto and Donatello and Botticelli, all are lost or destroyed. Most of the major works by Leonardo da Vinci either disappeared or, like *the Last Supper*, are slowly decaying on a church-house wall. The masterpieces of Cimabue and Michelangelo and Caravaggio and Raphael exist now only as stories. More is gone of Rubens and Vermeer than remains. The siege of Florence, a fire at the Doge's Palace, the Allied bombing of Europe, each destroyed hundreds of works, and thousands more have been lost in wars and accidents and thefts. We are left with only poor copies or historical accounts.'

'Secondary sources,' I said, though in truth I did not like the way she was approaching this. Something about it unnerved me, because, the more she talked, the more fragile the entire endeavour seemed. And also, I think, because I was thinking of the man inside the painting. For if all that remained of lost masterpieces were cheap reproductions and unreliable memories, then the same was surely true of the dead.

'Even more recent artists,' she went on, ignoring me. 'Consider Klimt and all his dazzling showers of light. You know what happened to most of his paintings? Confiscated from their owners by the Nazis, and taken to a grand castle, the Schloss Immendorf, so that they could be enjoyed by the SS. And you know what the SS did when they were finally forced to retreat from Austria in 1945? They burned the whole castle down, paintings and all. As I said, it is a miracle anything survives at all.'

'And then there's Van Gogh,' I said, completing her argument for her. 'I've done my research too. Six of his paintings were destroyed by fire during the Second World War. One disappeared after being seized by the Nazis and labelled as degenerate art. Three more were stolen from museums in the last twenty years – and once they're gone, they're unlikely to turn up again. That's before you get to paintings like Gachet, that supposedly still exist but that haven't been seen in years.'

It seems unlikely that you or I will ever see the painting in the flesh. I have studied hundreds of reproductions, of varying qualities. But that is not the same as seeing the physical flecks of paint on the canvas. It is not the same as pressing your face close to the picture the artist's hands once touched.

But perhaps it does not really matter. As a teenager I had a favourite song: a heart-squeezing, spirit-tugging song, that I recorded off the radio onto a crappy cassette that I listened to again and again on my Walkman. I never heard it performed live, never thought to buy the real album. And years later, when I downloaded a clean copy of the song from iTunes, I found I actually preferred the hissy, poor-quality version I had listened to for hours at the bus stop, or during all those walks home.

'It ought to be a crime to own such a work and not show it,' Professor Buckridge was saying. 'The same goes for manuscripts. I can never understand why some collectors hoard when there are so many experts who would give their right arm to study these items.'

She placed her mug down beside mine and leaned back in her armchair.

'It doesn't make sense to me, either,' I said. 'Why keep something that powerful locked up? What's the point? I mean, is a work of art still a work of art if there is no one to look at it?'

I blushed a little at this, for I knew as soon as I said it that she would not think much of such a question. She was interested in provable suppositions, and had no time for vague musings or amateur philosophising. And I was right, for I saw her purse her lips and push her glasses up to the bridge of her nose.

'You are beginning to sound like an undergraduate,' she said, and from the way she lingered warily over the last word I knew she meant it in the worst way possible.

'I know, I know,' I said sheepishly. 'But I was agreeing with you. My point was that locking it up and hiding it away is almost the same as destroying it. Van Gogh can't have wanted that.'

'Ah, but once again you are oversimplifying,' the professor replied. 'Artists have always painted for wealthy patrons, while collectors have always walked a fine line between aesthetics and investment. Without such a system of remuneration, without the financial speculation that comes with building a collection, the art world would not have been able to develop as it did, and our culture would be much the poorer for that. Your friend Doctor Gachet knew that – my research suggests his collection of Impressionist paintings grew to be exceedingly valuable. You, meanwhile, are not thinking things through. You are being as sloppy as the newspaper articles I read about the sale, and glossing over the real facts in favour of an interesting story. You know the reason all the reports fixated on the price?'

'Why?' I asked.

'They want to show the dichotomy. It makes for a good narrative: Van Gogh never sold a painting in his life, and now one has been sold for more money than any other work of art. Oh, the irony! Yes, it is a good story. But not an accurate one.'

'How so?'

'Van Gogh sent most of his works to his art-dealer brother, Theo, in exchange for money. At least two of these sold for decent prices, and there were probably more sales we don't know about. His uncle also bought a few. More importantly, those he did not send to Theo, he traded. He gave some to your Doctor Gachet in payment for treatment, which may otherwise have run to a great cost. Furthermore, he exchanged works with more established artists – for him, this was the very definition of success. If a Gauguin painting was selling for hundreds of Francs, and Gauguin was happy to trade one for a Van Gogh, then doesn't this mean Van Gogh was getting the equivalent of hundreds of Francs for his paintings?'

'Yes,' I leaned forward. 'At the very least it assumes they were worth roughly the same.'

'No, this is another common mistake,' she said with a sigh. 'Just when I thought we were getting somewhere! People always mistake value for worth.'

'Sorry,' I said, feeling chastened.

She brought her hands together in front of her. 'The worth of something depends upon the price it will raise in the market, depending on either the cost of production or the demand for such an item. A quick look at their sales at the time shows that works by Gauguin and Van Gogh were not worth anything like the same amount. But their value – well, that is something else all together.'

She peered at me over the top of her glasses, and in a second it made sense. I knew at that moment what Professor Buckridge had been trying so hard, in her own bumbling and pedantic way, to tell me.

I had misunderstood. Value was not dependant on anyone else. It could not be fixed by Sotheby's or Christie's. It didn't matter what some rich eccentric or stuck-up snob from the art world thought. What mattered was how it felt.

The painting's value depended only on what it meant to any person who might look at it. Its value was determined by how much comfort those sad eyes might give, how much solace might be found in that weary smile, how much of the viewer's own restless thoughts might be swallowed up in those restless skies.

We might give anything value by making it a part of our lives, by keeping it close. It needn't just apply to paintings. A pencil sharpener, an old keyring, a book or album, a favourite jacket, a seashell, a teddy bear, a faded blue stamp torn from the corner of a brown envelope, a rainbow scrunchie, a googly-eyed pencil-top monster, a used scratchcard: silly little objects that we might make valuable, as if through some act of magic, by charging them with the emotion of a certain moment and in this way making them a vessel for a memory. Value is something that, like love, we grant only to those things that exist not only outside us but within us too.

And more than that, value is something that survives. The worth of the canvas might rise with fluctuations in currency and inflation, or might tumble with changing fashions. Yet its value is something that carries on, no matter whether the canvas itself is destroyed by fire, or war, or bombs, or sieges, or battles, or travel, or mutilation, or theft, or decay. That it meant something to somebody is all that matters.

Only, of course, Professor Buckridge would not have put it that way. She was, like many Brits of a certain age, dismissive of anything that might be mistaken for sentiment. Her formal manner and academic exactitude made her suspicious of grand theories and unifying philosophies. She drilled her students that ideas had to be logical, rational, and soundly-supported by evidence. She disliked the abstract, the intangible. Those were not things she would have dared speak about in the cold light of day. But nonetheless I am fairly certain that this was what she had been trying to tell me.

This, I think, was the unspoken message behind each of our conversations: that what matters are the stories that speak to us, the stories we share, the stories that live on inside us. There is no value greater than this. And so I'll go on telling you the story that means something to me.

After a while Professor Buckridge got up and went ferreting in her drawers for biscuits she believed she had in there, some ancient custard creams that had probably last seen the light of day when I had been in here as an undergraduate. Meanwhile I steered the conversation round to her manuscript on medieval medicines. As she pottered around I kept one eye on the window, watching the students outside chatting, texting, smoking, drinking stray cans of Strongbow on the lawn, all ignoring their notes in favour of pretending that tomorrow will not come until they are ready.

# THE MINIMALISTS
## 1872

At first she assumed it was the house creaking. It did that sometimes, late at night, as if its joints were stiff after a long day and it needed to stretch back into shape, to flex out all the little knots and aches. Nonetheless, Blanche opened her eyes and sat up. Darkness covered everything like a thick layer of dust. She would not be able to sleep now. Even though she knew that the nanny would rush to the nursery and soothe little Marguerite if she woke with night terrors, Blanche's ears were too finely tuned to the sounds coming from the direction of her daughter's room. It was an involuntary reflex that had come with childbirth: the merest sniffle could cut through a dream. She waited a minute, maybe two, but heard nothing more.

Eventually Blanche snuggled back down, swaddling herself in her blankets. Even after eighteen months she still felt as though she might drown in the great expanse of a double bed all to herself. It did not seem right. She was still waiting. Sometimes the timber yawned, something in the walls sighed, the windows thumped against the catch, the drains gurgled, and once or twice a book had tumbled from the end of the shelf. But this was not one of those noises. She waited, waited, until at last it came again: a slow shuffling sound, like that of a chair being pulled to a table.

In an instant she was up, heaving on her dressing gown in the dark. Then, after much tired fumbling, she managed to make a light for the candle. She could have rung for the maid and roused the house to action. But something told her: no.

She tiptoed down the stairs and drifted through the sitting room, the dining room, the study, but all were empty. She checked the front door and the front windows, but all were shut for the night. Then once more: something between a sigh and a whimper. She knew now where it was coming from.

The kitchen was swimming thick in shadow, and the man sitting hunched at the kitchen table flinched at the candlelight she carried in. Blanche stopped in her tracks.

She could not move. Nor could she speak, though she realized with a jolt her mouth was open. She felt dizzy, as though the world had slipped from its axis and was spinning out of kilter.

She would not have recognized him were it not for his eyes, blinking up at her in the flickering candlelight. That strange sad wash of blue. The rest of his body, however, seemed to have been traded for that of a tramp. His uniform was ragged, and she could smell the sour stink of it from across the room. His hair was thin and greasy, his beard bristly and matted, while his skin was so pale his bones looked as though they had been wrapped in the most translucent gauze.

Both of them had been dreaming of this moment for months. It was the only thing that had kept Paul going this last year. Yet now, face to face, neither could summon the words they had planned to say. Paul wanted to go to his wife and take her in his arms, but seeing the shocked look on her face kept him rooted to the chair.

After a moment Blanche cleared her throat and set the candle down on the table between them.

'Paul,' she said.

He blinked, nodded, as though he was hearing her from across a great distance.

'When did you last sleep?' she asked.

He thought about it. He had probably averaged three or four hours a night – snatched fragments, broken shards of sleep – for weeks now. But nonetheless he smiled.

'I look that bad, eh?'

'No, I didn't...'

But her voice trailed off. For he looked unbelievable. Like someone had swapped her husband for a rag-tag beaten-down scarecrow. His hands were swollen, a purple bouquet of thorned callouses, and she noticed how unsteadily they reached for the cup of water he had poured himself.

'How is Marguerite?' he asked.

Even his voice sounded different, as though sand and shale had got stuck in the hollow of his throat. It made the hairs on her neck stand on end.

'She is good. Very good. But you know, she has missed you terribly.'

Paul nodded, thinking how ridiculous the idea was of the infant remembering him at all, but nonetheless he was grateful for the lie.

'Do you want to see her? We could tiptoe in if we're quiet?'

'No,' he said, and at once realized he had said it too quickly, too forcefully. He was not sure he could manage it, not all at once.

'In the morning,' Blanche said, trying to smile. But it could not quite settle upon her face.

He reached again for his water. She looked at the window, wondering what hour of the morning it might be.

She had followed the news, even when she could hardly bear to. Even out there in the countryside, the siege was all that mattered. Back in the winter, when the weather was calm, she had heard the distant thunder of shells raining down on the capital, and it had made her shake with fear for him. Once or twice when playing with baby Margo in the garden in the early morning, she had glanced up and seen a mail balloon drifting north across the sky, and she had prayed to the Blessed Virgin and all the forty-seven Saints whose names she could remember that it was not carrying bad news. But most of all she heard about it from the people she met. Young widows, mothers waiting for word of their sons, old men raging about the state of the war. And other women like her, desperate to believe that despite it all their own husbands might be spared.

It was no surprise to anyone when the country surrendered and the Prussians took the city. There can't be any French soldiers left by now, she heard the baker say, and she pictured the barbaric army marching in to Paris on a carpet of bones, their muddy boots going slipshod in the crunch. But still he didn't return, and with each day that passed she ate a little less, slept a little more fitfully. Then she heard the victorious army was gone, sated at last with its reparations, and rumour reached her of the commune.

Paul had seen it. He had left the makeshift surgery in the commandeered hotel and walked the streets amazed. It didn't matter that everything was rock and dust. It didn't matter that half the houses were now wrecks where rats ran wild. It didn't matter that each street now had its own glut of ruins and fire-gutted death-traps. Suddenly there was hope again. It was the kind of scene he had always been afraid to dream of: a new, fairer world rising from the rubble of the old failures.

After the occupants had left, the bitter and frustrated Parisians had taken over their city and set up a revolutionary commune. There would be no more sacrificing their young to wars that no one understood. No more crippling taxes to pay for the whims of their bloodthirsty government. No more of those rules that set each man against his brother. Paul could not believe his eyes. He could not go home now, not when there was so much work to be done.

The commune was an experiment in radical socialism. There was to be complete equality: no president, no mayor, no commander. Only brothers and comrades. They abolished military conscription, and set about the work of peace. They cancelled all the rents that were owed by those who had stayed in the city during the siege, wrote off the debts; they demanded that pawnshops return for free all tools and valuables pledged during the war; they abolished the charging of interest on any debts remaining from those dark days; they decreed that any business abandoned during the war could be taken over by the workers. In short, a clean slate. A break with the past. Paul would stay, help his comrades build something that would last.

It lasted about two months.

The authorities could not sit back and watch such a brazen display of socialism. When the troops of the humiliated Versailles Government reclaimed the city, they took brutal revenge on the citizens for trying to do without them.

It has been estimated that during 'bloody week' somewhere between 17,000 and 20,000 citizens were killed – many in mass executions – while around 38,000 were arrested and 7,000 deported.

But not Doctor Gachet. A doctor could still be useful.

And so they put him to work.

They don't need physicians, Paul had raged to Doctor Travere during the bloody purge. They need only undertakers. There are bodies twitching in ditches and they ask us to bandage wrists gone sore from firing too many rifle-shots.

But Doctor Travere had not replied. There was nothing to say by then.

Doctor Travere went missing soon after. His body was never found.

Paul had seen the firing squads. He was there when one-hundred and fifty shoving and sobbing men and women were lined up against Communards Wall in the cemetery. He had wanted to run forward, to stand between them and the soldiers, but his feet were frozen, and his mouth tasted of metal.

A coward, he thought. I am a coward and I deserve to die.

Tears had streaked his face, as foul and as fierce as the shit that streaked the quivering legs of the families cowering against the wall. Then the soldiers had fired. The army had to reload, once, twice, three times, four, again and again and again, to get all the bodies to fall.

He saw the mass graves, where thousands of corpses were tossed, some still squirming in the morass of blood and contorted limbs. He smelled the animal stink, and it got stuck in the folds of his clothes, in the folds of his skin. And he carried on.

Blanche had heard, but he had seen.

He had smelled.

He had tasted.

They would not talk of it. Not now. Not ever. Language is not made strong enough to hold the things he needed to say about it. Words are weak, fragile, brittle: they come apart in your hands.

So instead he swallowed them, let them grow hard like a stone in the pit of his gut. The place that sadness comes from. The place you put memories you do not want to remember.

The same memories you cannot forget.

Blanche tried once more to smile. Paul wanted to go upstairs and see his little girl, marvel at how she had grown and changed since he had left, but how could he now? How could he look at her without feeling that burning shame. Shame that he had stood by and done nothing. Shame that he had patched up the executioners, and left his comrades and brothers in those makeshift pits. She would see him, and be ashamed too. He knew it, deep down, with a certainty he could not escape. For how could it be any other way? So perhaps that is where the look comes from: it is an acknowledgement of the things he has seen, the things he could not do, the things he cannot say.

'We have thought about you every day, you know that,' Blanche said.

'And I you.'

But the words seemed forced. It was as though they had just been introduced – a potential match pushed together by well-meaning family but who, in truth, had nothing in common and little to talk about.

They fell back to silence.

The candle flickered.

Their shadows twitched, made nervy and uncertain by the ragged light.

Paul looked down at the table, at his cracked and battered hands, and wondered if perhaps a part of him too had been left there. If all that remained was a ghost. If somehow they had swapped places.

Blanche stared at the hands of a man she did not recognise, and wondered if perhaps there was no way back now. The past cannot be reclaimed. He needs a bath, she thought. A good meal, or two. Some comfort, some care. And in that moment

Blanche understood: love can be learned, and it must be re-learned. Love is a verb, it is an action. There was work to be done. She fixed her eyes on his until he finally looked up once more and met her stare.

'Are you back?' she asked.

At first he was not sure what she meant.

Was she trying to find out if he was back home for good or was just on leave?

Was she asking if he was there with her, or whether his thoughts were still elsewhere?

Or was she asking if it really was Paul underneath it all, if he might be able come back to himself?

'Yes,' he said. 'Yes, I am.'

They both smiled at one another, and he reached his calloused hand shakily across to her. She took it.

# A WAREHOUSE ON KOPERNIKUSSTRASSE

## 13 January, 1938

'Imagine a place where everything is backwards,' the Führer said.

They were gliding across Berlin in a sleek black Mercedes, though it felt like they were skimming through a cloudless sky, so small and distant did the world outside seem. Perhaps, therefore, it would be more accurate to say that a sleek black pterodactyl was swooping through the Reich Capital, and that, at least, would explain why the workers in their patched-up suits by the canal, the harried women running errands to the butcher or tailor, and the tousle-haired kids playing truant all stopped and stared as it drifted past, their dumbstruck faces reflected back to them in the blacked-out windows.

'Imagine a place where filth is celebrated and wallowed in,' Hitler continued. 'A place where strong and virtuous men are ridiculed, a place where able and loving mothers are spat upon, a place where the weak and the spastic rule. That is where we are going. For this, we must steel ourselves.'

They followed the police escort around the corner of Kopernikusstrasse, and the engine thrummed and purred as the car came to a stop. Hitler picked up his visor cap with the gold insignia from the leather seat beside him, placed it on his head, and waited for the chauffeur to open the door.

They were parked on a small patch of gravel with weeds nosing through. Nearby was a rusty water trough and a large warehouse with a tin roof. It was not an auspicious start to the afternoon.

Goebbels had been lurking at the entrance of the warehouse, talking in hushed tones with the armed guard, but now he came limping toward the car to greet the Führer (yes, Paul is not the only character in this story with a limp, and Goebbels' bad leg was also with him from childhood: he wore a special metal brace to correct his deformity, and though, in reality, he had been turned down for military service because of his ailment, this did not stop him telling those he met that his limp was the result of a war wound he had suffered while in heroic service of the Fatherland).

Hitler smiled at the short, pale man making his way toward him. Goebbels was stick-thin, with a long, haggard face, and empty eyes that seemed to have the power to look at a man and see straight through to the other side. With his Italian suit, slicked back hair and face that seemed permanently on the verge of sneering he looked like a B-movie version of a Mafioso snitch.

'Mein Führer,' he saluted. 'Are you ready for the grand tour?'

The Minister of Enlightenment and Propaganda led the way past the guards – hands stretching rigidly up toward the sky – and into the warehouse. Inside it was filled with countless metal stacks meant for storage of munitions and machine parts. The smell was musty, like the slightly sour musk of old books. Without the harsh light from the bare-hanging bulbs, the empty building might have been mistaken for some abandoned temple or tomb. As the two men strode between the rows the rhythmic thud and thwack of their heavy black boots, falling in perfect synchronicity, echoed off the tin walls.

They were there, of course, for the paintings. Thousands upon thousands of paintings, each one of them propped up and ready for inspection.

Though the war had not yet properly begun, the looting was already in full swing. These works of art had been confiscated from museums and private collectors alike and brought here, for they were, each and every one of them, morally reprehensible. They showed sensuality, individuality, wild and uninhibited joy. They documented the kind of unrestrained emotion that could only unhinge the mind and drive good people to irrational acts. They were corrupt and abnormal, and lacked self-control. They could teach the morally-upright citizen nothing. Therefore, they had, each and every one, been labelled as 'degenerate art'.

It was a working definition that came to include Impressionism, Modernism, and even jazz. What it meant in practice was anything that did not fit the racial ideals and strict conservatism of the Nazi regime. In other words, it was anything Hitler did not like; anything that showed a spirit that could not be brought under control.

The two men walked past works by Cézanne and Kandinsky, Picasso and Paul Klee, the bright and lustrous bathers of Matisse and the dream-like animal visions of Chagall. The Führer did not speak.

They paced on to the second row of the warehouse, glancing left then right then left at the paintings they passed. Goebbels was starting to grow nervous. Hitler still did not speak.

It is well known that Hitler was once an aspiring artist, just as the one thing most people know about Joseph Goebbels – the man who at that moment was running his cold and clinical eyes across each masterpiece in turn – is that he killed his six children before killing himself.

Let's be accurate: on the 1st May 1945, he told his five daughters and one son, then aged from four to twelve years old, that they needed inoculations to stay healthy inside their bunker under the ruins of bombed-out Berlin. What they were actually injected with was morphine; once they were unconscious, Goebbels had cyanide crushed into their mouths. After he was sure they were dead, he shot his wife, then turned the gun on himself. I am not repeating these gory details just to be lurid: this is one of the few men who touched the painting, who held it in his hands – he is part of its afterlife, and it is part of his. Besides, disturbing facts tend to stick in our minds, and more importantly I cannot help wondering what the tipping point is when death becomes more attractive than life. The war was lost by then, and Hitler had already committed suicide. Terrible rumours were circulating about the Soviet troops who were fast approaching the city: even if the children were spared rape, torture, brutal imprisonment or execution, then they would no doubt live the rest of their lives as pariahs, scapegoats for the fallen Reich. There was no way out. *Perhaps*, Goebbels's wife Magda said in the days before the end, *they would face a better chance through reincarnation*.

As a young man, Adolf Hitler applied twice for the Academy of Fine Arts in Vienna. Both times he was rejected. Nonetheless, despite his lack of success, he did not give up right away. In the years leading up to the First World War he lived off his dwindling inheritance in cheap boarding houses in Vienna and spent his time either painting watercolours and oils of postcard scenes (farmhouses, old buildings, fields of flowers), or else strolling round the city with a fancy ivory cane pretending he was a great artist. His paintings are decidedly amateurish, though this is no crime. What is worse is the startling lack of originality. There is nothing he painted that was not a cliché, that had not already been done to death. The tall castle from a fairy tale. The vase of flowers on a table. Meanwhile, his portraits resemble the cartoon caricatures that giggling children knock off in the back of classrooms. He had passable skills at depicting buildings – the flat vistas, the solid brickwork, the ornate battlements – but lacked the ability to bring people to life.

It is hardly surprising that he wanted to be an artist. The lonely, the misfit, the frustrated, all are drawn to the alternative reality offered by art. Sometimes whole tribes of outsiders emerge, like those dandies, beats, hippies, punks, goths, emos and countless others who have found in poetry, painting, or music some better reflection of who they wanted to be. The best art touches some unspoken need inside us. And it is true that those who are most captivated by art are often those who are dissatisfied with life as they find it, and, like Hitler, desperately seek to remake the world. I know that impulse, for right this second I want to do the same thing: I am desperate to rewrite this historical scene and have one of the heavier, badly-balanced paintings – a huge triptych with a thick, solid frame of oak or pine – suddenly come toppling forwards and smash into his head, falling at just such an angle that the hard corner cracks Hitler's skull and sends him into a coma from which he never wakes.

No. I'm sorry, but that wasn't quite good enough and I'm not happy with it. Because if I really could remake the whole world, I'd go just a little bit further: in the warehouse is a degenerate painting of blackbirds in the black branches of a twisted black tree, and suddenly the birds burst through the canvas and their furious beaks peck frantically at the Führer. Poor Goebbels looks on in horror as the blackbirds pluck out each of the hairs in Hitler's stupid little moustache, and then even the tree climbs out of the picture and uses its sturdy roots to clamp around his legs as it crushes him between its branches. Or, better yet, there is a straight swap: Hitler is sucked into one of the paintings and frozen forever, trapped in two dimensions beneath the surface of the canvas, while some bearded goat with a mandolin trots out into the world, made anew in skin and bone.

They rounded another corner and Goebbels had to fight the urge to clear his throat or dab at the dots of sweat now bubbling on his brow. Hitler had his hands clasped behind his back as he marched past another masterpiece. Neither of them spoke. Another handful of paintings. Another wrinkle of the nose and shake of the head.

*It is truly terrible*, Goebbels would go on to write in his diary. *Not a single picture finds favour.*

They kept walking in silence, following each row around to the next, passing hundreds of canvases stacked side-by-side.

There were prophets with mournful faces, lakes and gardens shimmering with sunlight, dancers with unrestrained glee on their faces, self-portraits of unremarkable men and ordinary women, pictures of smiling Jews, pictures of unsmiling Jews, pictures by Jews, pictures of men who can fly, fat nudes, hairy nudes, leery nudes, blotchy nudes, wimpy nudes, lumpy nudes, nothing-out-of-the-ordinary nudes, goats sitting on clouds, men with patchwork faces, collages where colourful triangles of newspapers flutter like birds, woodblocks of spindly trees at twilight, etchings from booze-soaked nights at seedy cabarets – and there, amid them all, was Doctor Gachet.

He had been confiscated from the *Städelsches Kunstinstitut und Städtische Galerie* in Frankfurt, where he had been hanging for the last twenty-six years. He was a recent addition to the warehouse, and now Adolf Hitler paused in front of him. Their eyes must have met, if only for the briefest second. Then the Führer turned on his heels and kept marching.

Gachet was lucky. Many of his neighbours in the warehouse on Kopernikusstrasse ended up on bonfires. In March 1939, the Berlin Fire Department set light to more than 1,000 degenerate paintings and close to 4,000 sketches and watercolours for a practice drill, while, in 1942, approximately 4,000 degenerate works of art were incinerated outside the *Galerie Nationale du Jeu de Paume* in Paris, among them masterpieces by Picasso and Dali. Yet somehow Doctor Gachet survived.

How do you get caught in one of the fiercest currents of history and still manage to swim away unscathed? Simple: economics. Herman Göring (morphine addict, commander-in-chief of the Luftwaffe, and big fan of old tapestries) realized he could make a little capital on the paintings Hitler hated. A few weeks after the leader's inspection of the collection of degenerate art, Göring commandeered some of the paintings from the warehouse and furtively put them on sale. He sold Gachet on the sly to Siegfried Kramarsky (who would take the painting with him to start a new life in America with his wife Lola) and used the profits to buy some antique tapestries to hang on the walls of his country house.

Hitler and Gachet exchanged glances. That much is certain. There is no record of the Führer lingering longer over this painting than any of the others, but nonetheless I cannot help suspecting that the two men saw something they recognized in each other's eyes. One in well-pressed uniform and full regalia; the other in a scruffy old suit that a peasant might wear. One precise, calculating and given to extremes of emotion; the other abstract, lost in thought, given to days of melancholy. I suspect neither liked what he saw. The dictator no doubt despised the weakness of a man who could not bring his emotions under a more rigid control. The doctor meanwhile would have been unimpressed by the fastidious philistine before him, though whether Gachet would have been more appalled by Hitler's bad taste or by his lack of empathy is a matter for debate.

The two men marched down the last row of the warehouse and toward the next appointment in the Chancellor's busy schedule. It would be foolish to think either Hitler or Goebbels were much changed by that disappointing afternoon. Despite what we would like to believe, art on its own cannot change the world. Or, at least, not as often as we would like.

But paintings do change. Over time, without care and attention they may crumble, decay, or wear away. Through exposure to extremes of light or temperature, the pigments fade, the tones warp, the layers of paint flake and crack, until after many years the painting may become unrecognisable. That is not what happened in the warehouse on Kopernikusstrasse. Doctor Gachet had always smiled sadly. Yet after that day – after their eyes met for those few seconds and they stared one another down – his smile was that little bit sadder.

# MOTION SICKNESS
## 1875

The stars, skimmed like pebbles across the night's murky canvas, bucked flickers of light through the bedroom window. Paul tracked their progress, measuring out the hours till morning. Every time Blanche as much as murmured in her sleep, he reached for her wrist and counted her pulse, and every time her eyelids began to beat in time to the depth of some passing dream he pressed the back of his hand to her forehead to check her temperature. If her leg twitched, or her stomach rumbled, or she rolled over and nuzzled her cheek against the pillow, he would sit up alert in bed, ready to pounce and take her blood pressure, to dab with a cool flannel, or to light the bedside candle and peer frantically down her throat and deep into her ears. He tried to lie still so as not to disturb her, but he could not help himself and so every few minutes he checked his pocket watch, or rose on tiptoes and paced across to the window. If he had been a praying man he would have prayed, but instead he stared bleary-eyed at the stars until they faded into dawn so that he could tick off another night reclaimed against the odds.

Although Paul had a horror of horoscopes and the quacks and cranks who pedalled them, the restless motion of the constellations across the heavens gave him comfort, for he recognized that he could no more give in and stop than the universe could. Like him, it was all jitter and movement. Like him, it spun on relentlessly into the darkness.

Sometimes her sleep was disturbed, and she would wake

with a start and draw fluttered, birdlike breaths, as though she was drowning in air. It was those moments he was waiting for, since it was only in those moments that he knew what to do with himself. He would run his hands through her bedraggled hair and hold a cold compress to her sweaty brow, and every time she would say the same thing:

'Where?'

Without a pause he would answer her. 'By the shore. Marguerite is collecting the prettiest seashells, and little Paul is playing in the sand. The tide is coming in, the waves lapping over our toes. The seagulls are picking off the last remains of our picnic – can't you hear them?'

And with that she would slip back into her hazy fog of half-sleep, both of them willing themselves to believe in the illusion that they were anywhere but trapped in that airless bedroom that stank of sweat and sour milk.

'Where?'

'Aboard a train, flying through the countryside. We have an important soirée to attend, which is why you are wearing the most beautiful, new, green dress. But I suspect we may play truant from the party and instead follow our whims through the Paris streets. In the meantime we are sitting together in the train carriage, racing towards the city, and we will surely be there soon. Can't you hear the steam-engine huffing away?'

She kept her eyes still closed, as though to stop herself from seeing that it was not real, and they remained screwed shut even during those fits when she would hack and cough and retch until she had covered his hankie with flecks of blood.

'Where?'

'On a hot air balloon, cruising above a grand palace built before the revolution. We are peering down at the tall towers and imagining ourselves the king and queen of the skies.

Flocks of birds soar past us, and the houses below have shrunk so small they might all fit inside a matchbox. Can't you taste the candy-floss clouds we're drifting through?'

She sighed and tried feebly to roll to her good side. He had moved their bed closer to the window so that she could be propped up on a mound of pillows and look down at her foxgloves, the sprays of violet and mauve, the curls of tiny trumpet mouths that looked, she said, as if they were about to burst into song. He opened the window to let in the smell of the flowers, but leapt up to draw it closed whenever the mere hint of a breeze whispered in.

'Where?' she asked, when she could summon the strength to speak.

But he never said what he wanted to say. He never said: *here*.

The nights were bad, as he lay in wait for signs of the fevers and chills that seeped into her dreams like drops of ink falling into clear water, but the days were worse. He was half-drunk with sleeplessness and worry, and he paced endlessly around the house, getting under the feet of the servants; in fussing and fidgeting he made such a mess in each room – by pulling down medical tracts and obscure journals in his study and throwing them aside in frustration when he could not find the hope he needed, or by upending cushions and blankets and bedding and rugs in his hunt to get rid of any lingering trace of dust that might impede her recovery – that the maids were forced to scurry always in his wake to keep any semblance of order and cleanliness in the cottage.

Meanwhile, Blanche slept fitfully upstairs, waking when the coughing overcame her and she had to claw at the sheets for breath. Other times she read, and when her red eyes grew tired or the pages shook in her hands, he read to her. Though he no longer took the train into the city each morning (he had shut his Paris practice until further notice), he still ran frequent errands to hunt for increasingly-obscure medicines, and each time he returned home bearing books – the latest Daudet, Gaboriau, Barbey, Zola, or Huysmans – so that, for a few hours at least, her mind might escape its cage.

There were books everywhere in their cottage, since Paul had long been convinced that art – by which he meant not only paintings, his first love, but also music, poetry, theatre, novels – would come to supplant religion in France. In the past, the stories told in church had helped people see beyond their own lives and catch sight of that invisible thread that joined each man to the next. For Paul, art fulfilled that same function. People could forget their worries in the lulling rhythm of a gentle melody, step through the pages of books into other people's lives, and travel through time and space in paintings of places they had never been. Paul would have said it is the same today: our inner lives and our imaginations are moulded more by iTunes and Netflix than by scripture.

After a hard day, we let our stress melt away in blockbusters, box-sets, or video-games. From these stories we pick up the ideas and motifs that help us get through life – the ultimate triumph of good over evil, the certainty of there being one true love for everyone, the hope of the happy ending waiting for us just around the corner. Paul said it himself: we are addicted to anything that reminds us there is more to the world than our private worries.

So he lived for paintings. She stepped into novels. And as proof that Paul was right, we can meet them there. We can travel across a vast and incalculable distance and find them in those stories: we can trace our fingers over those exact same words Blanche read in *Lettres de Mon Moulin* or the various books of *Les Rougon-Macquart* and find our imagination meeting hers, or we can look at the glowing brushstrokes of 'Soleil couchant à Ivry' and see where Paul's mind flew to. Or to put it another way, as long as the things they loved remain, Paul and Blanche are not completely dead. Part of them is right here, among us as we speak.

In short, Paul was always busy. There was not a single minute of the day when he was not engaged in some vital task. He kept going, because he knew that if he stopped, for even a second, then time would catch up with him and stillness would claim the whole cottage – but if he kept moving then he might somehow stay one step ahead, evade its grasp, keep her from its cold fingers.

For the same reason, he kept up a ceaseless flow of chatter whenever he was near her, as though to protect her from having to hear her own thoughts. 'I got another letter this morning, from Guillaumin. You won't believe what he has to say about Paris. It's almost unrepeatable! But he has saved us that one you adored from last summer's exhibition, 'Sunset at Ivry'. Do you remember? It was that one with all the orange light over the river. There were chimneys huffing out smoke in the distance, and you could see the clouds carried along in the flow of the water. I can collect it in a fortnight, and then I thought we might hang it in the bedroom. You know, it reminds me of those walks we used to take along the Seine, back when we were courting. Do you remember?'

She would nod her head, and occasionally smile at his rambling anecdotes and plans and reminiscences, but never too much, for even a giggle could shred her throat and lodge like a shard of glass in her chest.

On warmer days he would help her downstairs and settle her in a wicker chair in the garden facing the hills.

'Ah now, here we go. You know, if I only had the right palette, I think the view this afternoon would make the perfect picture. The trees just before they turn into silhouettes. It would be quite something. All those dazzling yellows and sharp greens. Can you picture it?'

She nodded her head. Outside she was swaddled in so many blankets she resembled a bulging cocoon fit to burst. For the most part she kept her eyes scrunched up, even under the shade of the parasol, like a nocturnal animal who had no memory of light and feared the way it picked out every startling detail.

'Promise me something,' Blanche said, that afternoon in the garden.

'Anything.' Paul had settled into the chair beside her, and was counting her pulse.

'This house...' She gestured at the cottage.

'*Our* house,' he corrected.

'Sell it,' she said.

At first he thought she was joking. Then he saw her face: her eyes now open and staring at him, sticky and pleading. Her clammy hand clutched at his wrist.

'Please.'

'You would prefer to return to the city?' he said. 'To be near your parents?'

'I do not mean now.'

There was a seasick feeling churning in his chest.

'This is foolish talk, we must not give in to –'

'No,' she said, her voice hoarse and cracked. 'Listen to me, Paul.'

He nodded, his hand covering hers, his tongue too hot to speak.

'Sell it. Move far from here.'

'We made a vow, and I will never –'

'Take the children, and find a house that is not stuffed to the attic with memories.'

'But –' he whispered. His voice sounded childlike and pleading.

'No! I mean it. I do not want my children – our children – to grow up surrounded by dust and ghosts. I do not want them to breathe in that stale air every day. It will suffocate them. Go, go anywhere, far from here. Find a wife, I beg you, for they will need a woman's softer touch – even more so now. Take yourself to –'

Her hoarse speech was broken by a fresh volley of coughing, and he hurried with his handkerchief and water.

'Come, you will make yourself worse.'

'Promise,' she hissed.

'This is silliness. You know as well as I that there is still –'

'*Paul.*' Her voice was a broken rasp. 'Have I ever before asked anything of you? Please, give me that little comfort. Promise.'

He sucked in his breath, and understood there was nothing else he could do.

'I promise,' he said.

And, almost instantly, he cursed himself for giving in, for not crossing his fingers behind his back.

Instead he ran his hands over the arched knots of her spine, both of them too worn down to carry on that stinging conversation.

Sometimes, during his restless rush through each day, Paul felt as though he was losing grasp of himself, as though his personality was being rubbed away, like the dark lines of a pencil sketch being steadily erased, until all that was left was smudges. Either he was fading, he thought, or else he was becoming overshadowed by the sickness. And though he did everything he could to fight against that feeling, there was a part of him that resented her for it, that hated seeing her skinny and wasted and almost translucent – and worse still hated her, viciously, for not getting better.

So instead he tried to focus on keeping her fit. She was pale and all angles by then, and it was all he could do to feed her soup, lifting the spoon himself and coaxing her on with gentle praise, just as he used to do with his son and daughter.

'I'm afraid this consommé is not quite right, Madame Baudin,' he would say, bursting into the kitchen and hovering around the cook. 'A little less salt, I think.'

'Very good, Doctor,' Madame Baudin would reply through gritted teeth.

'We need to get the lady of the house eating, you see.'

'Of course, Doctor,' the cook would answer, trying not to get flustered when he peered over her shoulder to check how she stirred the stew or kneaded the bread.

'Perhaps something sweet today would do the trick.'

'Of course, Doctor.'

'A warm dessert to revitalise her appetite.'

'Very good, Doctor.'

It was only when he started taking over her stove that Madame Baudin found she could contain herself no longer.

'Forgive me, Doctor, but is that a test tube?'

'Ah yes, but I will not be long. I just need to distil these sprigs of horehound – maybe add some fawn's milk, yes, yes, that would be good – get it all ready for the lady of the house, and then I will be out of your hair. Now, where's the honey?'

Once he had concocted his homeopathic remedies he would wander off, leaving a sticky mess and acrid smells in his wake, and Madame Baudin muttering about the indignity of dirty weeds and other muck being brought into *her* kitchen.

The children, meanwhile, stayed out of sight. A nanny looked after the tiny baby boy, while Marguerite at six had already learned to talk in whispers, to find hushed and secret kingdoms in the quietest corners of the house, far away from the echo of her mother's incessant coughing.

There was always something to do, something to check on, something to attend to. The local doctor visited (Paul had sought out second, third, fourth opinions, even though he knew the prognosis was beyond doubt), and ran the weekly tests. He was a timid, friendly colleague of Paul's, and each time he came he made various recommendations to save from having to spell out the obvious.

'How about a sanatorium? They're the latest thing for consumptives. Fresh air, enforced rest, may do her a world of good.'

'No,' Paul always replied. 'She must stay with me.'

'As you wish.'

There were times when Paul wondered whether he was being selfish, whether he stopped her going to a sanatorium or a hospital or a specialist ward because it was better for her or because it was better for him. At those times he wished he had not chosen to become a doctor, because all his meticulous learning, not to mention the decades of practical experience he had painstakingly accrued, meant nothing if he could not save her. He knew what was coming, and knew there was little he could do. He had never felt more lost.

This sounds, of course, like an exaggeration – like I am falling back on the familiar tools of hyperbole and embellishment. After all, he was a doctor. He had seen worse. He would have coped, surely?

I know what you want to say. Has he forgotten the last

few chapters so quickly? He was in a siege, for heaven's sake. He'd worked as a medic on the front line and seen the casualties pile up each day. Shouldn't he have been able to deal with a single case of consumption without falling to pieces?

And not only a siege. Paul had hung around Paris for the bloody aftermath. He had watched the firing squads do their bloody work. He had seen more than he could ever explain.

Yet this was precisely why he was now so lost. He had carried on, had done everything he needed to do just to get home – to get back to her. Is it any surprise that he became a man who fetishized the ordinary, the mundane, the everyday? He had learned how precarious each moment was, how powerless each of them were, how small – like twigs tugged along in the currents of history. He had come back home and clung to his wife and young children even more fiercely.

So it was no exaggeration: he had never felt worse. Because at some point the war, the executions, the teeming graves, all began to seem like a dream. They were not real in the way she was. It was one thing to see a stranger's body collapse, and another to feel the breath faltering in the body he had slept beside for a thousand nights. A body that he knew as intimately as his own, and loved far more deeply and passionately. Without her, he would not have been able to survive it.

Later that afternoon he was making his way from the kitchen with a pot of restorative tea. Blanche was napping fitfully in their bedroom, and since he had been unable to persuade her to take even a bite of food that day, he had decided the least he could do was make sure she did not end up dehydrated. Paul was halfway up the stairs when he happened to glance up at the painting on the landing. It was a landscape by Pissarro that the artist had given him a few winters before, when he had come to stay with them at the cottage: 'Chestnut

Trees at Louveciennes'.

It was a haze of milky-white snow. Three gnarled trees stretching out their skeletal limbs, their branches nuzzled by frost. In the background a red house, the sloping roof and chimney slippery with snow, cordoned off by a rickety picket fence. Everything on the edge of melting into light. The dazzle of the freshly-fallen snow forced the eyes to squint, and so nudged the whole day out of focus. In the distance the fuzzy silhouettes of evergreens. And from the gate came two figures treading carefully though the flurry. They were dressed in warm winter clothes, the woman in black and the little girl in an oversized coat with an orange scarf wrapped around her neck and head. They were holding hands and moving steadily forwards, as though walking out to meet the viewer.

Paul realized he had stopped, in the middle of the stairs, the tray of tea still in his hands. But he did not start climbing again. Instead he stayed where he was, his eyes fixing upon the painting. It had always been one of his favourites, but now it seemed suddenly different. There was something bittersweet about the fading light, the way winter hovered between hope and hopelessness. The girl could have been Marguerite's age, he thought – still just a baby really, all puppy fat and wild wonder at the world. The woman was as pale and thin as Blanche had become. And the more he stared, the more it seemed to him that those two figures in the painting were getting closer. It was as though they were almost within reach.

He heard a fuss of footsteps on the landing – the maid doing her rounds – but it was not enough to rouse him from his thoughts. He had been startled from himself, his worries suddenly lost in the picture. There was an unearthly quiet to the piece, a sense of time suspended.

He could dimly hear the maid fussing around the bedroom. Usually he would have called out and ordered her not to disturb her mistress, but he was too immersed to open his mouth. The branches of the trees were growing heavy with snow. Spindly shadows reached out towards the edges of the frame.

The little girl's features, though hazy, were just about discernable: dark eyes staring ahead, a thin line of a mouth. But the mother – for it has to be her mother, does it not? – had no face at all. There was nothing beneath her hood but a smear of paint. Her face was blank, as though it had been wiped away.

Then the frantic shouting brought him suddenly back to the present – the maid was screaming his name.

He almost let the tea tray fall clattering to the floor. The maid was screaming his name. He heard the call echoing down the stairs, and the sound of panic above and below as the house responded, but he could not move. He knew it instinctively, and with complete certainty, for in that instant he felt some part of himself gone, as though he had been pitted like a peach and his whole centre tugged out, and so he knew without moving that there was no longer any need to climb up the stairs, to find a way to put one foot ahead of another (if such a thing was even still possible) for it was already too late.

# REPLACEMENT

Let me tell you a secret: you are already dead.

In fact, your cells are continually dying and being replaced. It takes only seven days for your entire skin to regenerate, and in only seven years each and every cell in your skeleton will have died and been replaced. The person you were as a child, as a teenager, as a young adult, is already lost. You are not who you used to be. That person died many years ago. Every atom of your body has been replaced, utterly and completely. Even the wild alchemy of the brain, its soupy tangle of neurons and sparks, is not the same one you thought your first thoughts with. You are not who you think you are. That person is long dead.

So what happens to the you that is lost? These days, it is easy to find. Many of us are stored in pictures, kept in family photo albums or posted online, just as Paul lives on in that painting. We do not go anywhere. Click a button: you have been saved. Or, at least, a part of you has been.

But what happens when you become a painting, when you are caught in a photograph? You move from one place to another. A magic trick. A transference of something from body to screen. You are both that you far away and the you at the end of your fingertips. But you are also neither.

Is it a kind of splitting or a kind of doubling? Could it be that every time the camera clicks you are cleaved into another copy, sliced into another part, or rather, that with every doppelgänger you produce, you grow in power and in reach? You stretch to meet the ever-expanding edges of that ever-expanding digital universe. But are you lessened by this, or are you strengthened by it?

At any rate, though your cells are continually dying and being replaced, the same is not true of your double. Your body might take around a decade to decompose, depending on the coffin you choose – that is, if your ashes have not already been scattered and settled back into the soil, into the sea. A print photograph, unless kept in pristine, temperature-controlled conditions far away from sunlight, will soon begin to fade, and within a century will be impossible to recognise. But a digital image? As long as the servers remain active, your image may still be alive in five hundred years, a thousand years, or more. You will have been definitively replaced by your doppelgänger, your fake.

The same could be said of the painting. Like your own dying body, it never really disappears. Instead it multiplies. The original is supplanted by simulacra: posters, prints, and postcards become screensavers, 3D projections, holograms, memes. We are drawn to sadness like moths drunkenly circling a blazing bulb. And we also multiply ourselves, perhaps because deep down we know that our cells are continually dying and being replaced.

And so of course we die many times. We die a little every time someone forgets us; in some languages the word for memory is the same as the word for ghost. That's why we have to remember.

# THE HOUSE OF THE BROKEN PROMISE
## 1883

A country track curves round from the village. It is banked by tufty patches of grass and a low stone wall. Ahead, a few frail and lanky trees, and a couple of threadbare clouds in the blue bedraggled sky. At least, this is the view in Paul Cézanne's *La Maison du docteur Gachet à Auvers*. From the road we can see an off-white house, close to the colour of clotted cream. It squats in the centre of the canvas, stark and disjointed but with its own magnetic pull that draws in the eye.

Cézanne had been there many times, though for the most part only to visit Doctor Gachet's best friend, Camille Pissarro. The older artist was a charismatic teacher, his long salt-and-pepper beard sweeping down to his belt buckle, and he often held forth about the ways to free art from the stuffy academy. It was Pissarro who had taken his protégé into Paul's garden and shown him how to capture the light – how to do away with laborious preparatory sketches and pencil outlines, and instead to flick paint straight onto the bare canvas in rapid brushstrokes that would build into small bursts of colour. Find those feelings most alive in yourself out here, Pissarro had said to Cézanne, and get them down at all costs before they are lost.

*Simple*, Cézanne had sneered. He was cocksure and dismissive, and so, without a second thought, he got down to business: in Doctor Gachet's garden he dashed off a hurried and dazzling version of Manet's *Olympia*. *Look*, Cézanne had said. *It is child's play*. But, nonetheless, in the following years all his paintings were done outside.

*La Maison du docteur Gachet à Auvers* shows us Cézanne's subsequent abandonment of classical technique for something more free and exciting. This is not the perfect recreation of every finicky detail that you might find in a photograph, but the world as the senses experience it, from many different perspectives at once. It is the living landscape, messy and instinctive and daring us to admit we do not see things quite the same each time we blink.

But this was painted in 1873 (then given to Paul in exchange for medical consultations and a few of his trademark herbal elixirs), and after that Cézanne did not come back to the house for many years. This was not remarkable. His temper was as fierce and unpredictable as his experimental canvases, and he had a habit of changing his mind: he no longer spoke to Pissarro, nor to Monet, Degas, Renoir, or the rest of the old gang. Cézanne worked in isolation now, alone and increasingly obsessed by failure. However, he had also begun to feel uncomfortable in that whitewashed cottage. It wasn't the clutter and the chaos of it that bothered him – he was an artist, after all – but the feeling that the house was more like a mausoleum now, lorded over by a rambling old scarecrow with a pipe always between his lips. Something about the place made him uneasy.

He was not the only one. Renoir had also not been back to the haphazard cottage in quite some time. He had been somewhat disturbed by his last visit.

Renoir was an artist in love with the sensuality of colour, and the characters who populate his lustrous paintings are radiant and full of the warmth of life: their cheeks glow, their eyes spark, their smiles glisten. Yet the painting he had given

Paul was not like that at all. It was a small portrait of Renoir's model and lover, Margot Legrand, and it had been a gift in return for a favour.

This was by no means unusual. Paul was always more than happy to trade consultations for theatre tickets, or to swap medicine for books. He had a still life of chrysanthemums from Monet given to him as a repayment of a loan, and had received countless other works of art as gifts and favours: among his sprawling collection were dozens of paintings and prints by Pissarro, Guillaumin, and Cézanne, as well as a handful from Sisley, Gonzales, Monticelli, Guys, Delpy, Piette, and Cestero. He was not ashamed to admit he was an oil and canvas addict. He was swimming in paintings, like you and I might swim in songs – we hear something that makes us want to dance or shout or cry and we download it, so we might hear it again and again and bring that feeling whenever we need it. Like any addiction, it cannot conceive of limits. Paul's house was therefore not a house: it was a universe, and at any point he might step into one of the many worlds around him and disappear. It was the only thing that helped carry him through from one morning to the next.

The painting of Margot showed a sad-eyed girl with chestnut hair and a boxer's swollen pout. Renoir was besotted with her. Then suddenly she had been taken ill with a high fever. A rash spread across her arms and shoulders like ferocious blots of ink and turned her body into a canvas, so in his fear and despair Renoir urged his old acquaintance Doctor Gachet to call upon her. Paul of course agreed, and visited her sickbed. He helped clean the weeping pustules, and sat chatting with her hours on end, returning each day until the scabs and lesions began to turn to scars. In return for his kindness, Renoir had given Paul his most recent painting of Margot.

Yet the story does not end there. The smallpox was not gone, only biding its time. Soon the blisters bubbled back up and spread to her palms and the soles of her feet. There was nothing now that could be done. She died a few weeks later.

Renoir had therefore been a little shocked when he next visited Paul in Auvers and spotted – amid the mess of painting tools and old books and overgrown pot plants and boxes of rough tobacco and untamed papers and the many shelves of stoppered jars in the doctor's study – that small portrait propped up on his desk.

*Portrait dit de Margot* focuses on the young lady's head and shoulders – her body below fades into half-finished brush strokes. Renoir's usual portraits were awash with majestic blues and crisp whites and fiery reds, yet this is a painting composed from shadows. His lover is dressed in a black suit and a black top hat, with a white scarf knotted around her neck. In her sombre clothes and stiff pose it looks as though she is impersonating her own undertaker. She is seen in profile, her eyes half-closed and on the verge of tears as she stares off into the distance. She knows something terrible that she cannot share.

'Ah, please do not think me rude,' Paul had explained when he noticed Renoir staring at his own painting. 'I had it hung in pride of place, I promise you, but it is one of those that I turn to often. I keep it down here so that it can be a little closer to me when I sit at my work, so that I might have someone to talk to.'

Renoir had opened his mouth and then closed it again. He could be a shy and sensitive man, but was also full of a nervous energy that kept him always alert. It had taken him a while to find the words.

'I do not know how you could bear it,' he said at last, his

face turned away from the portrait.

Paul had set down his pipe. 'Do not think I do it for pleasure,' he replied. 'Though I must say it is certainly a beautiful painting. But no, I do it because I must. It is our duty to them.'

'I'm not sure I follow you,' Renoir said.

'It is basic logic. We remain, and so we have a responsibility. Come, my friend, you feel it too. We must keep them, sustain them.'

Renoir had looked at the bottles and jars upon the shelf and had in that instant a premonition of them all filled up with memories – the stuff from which spirits are formed, distilled to their primal essence – and he felt a shiver trickle down his spine.

'How often?' Renoir asked, gesturing at the desk.

'Every day. If I do not willingly grant them a little time, I fear they will take it anyway against my will, and leave me with nothing left over.'

Paul picked up his pipe and went searching for a pinch of tobacco to plug it. Renoir watched him potter about the chaotic study, uncertain as to whether he ought to feel grateful or resentful. On the one hand he felt a kind of jealousy, for she did not belong to this doddery old man, and yet at the same time he realized with a horror how terrible it would be for her portrait to be hidden away and her life forgotten.

'I could have looked at her forever,' he said.

'Ah, well, you see, you are not one of us,' Paul replied. 'All our friends prefer landscapes. Only you make pictures filled with people. You see right inside them. Those thoughtful faces, so lifelike – I envy you that power. You are a sorcerer. The champion of death.'

Renoir had taken a step back at those remarks. The doctor's sad passion unnerved him.

Gachet merely waved his pipe. 'Come, come. You know it too. The people in your pictures live inside that moment. She lives here.'

'It is not enough.'

'No,' Paul lit his pipe. 'Of course not. But we cannot expect more.'

Renoir had gone away feeling that he had left something behind – though willingly given or stolen he could not say. The old doctor seemed to him like a priest who had decided God was not up to the job and so had given up his faith, yet remained in thrall to those empty rituals no matter how sad they made him.

But Renoir left misunderstanding something vital. It was not Margot that Paul saw when he looked at the portrait. It was all of them. The faces of the patients he had lost in the asylum, in the cholera epidemic, in his private practice. The soldiers fallen on the front line, the starving in the siege, the hundreds he saw executed in the crackdown after the fall of the Paris Commune. Even his good friend Manet, dead only a month earlier from the syphilis that Paul had been unable to treat. Some nights, when he could not sleep, his insomniac mind attempted to add up how many that might be, but he could never complete such melancholy calculations. So instead he tried each day to look at the pictures, to keep them with him and so to carry on.

As for Renoir, he was not completely scared off. But from now on he troubled Paul only when he was desperate: when he caught pneumonia, Gachet was the first doctor he called. But his honesty could be a little frightening. *Things do not get better for those left behind,* Paul told him. For Renoir this was startlingly accurate. In time his rheumatoid arthritis would grow so terrible that his joints swelled up and he limped worse than Paul, then soon his body knotted so stiff he became wheelchair-bound and handicapped, while his hands seized into claws, leaving him calling out hoarsely each morning for his assistant to place the paintbrush between his bandaged fingers.

Paul had become a custodian of something whose glare was so powerful that Renoir himself could not stand to even glance at it. It is like the sun, he thought – stare too long at its savage blaze and your eyes will blot. But the doctor had been looking so long now his eyes had long since been forged into something new.

At the very least, this theory would explain why, on that lazy Saturday afternoon when they had no guests and the schoolbooks had been set aside, Paul let his son take a woollen winter scarf and tie it around his head as a blindfold.

'Now, is everything ready?' Paul asked.

Paul Junior giggled as he set up the chessboard upon the rickety table in the living room. Then his father reached forward, his fingers rubbing over the rough edges of each hand-carved chess piece until he found the one he wanted.

'Really,' he told his nine-year-old son, 'this is the only way to play.'

'You're being silly, Papa.'

'No, I am deadly serious. Now pass me my pipe,' he said, and then grasped around until he had picked up a paintbrush lying nearby. He placed it between his lips and pretended to take a puff, and though he did this every time they played, his son nonetheless fell about with glee.

And in those moments of glee, yes, right there, he felt it like a splinter pushing itself in the thin aorta of his heart.

On some occasions he claimed the blindfold was necessary

so that his mind did not wander away into the magical paintings that hung on every wall, and other times he told them his own parents had forbade such frivolous games and so he had been taught to play by a rebellious servant who gave him lessons at midnight after everyone else in the house was asleep, and since that day he could only play in the dark. But the truth was far simpler: he liked letting his son win, but he could not bear the big broad smile that lit up the boy's face when he claimed his victory, for when he smiled he looked just like his mother.

Marguerite, at nearly fourteen, peered over at the two of them in exasperation, then returned to her book. Like her mother and grandmother, her hands felt empty and awkward when they were not peeling through pages.

'Why not join us, Marguerite?' Paul called over through the blindfold. 'I can take you both on!'

'Really, Papa,' she chided. 'I am much too old for games.'

On afternoons and evenings like these, her work for the day done, she usually sat at the piano, and stumbled over some halting, jumbled melody, too shy these days to sing no matter how much they coaxed her, though occasionally she would forget herself and, her mousy hair falling about her cheeks, she would hum along in a voice as wispy and quiet as a breeze between branches.

She was a slip of a thing, yet newly gangly, all elbows and blushes, and already she was beginning to try to hide her beauty by hunching and keeping her eyes down whenever Papa's artists and their latest companions visited. In truth, he did not know what to do with her.

With Young Paul it was easier. He still knew all the tricks to make him snigger, could still race him round the garden, spend long hours lost in epic games of hide and seek or rum-

my played for piles of matchsticks, or lose an afternoon con-
structing Aladdin's caves and pirate hideouts from blankets
and boxes and then hunkering down together in an imaginary
world. The boy suffered from persistent nightmares – they
came crawling like insects into his ears, to lay little black eggs
in the hollows of his brain – and the only consolation was that
when he woke, breathless, his Papa would always be sitting at
the end of his bed, ready to lull him back to peace with outlandish stories: of an enchanted kingdom where the rain fell
hot, as toasty as marshmallows from a bonfire, where Christmas lanterns bobbed in the sky all year round and school was
always out, and where men and women ate cloud-cakes and
took tea with eagles, until the boy slept a sleep born on the
warmth of the old man's voice. In truth Paul felt disappointed
when his son slept the whole night through. There was a part
of him that longed to shake the boy from his slumber so that
he would have an excuse to be there telling tales.

Yet Marguerite was a different kind of creature, elusive
and impossible to second-guess. Everyone had muttered about
the problem of girls without mothers, yet there were few
missteps at first. For the first few years he had bought them
Christmas and birthday gifts from their mother, but in the end
this had led to too many questions about where she sent them
from, and why she couldn't be wrapped up and sent back to
them too, so he had given up that small tradition, though he
never succeeded in stopping the children making presents for
her, unopened packages that sat in the corner throughout the
festivities and so seemed to him a kind of accusation – he had
muddled on as best he could. He still kept only two servants,
the same old cook and maid, and taught Marguerite the same
history and algebra and grammar and music lessons he would
have taught a boy, but he had a sense recently that some switch

had been carried out while he was sleeping, for she treated him now as though she were the parent and he the child.

It was Marguerite whose hand he always felt upon his shoulder whenever he sat too long staring off into nowhere, Marguerite who roused him from sinking too deep, and Marguerite too who managed the servants and planned the menus while he fiddled with his etching press or went out to call on patients. She had asked him recently what her mother had been like – had *really* been like – and during his stammered and reeling reply, he sensed her looking at him with something akin to pity, that same look he had seen from couples and families in the village, the one that reminded him that the hole in his life was visible for all to see. Though he knew he ought to let her go out into the world instead of skulking around in the shadow of the past, every time she left the house he was gripped by a clammy dread that would not leave him until she returned, and so at home they made wide and complicated circles around one another, both father and daughter awkward and overly polite so as not to risk seeing too close into each other's lives.

'Why don't we go to the magic room before supper?' he carried on while groping for a pawn to move across the board. 'It is the perfect day for it. It would be a shame to waste all this light, eh? Let me show you how to etch. You would enjoy it, Marguerite. Maybe flesh out a scene from that book? Inscribe it in your memory so you don't forget it?'

She did not reply. Instead he heard only the swish of another page in her novel being turned.

The 'magic room', as her brother called it, was at the top of the house – its large window facing north so that the light that beat between the hills could puddle upon the thick-rugged floor. It was here that Gachet had taught Pissarro, and later

Guillaumin and Cézanne, the careful art of etching. He longed to teach her too, but she would not be drawn in. Would not now even enter the room. She had protested that this was because where art was concerned she was clumsy and unskilled (unlike her brother, who even now would ape Papa by carrying his sketchbook everywhere he went, scribbling out rough impressions of every face, landscape, or oddly-hewn object that caught his eye), though Paul could not help but think it was her way of showing that she would not follow, that her life was not the same as his.

Later that night, after supper had been cleared away and the lid on the piano set down, he climbed the stairs and wondered whether it was the floor that creaked or his own body.

Perhaps you are wondering why I have picked this day.

After all, I can pick or choose any day of his life I want. Why bother with a lazy Sunday when no one of importance visits? After all, I have already skipped the bulk of his formative years, avoided focusing too much on his time with his father and mother before he was fully formed, raced past his years of medical training, passed over his café conversations with the likes of Victor Hugo and Gustave Courbet, failed to mention his love of music and friendship with contemporary composers, stayed firmly outside the doors of his practice, ignored the bulk of his courting, and even let the Paris Commune and its bloody aftermath, perhaps the defining political and social event of his lifetime, happen off-stage.

OK, when put like that, I'm well aware that it could easily be argued I'm making a complete pig's ear of this attempt to find the point in his life where that melancholy look took root.

But on the other hand, to bring back every day would be an impossible project, and would fill more paper than exists upon earth. I want to travel to the place the sadness flowed from, and I have no reason to suspect we will find it in those grand public moments when he was forced to act a part or else sat in thrall to one of his many famous friends. We will find it when he was alone, when his guard was down, and the raw wound of his life was bared.

I have picked this Sunday because it was typical of that year, and the year before, and the year to come. It was ordinary, normal, banal, as each of our own lives often are. There was no explosive drama at all – but life is made of more than just those explosive moments. And the deeper currents of our hearts are set in those everyday moments, when we have nowhere else to focus but on the raw marrow of our minutes, hours, days.

Is it enough?

In the words of Doctor Gachet himself: *Of course not. But we cannot expect more.*

As he reached the landing Paul heard his daughter push her chair up against the closed door (there was no lock to her bedroom, so she had to make do). He sighed. He liked sitting at the end of their beds. He liked watching their chests heave gently up and down as they slept, their eyelids flutter, their bodies twitch and heave like sailboats trying to shrug free of their moorings. He liked being close enough to get a glimpse of their dreams.

He went in to Young Paul's bedroom, and found him at the first foot-twitching drift of sleep, the covers lumped around him like a camp. He stood for a while, watching the boy's breathing slow as he drifted deeper, keeping time. At last, when he heard the call of the clock downstairs, he tiptoed out.

He did not hurry to his empty bed – after checking on the boy, he always made sure he had something else planned. Many nights he ventured out, escaping from himself. Earlier in the week he had been to dinner with a palm reader and a Chinaman, and the previous evening he had been to a concert in the city – he went obsessively to every performance of work by the eccentric musician Ernest Cabaner, and even went as far as collecting all of the composer's scores, which he kept not by the piano but instead beside his bed so that a little of that wild music might seep in while he slept. Meanwhile every Thursday he attended the banquets of the *Societé des Eclectiques* in little restaurants in the Left Bank where he talked for hours about new science and old poetry.

But tonight he had no appointments, no invitations, and so after he had made his way back downstairs he slipped off his shoes and padded into the garden.

He needed to be away from the sound of the maid scurrying about the house, the hiss of guttered candles, the persistent metronome of the grandfather clock; he needed to be in the company of creatures he could talk to without fear of being pitied.

He curled his bare feet upon the damp grass, drunk with dusk, and began to converse with the animals he kept there.

'How have you been today, old Mr Turkey? Hmm? It's no good shaking that wattle at me. I know you've been up to no good!'

He left the clucking turkey and ambled on across the overgrown lawn, saluting each animal individually.

'Now where is my proud strutting prince?' he asked, hunting for the peacock. 'There's no use putting on airs and graces, you know, I'm much too old to be bothering with that.' Then he strolled among the hens, wishing each one a good evening and a good night. He walked over to the goose but decided against stirring it from its sleep. He picked up first a tubby ginger cat, and then a duck whose feathers he stroked, whispering to them good-naturedly as he continued his rounds in the moonlit garden.

He wandered amid his menagerie until his eyes could no longer make out either shape or form in the darkness.

And in that moment of blindness he thought of what everyone had told him in the first terrible weeks after it had happened. In time these feelings will lose their heat and fade to embers, to ashes. That was what they had all said. Things get better. It gets easier. But he understood now that this was a lie.

# GOLDFISH

When I was about five years old, I had a goldfish. He came home with us in a plastic bag from the funfair, and lasted about two weeks, a gobbet of rust lurking nervously at the bottom of a punch bowl. In accordance with British naval traditions, he received a burial at sea, which I later learned meant that my parents had flushed him down the toilet. On reflection, his death was probably caused by the fact that I fed him breadcrumbs and other scraps leftover from dinner, though at the time I was convinced, from the mournful way he circled the bowl, that he missed the fairground and his friends. It seemed obvious to me that he was homesick, and wanted to be back bobbing in his plastic speech-bubble beside twenty other goldfish at the coconut shy.

My parents did their best to assure me that was not the case. Goldfish, they told me, cannot hold more than five minutes' worth of memories in their heads. Therefore he cannot remember the funfair at all. But this did not make me feel any better – how much worse it must be, I thought, to miss something terribly and yet not be able to recall exactly what it was.

I was reminded of all this years later, in my first term at university, around the same time I first saw the *Portrait of Doctor Gachet*. I thought of the goldfish when two friends started arguing in the college bar. They were both Christians, both studying theology, and yet they took great pleasure in riling each other with their opposing views.

I have never been a particularly religious person, but nonetheless their argument interested me. When I sat down, Neil was proposing that, in Heaven, we will remember everything. Since the Almighty is omniscient, the afterlife must be a place of unbounded knowledge. It therefore makes sense that every tiny detail is reclaimed. Every minute of joy we have forgotten, every single second of human experience, is returned to us. We finally find the answer to every question. No matter what has happened to our bodies and brains by the time of our death, in Heaven our souls are whole again. Nothing is lost.

Ed shook his head. Don't be ridiculous, he responded. If you were to remember every second of panic, every twinge of pain, every misjudged word, every argument, every petty humiliation, every long hour of boredom, every sleepless night, every tiny worry, every moment of grief or heartbreak, then that would be Hell, not Heaven. It must logically follow, he argued, that in the presence of the Lord we are finally able to let go of all the little regrets that weigh down our life on earth. There is no time up there, and therefore no looking back. In Heaven, memory relinquishes its terrible grip on us. We remember nothing, and exist (if that is the right word, for by then we will surely be beyond existence) only and always in the present tense, like goldfish, free at last from our sorrows.

I have thought about that argument a lot since then. But it seems to me that if we no longer remember, then we are no longer ourselves. Not really. There is no way to wipe the slate clean without erasing something vital of our histories, our hearts. The reason most of us cling to photos, books, heirlooms, keepsakes, gifts, trophies, letters – all those vital old possessions – is to remind ourselves who we were, who we want to be, and who we might yet become.

Possession is a strange word. The verb form in particular is a double-edged sword: it has sharp edges. We possess things but we also run the risk of being possessed. The more we control, the more we might be controlled. The two meanings are intertwined: as much as we would like to believe it is only the big things – lovers, friends, children, schools, cities, jobs – that change our lives, the same is often true of objects, for once we give them value they have a kind of power over us.

Think of the *Portrait of Doctor Gachet*. Before it was confiscated by the Nazis in 1937, it hung for twenty-five years in the *Städelsches Kunstinstitut und Städtische Galerie* in Frankfurt. In 1911, when Georg Swarzenski (the director of the gallery) acquired the painting, the museum was devoted to old masters, its galleries filled with Renaissance art from France, Germany, and the Netherlands, along with Romantic and religious works from more recent centuries. It was a hallowed place, created to guide and elucidate the citizens of Frankfurt, all in keeping with the Kaiser's rigid focus on moral lessons and his hatred of modern art. The wild and kaleidoscopic image of the sad doctor must have stood out like a streak of lightning in those hushed rooms. A modern man contorted by grief and pain, staring out amid a sea of classical landscapes and old saints: he was a roar of ear-splitting feedback in a world of silence.

His presence changed the Städel Museum. When the shock died down, the walls around him began to grow more colourful in an attempt to compete with his explosion of light. Meanwhile, after the Great War stole half of Frankfurt's boys, and brought back the other half broken in either body or mind, the damaged old man no longer seemed so out of place. He was now the city's melancholy saint, and one by one his subjects and disciples came to him: by the start of the 1930s he was surrounded by canvasses howling with raw emotion, by the alienated and the shattered, and by the wild apocalyptic visions of the Expressionists.

The effect is not always so obvious. Take its previous owner, Count Harry Kessler. When he bought the painting in 1904, he was the director of a museum in Weimar, a renowned aesthete and a newly-minted aristocrat. During the seven years that Doctor Gachet was displayed in the house where the Count entertained artists and met furtively with his gay lovers, Kessler wrote papers on Impressionism, travelled around Greece, hosted fantastic parties, and even collaborated with the poet Hofmannsthal on opera librettos and ballets. He hung out in Monet's studio, dined with Degas, rode round town with Nijinksky, gossiped with Verlaine, traded jokes with Sarah Bernhardt, lent spare change to Rilke, and debated the merits of air travel with Count Ferdinand von Zeppelin. In short, he lived the high life and he loved it.

How strange then to think that only a few years after he sold the painting to the Städel Museum in 1911, this flamboyant and sophisticated art-lover suddenly had a change of heart: when the First World War broke out he enlisted as an officer in the German Army (even though he was in his late forties) and travelled to the front. Am I suggesting there is a direct link between the painting and this sudden change in his life? No, of course not. There is no way to know quite what effect the painting had on him, though I believe it is not that ridiculous to ask whether he would still have thrown in the liberal life of the connoisseur and social butterfly and gone instead to the trenches for the Kaiser if that sad old man had still been watching over him.

Or consider Alice Ruben Faber, the first owner of the portrait, who bought it from the Van Goghs in 1897. As an aspiring artist, she was drawn to its startling beauty, and as a free-living heiress she must have been delighted by its power to shock (she herself had already gone against the rigid social rules of her time by divorcing her first husband and sticking a finger up at her wealthy father by giving her support to a strike taking place at one of his factories). She was impetuous and forward-looking, but also suffered from tuberculosis and fought frequent bouts of crippling depression. It must have been a comfort then to have a doctor around, especially one whose melancholy expression suggested he had been through the same and knew how hard it could be. This might explain why, in a private photograph of her lying in bed, pregnant with her first child, the portrait is sitting close by on the bedside table. Doctor Gachet's sad eyes are keeping watch, reminding her that she is not the only one who has felt this way.

The objects we invite into our lives, the possessions we invest with meaning, sometimes come to have a strange hold on us. They help us remember, and for that we owe them a debt, because without them we would be goldfish, untethered from the past and so strangers in our own lives.

# EXCERPTS FROM THE CORRESPONDENCE OF VINCENT VAN GOGH IN THE LAST YEAR OF HIS LIFE

*From Theo van Gogh to his brother Vincent, Friday, 4 October 1889*
... the director of the asylum paid me a visit, and he seems to hold you in high regard. His kind face spoke volumes. He told me that he does not think you are mad at all. In fact, your crises appear to tend more toward epilepsy. He says that at present you're perfectly healthy, and if it wasn't for the fact that your last episode was so recent, he would have encouraged you to venture out from the asylum more frequently. Nonetheless, he advises caution. Yet if you can hold out and continue with your recovery, he sees no reason why you should not leave in the near future.

As to the question of where you might go when you are released, I have talked to Pissarro. I have the strong impression that his wife is the boss in that house, and so it was no real surprise when he told me yesterday that it would not be possible for you to stay with him. However, he has a friend in Auvers, a doctor who paints in his free time. He's close to all the Impressionists, apparently, and Pissarro thinks you could stay at his home for a while. He's promised to visit him and ask his opinion. If you could find something around there, that would certainly be a good thing...

*From Vincent van Gogh to Theo, Saturday, 5 October 1889*
I like the sound of Auvers, and I think we ought to focus upon that option instead of looking around elsewhere. If I travel up north, I'm sure that even if there's no room in this doctor's home, he surely would be able to help me find board with some local family or at the inn. The important thing is to get to know that doctor so that if, God forbid, I am overcome with another crisis, I have someone there who understands and can ensure I am not delivered into the hands of the police and dragged kicking and screaming back to the asylum.

*From Theo to Vincent, Saturday, 29 March 1890*
I truly wish I could be with you tomorrow on your birthday. Will you celebrate or are you still too awash in unhappiness for that? What do you get up to during the day there – are you able to distract yourself from your thoughts? Are you able to read, and do you have all you need?

After your last letter I was hoping you had started to recover, and I prayed you would soon write that you were feeling yourself once more. Dear brother, it is hell to be so far away and understand so little about what is happening to you. That is why I am happy that I can at least report some little success: I have met Doctor Gachet, the man Pissarro told us about. He seems like a man who understands such things. Funnily enough, he even looks a little like you. When I told him about your episodes he said he didn't believe they had anything to do with madness. If it was what he thought, he said he ought to be able to help you, but of course he needs to see you in the flesh before giving a more definitive prognosis. Have you asked Doctor Peyron about you leaving the asylum yet? What news?

*From Vincent to Theo, Friday, 2 May 1890*

I agree. I must go myself to visit this doctor as soon as I am able... You remember 6 months ago I told you that if I ended up suffering from another episode I would beg you to let me move? We have reached that point. I fear that the little reason and capacity for work I have left is in terrible danger the longer I remain in this place. Yet I am sure I can prove to this doctor that I can still paint, and therefore I hope he will look after me. Perhaps, since he is an art lover, we may even become close friends...

*From Theo to Vincent, Saturday, 10 May 1890*

Yesterday I wrote to Dr Gachet to find out when he will next be in Paris, for he gives consultations there. I have also asked that he find out about lodgings for you.

*From Vincent to Theo, Tuesday, 20 May 1890*

Auvers is a beautiful village, with a sky that skitters above many old thatched roofs of the traditional kind that are dying out elsewhere. If I might make a few pictures of this, there is a good chance I might recoup the costs of my stay. The countryside here is so beautiful it almost scares me.

I met Dr Gachet, who I must say seems rather eccentric. His medical experience must come in handy, for he is clearly fighting the same demons and ailments that have been afflicting me. He is suffering at least as seriously as I am!

I have found an inn for only 3.5 francs a day, and for now I will stay there...

You'll no doubt see Dr Gachet this week. He has an incredible painting by Pissarro, with two figures walking through the snow in front of a red house. And also a Cézanne of his house in the heart of the village. As for me, I will happily follow in their footsteps and turn my brush to this place.

Yet his house is stuffed to the rafters with odds and ends from many decades passed. It is dark, dark, dark, except for those sketches by the Impressionists I told you about. Yet though he is a decidedly odd creature, I have to say I am growing fond of him. When he talked to me of the days of the great painters, his grief-hardened face began to smile again. I do believe I will paint his portrait. He says I must keep working, and not think at all about what has come before. Only in that way will I escape the past.

*From Vincent to Theo, Monday, 24 May 1890*
... I only keep bothering you about my little nephew because I care about him. Since you wanted to name him after me, I cannot help but pray he will have a less anxious soul than mine – which, I am sad to say, is struggling to stay afloat.

I went to see Dr Gachet the day before yesterday, but could find no sign of him. Yet I have nonetheless been working hard and have made four painted studies and two drawings, and I am planning a larger canvas.

Let me be frank: I believe we cannot count on Dr Gachet. For a start, he is far sicker than I am, and that is saying something. When the blind lead the blind, they will both go tumbling into the ditch. My last crisis was due in large part to the influence of the other patients, and the doctors in the asylum left me to rot along with the rest, who were already cankerous. I do not know what else to say.

*From Vincent to Theo, Sunday, 25 May 1890*
I saw Dr Gachet once more today, and I shall go to paint at his house on Tuesday, then lunch with him and show him my latest pieces. Perhaps I misjudged him. He seems more reason-

able now, but is as dispirited with his work as a country doctor as I am with my painting. I told him I would happily swap places with him! But I think we will in fact end up being good friends. He told me that I should not be ashamed to speak to him of my darker impulses, for if the melancholy takes hold he could do something to make it loosen its grip. I fear that moment may come, but today at least all is well.

*From Theo to Vincent, Monday, 2 June 1890*
I am certainly most interested by all you write about Dr Gachet. I do hope you will become close friends. I would love to have a doctor as a friend, for every day now I find myself wondering where illness comes from.

*From Vincent to his mother, Thursday, 5 June 1890*
Do not worry, the doctor here is most kind. I visit his house often, and he tells me all the latest gossip about what is going on among the painters these days. He suffers from some nervous disorder himself, no doubt due in part to his wife's death, and so he understands. He has two children, a girl of 19 and a boy of 16. He assured me that if I keep working I can conquer it. Besides, I can pay him in paintings, which is a blessing, since everything is ridiculously expensive in the village here.

*From Vincent to his sister Willemina, Thursday, 5 June 1890*
Returning to the north has been most beneficial. Dr Gachet has become something like a brother to me, for we resemble each other not only in our appearance but also in our outlook. He has his own nervous tics and odd habits too, and has helped and befriended many artists of the new school. I painted his portrait a few days ago, and I also plan to paint his daughter. He lost his wife a few years ago, and I think it is this which

broke him. We became friends as soon as we met, and I spend a few days each week at his house, working in his garden and painting all the cypresses, roses, marigolds and vines that grow there.

Yet what I care most about right now – far more than anything else I have worked on – is the portrait. I seek it through colour, and I am not alone in doing this. I dream of making a portrait that would appear to people living a hundred years from now as something akin to a ghost. I do not mean to do this by creating some photographic resemblance, but by bringing out the passion in a man's expression. Thus my portrait of Dr Gachet shows you a face the colour of sun-blazed brick, his hair all flame, his cap white, with deep blue hills behind him that melt into his deep blue suit. He has a surgeon's rough and heavy hands. Upon the red table he has some novels and a purple foxglove picked in his garden...

*From Theo to Vincent, Thursday, 5 June 1890*
We are delighted to hear that you are doing well and that the countryside has had a beneficial effect upon your health. Dr Gachet came to visit me yesterday. We could not talk for long as there were many people around, but he did tell me he believes you are much better and he sees no need for any of it to ever happen again.

*From Vincent to his sister Willemina, Friday, 13 June 1890*
... In the portrait Dr Gachet has that look of startling heartache that one might at first mistake for a grimace. Compare it to those calm and placid ancient portraits, and see how much expression we have in our heads today – these days our minds are aflame with passions and it is all we can do to stop them running wild. Sad but gentle, clear and intelligent, that is how

the portrait must be. It is a head that people will look at for a long time, and centuries from now it might still seize them with regret...

*From Vincent to Paul Gaugin, Tuesday, 17 June 1890*
It is really uplifting to hear you liked the portrait I did based upon your drawing... my good friend Dr Gachet looked at it for some time before saying: 'How hard it is to be simple'. Isn't that the truth! I am going to etch it, then I will be done with it. Whoever wants it can have it.

In addition I have recently done a portrait of Dr Gachet with the heartbroken expression of our time. Perhaps it is as you said of your own painting: some things are not destined to be understood.

*From Paul Gaugin to Vincent, Saturday, 28 June 1890*
... I have not met Dr Gachet, but I have often heard Pissarro speak of him. It must be a great joy to have someone nearby who understands what you are trying to do, and who feels your ideas as keenly as you.

*From Theo to Vincent, Tuesday, 22 July 1890*
My dear Vincent, I pray that your health is good. You said that you are having trouble writing, and you have not told me anything about your work in some time, and so I cannot help but worry that something is upsetting you or that circumstances have changed. Please take yourself to Dr Gachet, and perhaps he might give you something that can restore your spirits. Please send me news of your health as soon as possible!

*Doctor Paul-Ferdinand Gachet to Theo, Sunday 27 July 1890*
It is with the utmost regret that I must disturb your day of rest, yet I believe it is my duty to write to you at once. At nine o'clock this evening – Sunday – I received message that your brother Vincent needed to see me without delay. I went to the inn and found him most sick. He has wounded himself...

# RESURRECTION OF THE FLESH
## May 1890

The hens shuffled round in mad and loping circles, backtracking and crisscrossing the worn patch of garden around their coop, hugging tight to the border where the claw-gashed dirt turned to tufts of grass as though some invisible line forbade them crossing. Paul watched them for a while, then reached again for his pipe.

The old doctor and his new acquaintance sat a few feet back from the birds, in the shade of a crooked cypress as old as the house.

'So you are saying all remedies would be useless for me?' the young man asked once more.

'Not at all,' Paul replied. 'Some herbal teas will calm your spirits and aid your digestion, some valerian may help you sleep through the night, and I have many homeopathic medicines we might try to keep the attacks at bay. But on their own these will only temper it by degrees.'

Paul continued to suck on his pipe, occasionally pulling it from his mouth and using it to punctuate his advice, gesticulating in movements so generous that clumps of ash fell upon his scuffed blue suit.

'You see, some sicknesses are in the body,' he continued. 'The virus, the disease, the contagion. But many others are conjured by the mind. When my wife died, I spent a year in the kitchen. I brewed up wild herbs and shrubs, I distilled elixirs and new medicines. I kept my test tubes bubbling at the stove for many long nights. Nothing helped.'

The younger man leaned forward, his fingers drumming restlessly on the table. 'Then what worked?'

'For me?' Paul looked somewhat confused at the question, as though he had been asked how he kept the sun in the sky.

'Yes.'

'Time,' he said at last. 'I carried on. Because what is the other option?'

'I have wondered that.'

'You keep going, because you must.' Paul sighed. 'It is both exceedingly simple and agonisingly difficult. But you must also find distraction. I can see that you do not go many nights without the bottle – do not deny it. The signs are clear. You must try to stop, or you will never bring these fits under your control.'

'It is not easy.'

'I do not expect it to be. But I can help you learn temperance. And, yes, some compassion. You must care for yourself. We must summon the will to believe there may be some better future ahead of us.'

'Yes, yes,' Vincent began to get quite excited. 'The future, that is why I paint – that one day a man might see my paintings and understand.' His hands were like the fluttering wings of an agitated bird, and since he could not keep them still upon the tabletop, he raised them to his bearded chin. He was afflicted by all manner of tics and twitches. His hands flailed, one moment thrust deep into his pockets and the next swinging helplessly at his side or reaching up into his sunblushed hair, trying to tame a strand that had fallen loose over his eyes. He seemed absorbed in something more pressing than the conversation between doctor and patient in that rambling and unkempt garden, but Paul paid this no mind, for he had seen worse, and he himself had come to learn how much the body can be a stranger to the man.

Paul reached across and put his gnarled hands over Vincent's own. Within a second they were still, but nonetheless he kept them there, pressing tight, feeling the warm, clammy skin against his own.

He understood it then, that the two of them might have been brothers. Two rough stones rubbed down to the rawest nub by the constant eddy of unstoppable currents. He recognized in the younger man that sense of a life disjointed, of feeling like the clock is always five seconds behind no matter how often it is wound – because he felt the same. Two men who found the world only made sense when caught inside a canvas.

'And that is why you must put all your energy into the work. That is the only way. The idle brain latches onto any small concern until it has magnified it beyond all proportion. So you must focus upon the task in hand – I have all the supplies you might need, and they are yours whenever you want them. There is even a printing press upstairs. We could work in my garden together here, what do you say?'

A gaggle of ducks came waddling past them. Paul removed his hands from the painter's and sat back in his chair. The sun was skimming an arc towards the hills, and he pulled his cap on tighter to keep the light from his eyes.

'I would like that,' Vincent replied. 'But I do not know how much my brother told you. Whatever happens, I wish to continue working, for without that there is nothing. But sometimes I lose hours, days. My head sometimes feels as though it is full of echoes.'

Paul nodded patiently as the younger man took a deep breath to calm himself.

'When you cannot bear the world in your head any longer,

turn to the outside world, and paint. That is all we can do.'

For a while they did not speak. The ducks honked from the other end of the garden. The sun dipped quickly beneath a corner of frayed cloud, then appeared again remade. But soon the younger man was fidgeting once more in his chair, and Paul leaned forward to try to catch his eye. Vincent looked up and stared hard into the doctor's pupils.

'You do not know how it gets. I fear it will return at any moment.'

'I have been to war. I have seen far more hopeless cases.'

'And this?' Vincent's hands swept nervously towards the left side of his face. 'You cannot keep pretending it is not there.'

'Oh, I never pretend,' Paul said patiently. 'It is beyond my ability. But I have not asked because I do not care about how or why. The past is behind us. Try to carry it all with you and the weight will slowly crush you. But for the purpose of a full diagnosis, let me get a closer look at the scar tissue. Come now, do not be ashamed, I have been where you have been and I know the way back. Yes, that's it.'

Vincent raised his straw hat for a moment and Paul leaned forward.

He peered closely at the mottled petal of curled and ruined skin where the lobe should have been.

'Ha,' he said. 'It is nothing. Barely the bottom nub. Oh no, I doubt losing that tiny bit of cartilage will have affected anything. You know why our ears stick out like that, don't you? To catch sound before it rushes past. But between you and me, I think we missed a trick. Wouldn't it be wonderful if we could move them? Think of a dog, or, better yet, a wolf, pricking up its ears to hear a call coming from a great distance. Imagine being at a symphony and turning your ears towards each player in turn! Ah, well, such are the quirks of evolution. Still, perhaps in the future our species may develop such skills.'

Vincent bristled at this and set his hat back down. 'You do not give credence to such poppycock?'

'I consider myself Darwin's disciple. I cannot think of a better theory to explain how we ended up stranded in this hopeless state. Yes, I believe it, my friend, most certainly. There is no more rational explanation as to how we have come to be here.'

The painter smiled a crooked smile. 'I cannot agree. Suppose I put on a blindfold and flicked paint at a canvas. Would the end result be a portrait filled with passion, with life, with energy?'

'No, of course not, but –'

'It is the same,' Vincent went on. 'The world is greater than any canvas, and like the best works of art, it was created by a compassionate eye. It had life breathed into it by One who understands. Look around you, at the starry night, at the wind bending the wheat in the fields, at the expressions on the faces of your fellow man, and you will see the artist's signature, His Divine fingerprint.'

Paul nodded and smiled, 'Surely a work of art can only become a masterpiece when the artist has ensured his work is free of imperfections. And yet that is not true of the world in which we live. Nature is a work in progress, just like our beloved Republic, and like the Republic we must hope it gets better with the years. We can adapt, we can change. Yes, I believe we must. Over time, by imperceptible degrees. What other hope is there for the future than that one day there will be better men than us?'

'Indeed. But do not forget another hope for the future

that the Lord has planned for us: the resurrection of the flesh.'

'No.' Paul set down his pipe.

He wanted to say that he had seen more corpses than he could count. On troubled nights he still saw those men and women with eyes dripping from the sockets, with limbs ripped from their bodies, with their stomachs come unstitched, with great jagged holes of blood and bone where their faces should be, and so he could not believe there was any way they could be put back together again. Were he at a dinner party, he would have taken great delight in shocking the assembled guests with his macabre opinions, but now was not the time; he did not want to upset this more sensitive friend.

'No,' he went on. 'We shall have to agree to disagree. But it is enough that we are both optimistic for the future. That is the important thing, to have hope that there is something better ahead. But I am being a poor host. There is something I want to show you inside before you return to the inn.' Paul rose creakily to his feet. He offered his hand to Vincent, who stood as straight as a new recruit called to attention. Shooing away the old turkey skulking by the backdoor, he led his new friend into the house. Inside was dark and dry. Here and there, light managed to slip between the curtains and blinds; Paul was well used to it, but he could see Vincent squinting blindly as together they picked their way through the cluttered room.

'Sorry, but I must keep the shutters closed,' Paul explained. 'Too much light can daze the eyes, I find, and make it hard to think. Besides, a little darkness helps train the eye.'

Vincent did not reply, for if it was a joke then it was one that did not sit well with him, and if it was not, then that was something else altogether.

Though Paul knew by heart the best path through, Vincent found himself forced to tread carefully to avoid stumbling over the jumble of objects strewn across the darkened room. There were canvases, yes – upon the walls, of course, but also propped against the door, the cabinet, the bookshelf, and one even lying upon the table. But, more than the art there was a vast collection of odds and ends: books piled upon the rug, paintbrushes and sketchpads sprawled across the settee, the piano littered with the loose pages of musical scores, withered pot plants sulking in the corners, a chipped teapot on the table along with a handful of burned-down candles and pouch of tobacco spilling out its bristles, a trio of china geese parading across the floorboards, a battered jacket folded over the back of a lopsided chair, a moth-eared slipper filled with blunt pencils, and bookshelves stacked with wine glasses and gargantuan jars full of frothy concoctions.

Paul followed Vincent's glance to the floor. 'Books are a little like cats, I find,' he said, by way of explanation. 'They follow their own whims and turn up where you least expect them.'

Paul carried on, leading the way into the hall and towards the stairs. Yet when he turned around he found the painter had stopped near the front door. Vincent was watching the servant girl move her feather-duster softly, reverently, over the old mink coat and summer hat hanging on the hat-stand. Vincent's features hunched into a frown.

'They belonged to my wife,' Paul said.

Vincent nodded, as though he understood, and the two men turned to ascend the stairs.

It was not that Paul thought she would at any minute return and need her things. He hadn't gone mad. At least, as he himself was prone to say, not entirely. It was rather that he thought her old clothes, her books, her trinkets and bracelets all kept the house from falling into ruin, as though those few talismans safeguarded its inhabitants, and also helped them feel that she was in some way still among them. For Paul and the children it was still her house, as though the walls and floors and bricks themselves were suffused with her, and her memory washed over everything, like a slick of oil sloshing above the slower tides and currents of their daily lives.

'May I ask,' Vincent said as they climbed, 'where it is you are leading me?'

'Ha! Yes, of course. The north room, at the top of the house. That is where I keep my pièce de résistance: a press for printing etchings. It is a marvellous thing. A machine that stops time, my son calls it. Tell me, do you know how to make an etching?'

'I am afraid not.'

'All the better,' Paul said. 'For you know, I quite enjoy playing the role of teacher. I imagine you are a fast learner. Your brother tells me you are completely self-taught?'

'He exaggerates. I have sat in front of masterpieces until my eyes felt raw and my head spun. I have worked for months on pencil sketches, then watercolours, then oils. I have given the best part of my life to it. And I am still learning.'

'Astounding. By the way, I think you'll like the view up here. The hills, the thatched houses of the old village cottages, the church in the distance.'

When the younger man did not reply, Paul turned to see what had happened. At the top of the stairs Vincent had stopped once again. Paul was grateful of the chance to pause and catch his breath. Vincent was staring at the painting on the landing, squinting hard at the figures in the snow. He tilted his head, as a lizard might when considering a fly, and his hands started flapping up towards a frenzy.

'This is Pissarro's work, am I right? It is uncanny: despite the beads of sweat on my back I can almost feel the sharp sting of winter.'

'Yes,' Paul said, though he chose not to look at the painting but kept his head turned towards his new friend instead. He did not dare glance at it directly any more. 'It is a great privilege, is it not, to be able to step into another world when this one becomes too much to bear?'

'Some might call it a miracle.'

At this they were disturbed by the sound of footsteps from the landing. They turned to see a gangly young lady, her ruffled-blonde hair pinned up above her head. She was dressed in a pastel jacket that matched her long pastel skirt and was clutching a novel to her side. She broke into something of a smirk when she saw them.

'Marguerite, come and welcome Monsieur van Gogh, the great artist I have been telling you about,' Paul said. 'He will be joining us for dinner, and I pray we will be fortunate enough to see a lot more of him, since he will be residing in the village. Vincent, it is my pleasure to introduce my daughter, Marguerite.'

'No, the pleasure is mine,' the painter stammered, raising his hand to politely tip his tatty hat to the lady, and also to shield his scarred ear from her gaze.

'I see you are admiring the snow,' Marguerite said, the spark of a smile still playing about her lips.

Vincent nodded. 'You have an impressive collection. One of the best I have seen. All the Impressionists together, in one place. Your house could be a gallery.'

Paul rolled his shoulders back in cat-like pleasure. 'You are too kind. Marguerite, he was just calling this one a miracle,' he beamed.

'No, you have misunderstood me!' Vincent turned to

Paul, his face flushing, suddenly fierce. Paul took a step back, confused.

'They are all miracles. How can you not have faith in the incarnation when you look at works like this? It is the same principle at work. Inanimate materials – canvas, cloth, oil – suddenly imbued with soul and brought to life. The spirit made real. This is what proves the Resurrection of the Flesh. For if mere men can fill a canvas with living spirit, think what the Lord can do for us!'

There was spittle on the painter's lips, and he wiped it away with the cuff of his shirt. Paul opened his mouth to speak, but then found he did not know quite how to reply. He had seen something of himself in this younger man and jumped to conclusions: *at last, someone who understands. Who sees the world for what it really is. Who can paint exactly what I feel: the turbulent, restless universe that churns us through its depths.* Only to find, in the next moment, that there was a gulf between them that could not be bridged. Perhaps that is why he looks so knowing, so sad. But then again, perhaps by now he is used to coming close to joy, then having it snatched from his trembling hands. At any rate, as he stood there on the stairs, for once he did not know what to say.

His daughter, however, had no such qualms.

'I am afraid you will not get very far with my father, Monsieur. Papa is far too stubborn to admit he might be wrong when it comes to the afterlife. Didn't he tell you about the little group he founded?'

'Marguerite, really, now is not the time,' Paul said, seeking to avert a disaster. But she would not be so easily dissuaded.

'The Society for Mutual Autopsy, they call it.'

'Is this some kind of joke?' Vincent asked.

'Oh no, it is deadly serious,' Marguerite replied. 'All who sign up agree to have their bodies cut open after death so that their remains can be examined.'

'It is not as gruesome as it sounds –' Paul protested.

'He will try to convince you to join if you are not careful,' Marguerite went on. 'He was trying to convince Renoir to volunteer last time he visited, so that they might one day have an artist's brain to examine. They want to heft it out of the skull and slice it up and determine exactly how it works!'

'Marguerite, that's quite enough!' Paul said. 'Where are your manners?'

He took a step closer to the painter, as though to contain any possible explosion, but to his surprise, none was forthcoming.

'It is fine,' Vincent said. 'I don't begrudge any man his beliefs. But you will not convince me. You may dissect the body, but you will not find that spark that makes life, that makes art. It does not live there.'

'I am sorry if we have offended you,' Paul said.

'Nonsense. Talk of death does not bother me. It is life that is difficult.'

'Ah, but we would not want it to be too easy,' Marguerrite replied. 'And now, please excuse me, sir.'

Vincent stepped aside and watched as Paul's nineteen-year-old daughter made her way down the stairs.

'Please accept my apologies,' Paul said once she was out of earshot. 'She is strong-willed, opinionated, and far too brash for a lady. Just like her mother was. It is my fault, I'm afraid. I fear I have kept her too closeted and she feels herself empress of this whole house.'

'On the contrary, she does you credit,' Vincent said. He stared back towards where she had passed, as though some invisible trace of her still lingered there.

Paul said nothing, but carried on down the landing, past a few paintings leaning against the wall that he had not yet found time to hang. The air up there was thick with memories, as though they spun through the musty afternoon like motes of dust. And yet Paul felt suddenly hopeful, for he had a sense of this nervous man as a kind of double, a doppelgänger of sorts: someone brimming over with the same passions and the same doubts. If he could just steer him away from his own mistakes, then perhaps, just perhaps, there might yet be a way to pour all of it into pictures. If they could only manage that, then everything else would have been worthwhile. If they could turn that sadness into something beautiful, then perhaps it would all make some kind of sense.

They continued past the bedrooms and on to the room at the top of the house. Paul could not stop himself from a little flourish as he opened the door: he swept out his hands and gave a theatrical bow.

'Now, this is what I wanted to show you. Come in, and together we shall stop time.'

# DOPPELGÄNGERS

Wake up.

It is still early. Too early. You snuffle and twitch, wriggle off the last sticky threads of sleep, reach over bleary-eyed to check your phone, then throw your legs over the side of the bed. You are cotton-mouthed, and so you glug stale water straight from the glass. Shuffle over to the window and open the curtains. Then something catches your attention and – instantly – you are alert. Down in the street below, you can see someone walking quickly through the early morning mist. You rub the dream-dust from the corners of your eyes and look again. You peer so close your nose presses against the cold glass. You can see someone wearing your face.

You feel dizzy, suddenly uncertain of yourself. Maybe you pinch your arm, just to check you actually are awake. Perhaps you check the mirror, gripped by an irrational fear that you are not really who you thought you were. Maybe you run downstairs, out of the door, chasing your double down the street – but by the time you reach the corner they are gone.

You feel dizzy, suddenly uncertain of yourself. You sense your own identity slipping from your grasp, because in that instant you are no longer unique, individual, one of a kind. You are not the only one. And that is how I felt when I came across the second portrait.

Yes, there are not one, but two paintings of Doctor Gachet. And like all doubles, it leaves almost everyone who sees it feeling uneasy. I came across a description of it in one of the books Professor Buckridge had found for me, and straight away I searched for the image, only to sit and stare at it in profound disappointment. It was like seeing one of those Hollywood beauties who have ruined themselves with plastic surgery: the face is familiar but strange, unnatural, out of place.

It's not like it's terrible. I mean, I certainly couldn't paint anything like it. It's not a train wreck. It's the kind of painting you might stop and look at for a minute or two in a gallery (and if you want to do that, it's not difficult: unlike the elusive and well-travelled original, this one is still in France at the Musee d'Orsay, and is sometimes lent out for exhibitions). But it's not the kind of picture you would keep beside your bed. It's not the kind of painting you could lose yourself in. It's not the kind of painting that speaks. Perhaps that's the problem. It is not terrible at all. It's mediocre. And somehow that is far worse.

In the second painting the sky is still blue, though it is not the same wild and agitated blue, but something staid and stodgy. It is a murky pond of water. It is too still, too heavy, too flat.

Paul still rests his head in his hand, but his look now is less melancholy than exhausted. His eyes are no longer piercing but distant: they do not stare at you. He is distracted. He has had enough and cannot take any more. The smile is not heartbroken. It is simply worn out. His sympathy is ebbing away.

The foxgloves are still laid out on the table, but those familiar motifs no longer prickle up and spike out from the canvas. Perhaps that is because they no longer have anything to rest upon, as all his books are gone. He has no time for reading now, is not searching for explanations.

In short, there is something about it that is not quite right. It is profoundly unsatisfying. It is the evil twin, the black sheep, the poor relative. And it is not just me that the other portrait confuses. It is almost universally agreed that this version was painted second: that it is an imitation, probably rushed, made from the original. No one can agree, however, about who painted it.

The commonly held view is that Van Gogh made it to give to his friend, while the artist kept the original. Others argue, however, that it was knocked off either by Doctor Gachet himself, or by his son, the younger Paul. It is certainly distinctly amateur-ish in comparison with the majestic, hypnotizing power of the original. But could it really have been a copy?

Paul and his son certainly wouldn't have been past trying something like that. Paul quite openly copied paintings by Cézanne and others, aand his son continued to work on copies after his father's death. These facts have made a corner of the art world very sniffy about the Gachets, and also more than a little suspicious. Paul is accused of ripping off his friends and betters, of acting unethically by exploiting the works of art he bought from them, and also of a kind of morbid voyeurism in the sketch he made of Van Gogh on his deathbed. But I think this is over the top. It was common practice to learn from imitation. Paul spent most of his life hanging around with the great Impressionists and staring entranced at their masterpieces. He would have done anything to paint as they painted. It was natural for him to copy, for how else would he pick up their tricks, how else would he be able to master their prodigious skills?

However, in this particular case, it seems unlikely. Put simply, he was not good enough to make a copy this convincing. He knew this, and would have been the first to admit it, no matter the sadness it caused him. He was passable at blurry landscapes or hazy rooms, but not so good at detail. He could just about manage a foggy landscape. He was an expert at etching, and taught the skill to many of the artists whose work he longed to emulate. But something this free-flowing? Beyond his capabilities, let alone his son's much-mocked abilities (which depended on creating an outline and then filling in the colours, rather than Van Gogh's quick and unrestrained method of painting with no safety net). Besides, Gachet was relatively well-off, and spared no expense when forking out for expensive canvas, the finest oil paints, his beloved etching press, and any other materials that took his fancy. Both of the portraits, however, were done with the cheapest paints available.

The Van Gogh Museum in Amsterdam certainly believe that this second portrait is by the artist himself, and I am inclined to agree. It was an afterthought, then, a hasty favour for his friend – rushed through rather carelessly, as a souvenir. After all, it is made up of Van Gogh's signature sweeping brushstrokes. It may be a little clumsy, but perhaps that was simply because after the frenzy and passion of the original, he had lost interest. He must have known that he had achieved something as close to perfection as he would ever get, and so there was little chance of matching that original magic.

Maybe that is what bothers so many people: that Van Gogh could paint something so sublime followed by something so unexceptional; that his last weeks were not entirely filled with frenzied works of passionate genius; and that he had no qualms about hurrying off a second-rate painting. It goes against the myth of the tortured perfectionist. That would explain why so many people have suggested it is a forgery. But there is one key detail those people overlook: the foxgloves. Research done by the French museums directorate suggests both paintings have aged in exactly the same way.

Both the first and second portraits contained bright mauve flowers. In the century since they were created, the foxgloves in both paintings have faded to the same pale blue. They must have been done, therefore, in exactly the same tone, from exactly the same palette, at roughly the same date. It is not clear, however, whether the promise the flowers signify are also apt to warp over time.

Curators and art historians will continue to argue about the provenance of the other Gachet, because like all doubles and doppelgängers it is unsettling to think that there might be more than one. But this shouldn't worry us. There's hardly any point getting worked up about a second portrait when the original only exists to us now in the form of copies and clones. Copying, after all, is an act of love as well as an act of commerce, and in this way Paul was startlingly ahead of his time. For we are like him: we do not fear copies anymore. We embrace them, participate in their creation and, like the old doctor, sometimes we escape into them.

Almost all of us now exist in other versions. We have been wilfully cloned, and by our own hands: our lives multiply, and in this day and age there is no end. There are different versions of us on Facebook, LinkedIn, Twitter, Spotify, Instagram. Our images proliferate, and our selves diverge. We are everywhere at once. Just as Doctor Gachet leads a second life in the painting, so the rest of us exist apart from ourselves, reduced not to splashes of colour and light but to a pulsing stream of zeroes and ones. We are code, we are encoded and we are alive online, outside our bodies. What's more, none of this seems strange to us anymore.

We are everywhere at once. Perhaps we leave parts of ourselves in the world to prove that we are really alive. That we lived once, and are living now. Proof that, like Paul, we have been born in strange times, and somehow against the odds we are still here, we have (for now) survived.

# UNDER CLOUDED SKY
### June 1890

Let us try to make a little sense of this so-called madness. Van Gogh arrived in Auvers at the end of May. He stayed in a cheap attic room at the Ravoux Inn, but he took dinner frequently with Paul: he admired his new friend's huge and ramshackle collection of Impressionist paintings, argued with him about new ideas and new projects, and listened to his daughter play the piano in the evenings as the light grew faint and the candles flickered.

But more than anything else, he painted. During his time in the village, he completed more than 70 paintings, as well as many drawings, sketches and even etchings (as taught to him by Doctor Paul-Ferdinand Gachet in the top room of the tall white house). That meant he averaged more than one a day.

He catalogued his new life with a zeal that tended toward the obsessive. For, make no mistake, these are not flights of fantasy or elaborate dreamscapes. He painted, as ever, the world as he found it, in all its strange and sacred wonder. Yet he depicted not just what he saw, but also how it made him feel – his last works are startling because when you look at their wild mix of colour, sense and emotion you feel it too. His paintings from this time are a diary of his inner life, with ecstatic moments of clarity and also crushing moments of despair. He spent days wandering around the village, and on these trips he painted the *Village Street in Auvers*, the *Thatched Cottages*, the *Houses in Auvers*, and the *Farmhouse with Two Figures* out where the roads turned into muddy tracks. He painted the *Cows (after Jordaens)* in the fields, and a *Child with Orange* he met during his afternoon walk, a ruddy-faced toddler hunkered down in the sun with a daydream and a fat globe of fruit. He painted the *Church at Auvers*, the *Chateau of Auvers at Sunset*, the *Vineyards with a View of Auvers*, and also *Landscape with Carriage and Train in the Background*, in which a black steam-engine tears across the horizon, rushing away from that little village that the painter himself would never leave.

Paul was over the moon.

'He is surely cured,' he said to his daughter that evening, after Vincent had finished dinner and returned to the inn.

Marguerite had nodded curtly. 'Indeed, he seems full of a certain vigour.'

'It is the painting. I think he has found it, that spark of light that chases away the shadows. If only he can cut down a little more on the drink – but we must be patient there, I fear. Yet if there is hope for him, then there is hope for all of us.'

But with hindsight we cannot, of course, be so confident. And so the question remains: Was he frantic or simply prodigious? Was he painting so much because he felt so much better, or were the paintings a reflection of his increasing anguish? After all, most of his best loved works date from times of desperation and despair: he painted his *Self-portraits* and his *Starry Night* while staying – against his will – in the asylum in Saint-Rémy, and painted his *Sunflowers* and his *Chair* and his *Yellow House* while rowing violently with Gauguin and hurtling towards crisis.

But it would be too simple to say these paintings – these wild, swirling bursts of colour that leap from the canvas as though they are made not of paint but flame – were products of his inner turmoil. It would be easy, it would be trite, and worst of all it would be wrong. It's a cop-out: the tired old cliché of the lonely, insane artist. Yet it is a myth we turn to again and again. Why is that? Why do we demand that great art must come from suffering?

Is it because in the Christian tradition suffering is redemptive, because it cleanses the soul and brings us closer to God? Is it to make us feel better about our own mediocre lives, to comfort us with the idea that it is impossible to both achieve greatness and be happy? Or are we all, secretly, a bit like Paul Gachet, wanting desperately to believe that our suffering is not meaningless, that if some great joy – a song, a canvas, a book – can be salvaged from our sadness then it is not in vain?

I do not know the answer. But I know that this idea of the tortured genius is destructive, for it is a one-note stereotype that allows us to lump together such intriguing and diverse artists as Sylvia Plath, Franz Kafka, Kurt Cobain, Virginia Woolf, Jackson Pollock, John Keats, Amy Winehouse, and poor old Vincent, patron saint of the lot of them. Besides, does it really matter? Why should we care what the artist was feeling when we look at the painting?

It shouldn't matter. We ought to be able to separate the dreamer from the dream. To love a song or a picture or a book or a movie regardless of where it came from. It shouldn't matter at all. But it does.

Because we get that familiar spine-tingling feeling when we stare at those landscapes, at those churning waves of light that make up his last turbulent pictures. Because so many of us have felt the same.

But nonetheless, I believe Van Gogh was, at least for a time, starting to feel better. He wrote as much to his brother – though this could simply have been to stop Theo worrying – and gave Paul every sign of emerging slowly from his dark days. He had a new sense of purpose. When he was younger, he had tried being a teacher, but had struggled to inspire his students. He had worked briefly as a Pastor, but had been forced out. He had dreamed of an artist's commune, but after his bitter experiences with Gauguin he realized he could only work alone. Yet he had not given up. On the contrary, he painted now with a new sense of determination. He was convinced, with Paul's encouragement, that in the future there would be an audience for his work, and that in time people would look at his paintings and understand what he was doing. He believed he was communicating something across a vast gulf of time.

What is most surprising is that, unlike many of his other fantasies and delusions, this time he was completely correct.

Paul plugged his pipe and, leaning back in his chair, patted down his pockets for the matches. Outside, the late summer evening still burned pink at the fringes of the sky, and the one-eared scarecrow-like figure with his tatty straw hat had only just started off home along the country path. Paul Junior had retired upstairs. Half-empty cheese plates littered the table, and only dregs swam in the bottom of the wine glasses. Marguerite was looking at the open window, her scrunched-up nose turning her face into a scowl.

'Come now, I see you don't agree with me,' Paul said. 'Out with it, Marguerite.'

Marguerite looked across at her father as he lit his pipe. 'Well, he seems a man who is either all light or all shade. There is no in-between.'

'Ha,' Paul said. 'You know what that is? It is a mark of integrity.'

'Really, Papa, it is quite the opposite. It's a lack of refinement, surely, to be so excitable one moment and so sullen the next.'

Paul took his pipe from his lips and pulled an exaggerated grimace. 'Oh, my dear, have I really brought you up so badly to prefer manners to sincerity? Would you rather spend your day around fakes? Tell me that you yearn for the affectations of the higher classes and I will have definitive proof that I have failed as a father! Here is a man who shows what he feels, a man who cares more for authenticity than fashion, and you damn him for not being haughty enough!'

'It is not that. You know I don't care for any of the ridiculous fops who lord it up in the village or play at being fashionable in Paris. It is just that he is, well, unlike any man I have ever met.'

The serving girl came in to clear the plates and bring more of the night lamps, and Paul set down his pipe and leaned forward towards his daughter.

'I have never met anyone like him, either. But each of us sometimes seems strange to one another. He is not so different from you: an old soul in a young body. So let me be clear: you must be kind to him, for my sake.'

'Of course, Papa. I would not dream of being otherwise.'

Paul reached for his wine glass, only to find that the serving girl must have cleared it away. He could not help but feel that his daughter's tone was a long way from sounding sincere.

'Don't, please, embarrass me. He may seem strange to you, but he is still our guest here in Auvers, and more importantly he is that rarest of things: a true and honest man. I will not have you turning up your nose at him.'

'As you wish, Papa.' Marguerite kept her eyes lowered as she rose from the table and made her way up to bed, for she recognized the sudden shift in her father's mood, and knew that it would do neither of them any good if she continued arguing with him.

But Paul, as ever, stayed up for some time. In truth he had half given up on sleep, for it did not come easily to him, and when it came it was as slippery as an eel and just as electric, for it shocked him in fits and starts from which he woke clammy and panting for breath. He had tried countless herbs and homeopathic remedies, but the sad secret (which, it goes without saying, he kept to himself) was that he was no longer sure he held any faith in their power.

Instead, he took to the garden, and stood awhile in his bare feet, his thoughts flitting along the ridges and fault-lines of his usual fears and worries without ever quite tumbling into the cracks. The stars crept out across the cloudless night, the hens clucked in the henhouse, and he tried to focus on something, however tiny, that would tide him over till sunrise. And it was there, in the garden, that Vincent came upon him the next day (though he had by then changed his shirt and, without a doubt, the contents of his pipe).

The afternoon was clear and bright, the sky blue enough to make a pair of sailor's trousers, as his wife used to say, and Paul pulled his cap tight over his head to keep the blazing sun from his pale skin. It was the kind of fierce summer's day that seems made for those who have someone to share it with. He was picking a few flowers for the dining room when he spotted the unshaven painter loping towards him, so loaded down with brushes and canvas and paint box clutched beneath his arm that he resembled a travelling salesman desperate to make a pitch.

'Are you quite sure?' Paul said.

'Without a doubt,' Vincent answered. 'Today is the day. The light is perfect out here. I cannot bear to paint indoors when I have the chance to be in the thick of it. Too much time indoors is bad for the soul.'

'I quite agree. But I did not mean the setting. Perhaps you would prefer to take on my garden again instead? The natural world offers so much more than people, don't you think?'

Vincent shook his head, unwilling to concede to the doctor's point of view that the trouble was always mankind. Like a plague of insects that has overrun this planet, he had heard the older man say, and he felt that to agree would, in some vital way, be the same as giving up.

'No? Well, I still think it one of your best. All those billowing reds and greens, it was as though my whole garden was full of light and joy! I have to tell you how pleased I was to see such a positive work. It is a good step for you!'

'Perhaps,' Vincent said as he set the easel on its wobbly legs. 'But they are not that different from people. The landscape changes with the seasons; so, too, our faces change as we age.'

'Ah yes,' Paul said. 'The slow sagging of the skin, the entropy of the muscles.'

'The accumulation of experience,' Vincent replied. 'For better or worse.'

'Experience is another word for having made countless mistakes,' Paul said. 'You know, you are lucky. To be an artist, to have the liberty of honesty. I envy you.'

'Ha. I was thinking the same about you,' Vincent said as he steadied the easel. He checked the angle one last time, then opened his box of paints and started unpacking them upon the small garden table.

Paul took the flowers he had picked and sat down at the table.

'Honesty in the medical profession? It is rarer than white diamonds. Do you know the function of a modern doctor? You keep people going, just a little longer. I have a patient in Paris with gout. It is not uncommon. He comes to see me every few months, when his toes are so swollen he can barely walk. I give him medicine, and tell him he must alter his habits. And every time – every single time – he swears he will change. Sometimes he does, for a week or two. Then as soon as he's feeling better he slips back into his old ways: reaching for steak and shrimp and beer until he is sick once more. He cannot stop himself. And in truth we are all a little like that. We are architects of our own undoing.'

'Not all of us.'

'You know, I am often called to visit those suffering from syphilis, or from consumption. Some of them cannot move, others do not know who they are. And I cannot help but wonder what we are doing. To keep men living, though they are wracked with pain. To keep them clinging on to life, no matter the cost. As a doctor it is my duty to heal them, and all the while to keep my mouth closed and never ask that most vital question: am I not just prolonging the misery? Am I not just making matters worse?'

'These are questions only the Lord might answer.'

'Then how dare he stay silent?' Paul asked.

Vincent looked at him sadly, but said nothing.

Paul took a deep breath. 'Please forgive me. I get carried away... I see you are ready.'

Vincent nodded. 'Yes, it is time. But it is not quite right yet. That flower you have been twirling between your fingers, please set it on the table.'

'This?' Paul said, holding up the bright and wiry sprig. 'I hadn't even realized I was still holding it.'

He set the flower down upon the table in front of him, next to the yellow-backed novels he had been reading (borrowed from his daughter's ever-growing library).

'Digitalis. Am I right?'

'You have a good eye. Yes, foxgloves,' Paul said, and before he could help himself he added, in a quieter voice, 'her favourite.'

'I have heard many physicians prescribe it for problems of the heart. Do you believe it effective?'

'Ah, well, it depends how badly the heart is broken,' Paul replied.

Vincent nodded, understanding, and turned to ready his palette.

Paul rested his head on his hands, and remembered at that moment that they meant something else besides, in that strange old language of flowers.

Vincent reached for his oils, squeezed out the blue onto his palette and began dabbing his brush into the thick of it.

Paul raised an eyebrow.

'Is all of that meant for me?'

'You should know that I do not plan to just paint your appearance. I will paint you. And besides, it is not what you think. Blue is not meant for melancholy alone.'

Paul raised an eyebrow. 'No?'

'It is also the colour of infinity,' the painter said, with a flourish of his brush.

Paul smiled sadly.

Vincent leaned forward, and flicked the first fleck of bright blue paint across the bare canvas.

And that was it.

I could tell you about the painting, but I suspect by now you know it as well as I do. That jutting body looming large in the centre of the canvas. The eerie calmness of that pale face. The wash of swirling blues crashing across in restless waves: the stark blue suit, the sad blue eyes, the cobalt blue hills, the azure blue sky. The tilted head, the look that has seen it all, that affirms the depths to which we test ourselves.

Should I try and describe how Van Gogh does it? It is enough to know he works in a mad and skittish flurry of criss-crossing brushstrokes, not even pausing once, tilting at the canvas until his hands ache.

Should I try and describe the thoughts going through Paul's head? You know them already. You have followed his life, with me, and know how this look was forged.

This is where everything has been leading. Paul was almost 62 years old, had spent exactly 22,630 days on earth, had lived out each minute of more than half a million hours: all those moments that make up a life, everything that has added to his sadness and everything that has kept him going, distilled in a single afternoon into something set free from time.

And so, really, this book should stop here. Or, at the very least, we should draw this part to a close. Paul is no longer any use to us. Everything he had to give has been given. His life has been poured into the canvas, and from this point forward the painting has its own story for us to follow.

Some might go as far as saying that after that day Paul becomes a husk, a shell, whose soul no longer resides in his body but in the painting. He begins to fade, while the picture stays as haunting and vivid as ever.

But that will not do. It may be poetic – if a little pretentious – but it is not true.

He is not dead yet, and I have grown to like him. Besides, there is something else to consider. One more reason for that melancholy look in the painting. Maybe he was sad for precisely this reason: that he knew what was going to happen next, and knew he would not be strong enough to stop it.

# THE STARRY NIGHT

And then I woke up, and it was all a dream.

When I was a child all my stories ended that way, with all the wrongs turned right, all the tangles unpicked, and everything returned to its place. I wish it was that simple. If I could, I would do it now, and turn everything back to how it should be: the old doctor, stirring in the night and reaching out to find his wife lying beside him; the artist in the wheat field, moving his fingers to his chest to find the shot misfired, his heart still whole.

Yet in a sense it is already a dream: from a distance the past often seems hazy and dreamlike. Maybe that is all it is. After all, we can never really know for sure. The life that makes up that look that burns inside the painting is little more now than guesswork and conjecture. The past is a story we tell ourselves to make sense of the present. Our lives, too, are made of stories. But the difference between a story and a fantasy is not always clear.

The last time I saw Professor Buckridge, she had given me the usual warning about double-checking and cross-referencing my sources. How, in historical study just as in detective dramas, you should be careful: everyone has a motive.

For my old teacher, the study of history was full of dangers. Every account was to be treated with suspicion. Van Gogh, in his letters, might just be telling his brother what he wanted to hear. Or perhaps trying to convince himself, by the act of writing down those difficult ideas, that this was how he really felt. After all, sometimes it is only by putting something into words that it becomes real. Meanwhile, for each person we meet, we reveal a different side of ourselves. Imagine: something funny happens to you on the way to work. You meet your friends at the pub and tell them what happened, and no doubt you exaggerate a little, play it up for laughs. You tell that anecdote again in the office, standing around with your colleagues during a coffee break, and this time you cut down on the swearing, edit out the parts that make you look too silly. You tell the anecdote one more time to family back at home, stripping it of any extra details and focusing more on how you felt than what you did. Each time the story has changed. The question remains, is one version more true than the others?

Take Paul. To his childhood friends he was annoyingly righteous, a limping pain in the backside. To his teachers he was often an insufferable know-it-all. To his wife, the gentlest and silliest man she had ever met. To painters, either an annoyingly frenetic and obsessive amateur, or a welcome source of kindness, understanding and, most importantly, favours. To his daughter, a well-meaning old man with unpredictable mood-swings. To his son, a source of magic tricks and good advice. Which is his true self? Or, to put it another way, which of these is the Paul that we see staring back at us from the portrait?

For Professor Buckridge, the only way to find out the truth was by painstakingly uncovering, analysing and cross-referencing primary sources. Ideally eyewitness accounts – the more unguarded the better. But everyone knows that eyewitnesses get muddled all the time. You see it in court every day. Two eyewitnesses, two contradictory accounts. Everyone sometimes makes up stories to impress people. Paul certainly did. He exaggerated for effect, or to make himself look good.

Or twisted things to make others look bad. Every source, like every person, is a hodgepodge of bias, a rattlebag of judgements and hidden agendas. No one can be fully trusted.

By this logic, the best kind of source to use as a basis for historical enquiry is a diary. Because, according to my old teacher, it's not trying to impress a particular audience, it's not aimed at anyone but the writer. It's a direct and unfiltered statement of experience. Think of Pepys, Boswell, Marcus Aurelius, Anne Frank. Those private voices speaking their thoughts to themselves are some of the most valuable sources of all.

But if you ask me, the whole idea is a sham. Sometimes, the kind of people who keep a diary are exactly the kind of people who long for someone to steal it and read every page. At any rate, you can't trust diaries at all. We watch what we say to others, for sure. We tell people what we think they want to hear. Twist events until they fit the version of truth we're trying to peddle. But we do something else as well. Every second of the day we play tricks on ourselves, we look the other way, we convince ourselves to believe in falsehoods that help us sleep at night. Yes, we lie to our bosses, our partners, our families, our friends. But not as much, no never as much, as we lie to ourselves.

# NOT A QUESTION OF LOGIC
## July 1890

It is not entirely clear what happened next, nor why.

This much at least is beyond debate: it was Sunday night. The sun was still flush late in the evening and rippling out in shades of crimson across the crimps of scattered cirrus. The old bell in the village church had long ago rung out its evening mass, and Paul was sitting down to supper. More specifically, he was peeling a tangerine. He had grown impatient waiting for the serving girl to bring in the fish they had caught in the River Oise that afternoon, and his aperitif had left him ravenous, and so his heavy fingers wrestled with it until he managed to tear off all the strips of peel to get at the slippery fruit beneath. Marguerite had, despite her father's protestations, brought a book to the table, and she looked so like her mother when she was absorbed in a story – her lips sometimes silently mouthing the words on the page, her brow furrowed with intense concentration – that he could not bear to disturb her. Paul Junior, fishing with his father all summer Sunday long, was now snoozing in his chair. Paul had just popped a plump segment of tangerine into his mouth when the serving girl burst in, flushed, with a note from a boy at the door.

Paul held it close to his face and squinted at the hurried scribble. He felt his throat tighten. After he had read it twice he carefully folded the note in two and placed it in his breast pocket.

Marguerite looked up from her book as her father wiped his juice-sticky hands on his napkin and then rose from the table. 'I must attend to a patient,' he said.

'Now? But, Papa, *supper*.'

'Don't worry, I will be back soon. Start without me.'

In the hallway he found his hat and medical bag – complete with a couple of his homemade remedies and his electric coil, just in case – then stepped outside and closed the door behind him.

The dirt track that skirted the fields behind his house was deserted. Thoughts were tumbling, one after another, through his head. As his breath grew thick a pair of rowdy crows cawed from the wheat fields, and he turned to see the sunset about to break.

I know what you are thinking: did he really pass the wheat fields, or have I just thrown them in so I can draw your attention to Van Gogh's last works? Honestly? The answer is, a bit of both.

On the one hand, there is no other way to get to the main village street in Auvers, so Paul must have passed them.

But also, I wanted to return to the wheat fields. Because besides the still lifes, the portrait of Doctor Gachet, the farmhouses, cottages, and streets he passed, the gardens he sat in, and the children he met, Van Gogh painted wheat fields. He painted them again and again and again. Just as he had done when staying in the asylum. In distress, it seems, he turned to wheat.

He was a fervently religious man, a passionate believer in the resurrection, and so it is inconceivable that the Bible verses were not in the forefront of his mind. *Be not deceived: whatsoever a man soweth, that shall he also reap*. Something about this calmed him and, for the most part, these last empty landscapes are remarkably tranquil. They are pure light, pure spirit.

But what do they mean?

That is not for me to say.

But in his last few frenzied weeks he completed the following canvases:

— *Wheat Fields* – which is empty of humans, and so is startlingly quiet.

— *Wheat Fields with Cornflowers* – where all is haze and burning rust.

— *Wheat Fields with Auvers in the Background* – where the world of people is fading out of focus.

— *Wheat Fields Under Clouded Sky* – twice, for though it was high summer he sensed the weather ready to turn at any minute.

— *Wheat Stacks with Reaper* – with just a single figure in the middle of the field, engrossed utterly in his work.

— *Wheat Fields with Crows* – the wildest of the lot, with the sky disturbed by birds and the fields cut by paths: everything in flight towards the distance.

It took Paul a quarter of an hour to make it to the heart of the village, and he hurried down the main street past La Poste and the butcher's until he arrived at the Ravoux Inn, next door to the little wine shop.

Monsieur Ravoux, a stooped carthorse of a man with rolling shoulders and bristly whiskers, met him at the door.

'Gachet?'

Paul recognized that quizzical look in the man's eyes, a look he saw more and more these days – a look that asked whether this doddery old man was actually capable of carrying out the job.

'What happened?'

'We'd just finished eating – it wasn't like him to miss a meal – then we came out to take some air. That's when we saw him. Stumbling up the road like a drunkard. He went straight inside. My wife went up to check on him but the door was locked, so I had to get the spare key. When I went in he was on his bed, holding his side. His shirt was something rotten. He said he'd shot himself.'

Doctor Gachet sucked in his breath. Monseiur Ravoux shifted his weight from one foot to the other, waiting for the doctor to say or do something. Paul pressed his hands to his head to try to stop the world from spinning.

Did he ask the question?

He must have.

*Why did he do it?*

I cannot answer that. It is easy to spin theories, but they do not get us very far. Better, perhaps, to leave well alone: to try not to cheapen the life before by focusing solely on the last day.

Nonetheless, there is plenty of macabre speculation out there, and it continues to this day: that he was bipolar; that he was crippled by depression; that he could not cope with the thought of another epileptic attack or another enforced stay in the asylum; that now his brother had a child he could not bear to be a financial burden on the family any longer; that absinthe had shredded his nervous system and left his hands so shaky he would soon be unable to paint and that possibility was one he could not live with; that life was just too much for him; or that two boys from the village shot him by accident and he decided to keep quiet to protect them from the police – each one is true, and none of them are.

I wish I could be like Paul, who never even thought to ask his friend why he did it, who never sought an explanation. He seemed to have understood that some questions cannot be answered.

'Well,' Paul said at last, his hand kneading his temples. 'He was able to walk, that at least is something. Did he say anything else?'

'What?' Monsieur Ravoux's face scrunched into a frown. 'Wait, yes, actually he did and all. He said he hoped this time he'd succeeded.'

Paul felt another wave of dizziness sweep over him. He tried to breath but his throat was suddenly knotted. 'Where is he?'

'He has the attic room. You'll need a light.'

Monsieur Ravoux retrieved a candle from the bar and then started up the narrow staircase, the light from the candle leading them all the way up to the very top of the house.

Monsieur Ravoux nudged the door open then slunk back, towards the safety of the stairs, as though to enter the little room in the loft would be to risk something terrible – if not contagion, exactly, then something equally unspeakable. And there he hovered, watching as the doctor made his way inside.

Paul took a few steps in then stopped, and remained motionless for a moment to let his eyes grow accustomed to the gloom. For an instant he was held still by the ridiculous notion that if he did not move forward, if he did not see it for himself, then perhaps it would remain forever unreal. Then he shook his head and started across the loft.

He had to hold the candle close to his face to guide him, and as he crept over the dirty floorboards it threw flickering shadows upon the little wooden chair where rested that familiar straw hat, then the cabinet, and the desk on which his most recent paintings were stacked. The attic was burning hot, musty with the stink of stale air. It was a cramped room of the cheapest kind, a mean storage space turned into a makeshift cell, with the low roof sloping down at such sharp angles that Paul was forced to hunch himself in half as he moved cautiously toward the bed.

The cobwebs thrummed and shimmered. It was so stifling that it felt as though all oxygen had been wrung out, as though – Paul thought – the bright canvases on the desk had sucked all life from the room and were hoarding it all for themselves.

The man on the bed in the corner twitched at the sound of the creaking floorboards. He was lying flat upon his back, his bare and dirt-scabbed feet tipping over the edge of the short bed, his hand resting on his side. Paul set the candle on the chair. Then he bent down, close enough to be overcome with that cloying, sour reek of sweat, an animal stink that stuck in his throat. The sound of a thumping heart seemed to echo around the loft, though Paul could no longer say whether its relentless beat belonged to his patient or to him.

There was no mistaking it. The thick stain upon the painter's shirt looked to have only recently turned crusty, and had curdled into a map of some unknown country. The shirt would have to be removed. But as soon as Vincent felt Paul's hands upon his chest his whole body flinched and his eyes shot open. Yet he did not turn his head to look at the doctor, but instead stared straight up at the ceiling. Neither man dared catch the other's eye. Neither man spoke.

Why was this?

Many years later, Monsieur Ravoux's young daughter would remember her father saying Gachet and Van Gogh did not exchange even a single word. He assumed they did not know each other, and had never met before that day.

And since this is Vincent van Gogh we are talking about, there are naturally countless conspiracy theories that seek to explain this silence. Just so you don't think I'm trying to hoodwink you with my own interpretation, let's reel them out and try to be objective:

## 1. Marguerite

You may remember that in a previous chapter Paul told his daughter to be kind to Vincent. She would never have disobeyed her father, and so when the painter asked, she agreed to sit for him. He painted her twice, for *Marguerite Gachet at the Piano* and *Marguerite Gachet in the Garden*. In the former she is careful, poised, elegant and intense as she plays to him. In the second, she is radiant: a calm and gentle presence surrounded by bright and glowing flowers.

One theory has it that after Paul arrived back from his practice in Paris and found out about these two portraits, he panicked. Van Gogh had a habit of falling madly and passionately in love with women he barely knew, and many of his crises had been precipitated by wild and uncontrollable infatuations with young women. Furthermore, it has been pointed out that in the painting of the garden, the nineteen-year-old Marguerite is wearing a wedding dress, while in *Undergrowth with Two Figures* there appears to be a bride and a groom emerging from amid the trees. Paul ordered Van Gogh to break off contact with his daughter before their relationship got out of control. Van Gogh was heartbroken, and the two men never spoke again.

Some go even further and suggest Gachet had something to do with the incident in the field – perhaps it was he who shot Van Gogh, after he found out about a love affair between the painter and his beloved daughter. That would explain why the gun was never found, and would cast some light on the fact that Marguerite never married, why she was overcome with depression after the painter died, and why for the rest of her life she never left the family home in Auvers.

There's only one problem with these theories: there is absolutely no proof for them. True, Marguerite is wearing a white summer dress in one of the paintings – but that's hardly surprising for the middle of June. And that's as far as it goes. The rest is nothing more than conjecture. And the facts are muddled, for Paul knew all about the portraits. In fact, he actively encouraged them. Van Gogh wrote to his brother after completing *Marguerite Gachet at the Piano*, and noted that Doctor Gachet 'has promised to make her pose for me again at the small organ.' That's not the kind of promise a father would make if he fears something stirring between his friend and his child.

So that cannot be the reason. This leads us to the second theory:

## 2. The Argument

It is no secret that Van Gogh had a volatile temperament. He ricocheted between extremes of happiness and melancholy, and it has been suggested that he may have suffered from what we would now diagnose as bipolar disorder. One week he wrote to Theo that Paul was the best friend he had always wished for, a man who understood him perfectly, and noted the deep understanding between them. The next he was writing that Paul could not be trusted. What might have happened?

Many accounts suggest the two men had some kind of argument about a painting. On one visit to the house, Van Gogh had seen a nude by Guillaumin unframed and leaning against a wall. He had upbraided Paul, and told him that such a work ought to be treated with the respect it deserved. Paul had agreed, and explained that a carpenter in the village was currently working on a frame for it. A week or so later, Van Gogh spotted the same painting still unframed, and exploded with rage. He cursed his friend, shouted and ranted in Dutch, and screamed until he was hoarse. Paul did his best to stay quiet and calm until the painter grew exhausted and left the house, slamming the door behind him. After this strange incident, Paul was left shaken, and as he was aware that such manic episodes might easily spill over into violence, he avoided Van Gogh from that point onward. The painter felt abandoned and distraught, for he was lost without the new friend who had kept him going that summer. They never spoke again.

This theory is at least well-supported. There was certainly some kind of disagreement regarding the painting, though its nature is not clear. And it is true that in one of his letters Van Gogh indicates that he is becoming disillusioned with Gachet, who is 'at least as sick as I am'. Yet within a week he was writing once more of how Paul was like a brother to him. Is that suspicious? No. That's how most relationships work. We're mad with someone one second, and forgive them the next. We have tiffs, spats, upsets and quarrels, and in the end we get over them. Paul and Vincent were no different.

Like any friendship, theirs had its peaks and troughs. The two men certainly argued, and they just as certainly made up, as Van Gogh's letters clearly show. If they fought about something, it was soon forgotten, and they went on to discuss future projects together. Therefore, there can only be one explanation:

## 3. The Truth
The silence was not because they had fallen out. It was not an angry silence, or one filled with recriminations, regrets or mis-

givings. It was a silence that can only exist between friends, a silence that reminds us that we are connected by something deeper than language, a silence that acknowledges that sometimes no words will do.

In short, it was a form of kindness.

Paul wiped his brow with the back of his sleeve. It was so stuffy the whitewashed paint was curling from the wall. With as gentle a manner as he could muster, Paul tugged the unbuttoned shirt away from the painter's chest. A swirl of strawberry-blonde hair trailed across his bare torso, and Paul was relieved to see that dimpled plain from nipple to nipple was untouched: there was no damage to the heart. However, his relief was short-lived: as he pulled the soggy shirt away he saw it. It was down at the lowest curve of the lowest rib. The wound was a ragged circle, not much bigger than the fiery tip of a cigar, surrounded by a burned ring of mottled purple flesh.

As his fingers pressed close to it, he heard the painter's breathing quicken. Nonetheless, he did not stop pushing down against the abdomen, testing it, until he was certain: the bullet was buried deep. It must have lodged somewhere near the spinal column. Depending on the trajectory, Paul thought, it would either have ripped through the spleen or the left kidney. Why did he not remove the bullet?

Over the intervening years Paul has been called a quack, an eccentric, a bad doctor and a worse friend. He has been blamed for not trying to save Van Gogh's life. But the truth was it would have been impossible for him. Surgery of the lower body was rudimentary at the time, and without modern medicine and medical tools he would likely have caused massive internal damage and killed his patient within hours. Especially when you consider that he was working by candlelight, and that the last time he had operated on anyone was close to twenty years previously, during the war. He was no surgeon. He knew he could not save his friend. So instead Paul spared him the final agony of clumsily cutting him open, and kept him going long enough to see his brother once more and say his goodbyes.

More damning is the judgment that Paul was negligent in not getting Vincent straight to a hospital, since there was one in the nearest town, not much more than half an hour away by horse and trap. For, make no mistake: Van Gogh did not die quickly. He remained lucid for more than twenty-four hours in that cramped and airless loft, only dying in his brother's arms early on Tuesday morning. So did Paul misjudge the severity of the injury, or did he simply abandon his friend to fate? Both are possible – he may have deluded himself that the 'miraculous' painter could turn one more miracle and somehow recover, or alternatively he may have thought he had no right to interfere with his friend's desire to end his life – but I suspect the truth is a little more complex.

As a doctor, Paul knew one thing better than most: no one wants to die in a hospital bed. No one wants to die in a strange place, wracked by pain and fear, all dignity stripped away, surrounded by strangers. I do not think Paul misjudged anything. He knew there was no way Van Gogh could survive. Say what you like about me having grown too close to this eccentric old man – I admit it, he has become important to me – but I think Paul's decision to let Vincent stay in the village he had come to love, surrounded by familiar faces and his cherished canvases, was an act of mercy.

The attic room was growing hotter than ever, and Paul could feel the sweat slithering between the folds of his shirt as he dug into his medical bag. He found the saline solution and tipped a little onto a cloth, which he rubbed around the wound to clean it. He then dabbed on some antiseptic ointment, the painter hissing at the sting of it as though shocked by an electric current. Finally he cut and folded a long strip of gauze, which he taped across the abdomen. By then his brow was wet and sticky, with sweat dimpling in the folds of his eyelids. He packed up his medical bag, and tucked the shirt back into place to cover his patient's chest.

Then he rose unsteadily to his feet. He had to write to Theo, to summon him at once. The police, too, would have to be called (Van Gogh would stubbornly tell them it was none of their business, that he was free to do as he wished with his own body). Once again, Paul felt dizzy, his thoughts tumbling away from him.

Yet just as he reached for the candle, the painter raised a finger. Paul turned to see where he pointed. Then Vincent shuffled on the bed, and with a few grunts and gasps he pulled himself up until he was propped on his elbows. Paul nodded. He understood.

Under the sloping wall was a little wooden chair, and on its back was slung an old blue jacket. Paul rummaged in the jacket pockets, until he found the pipe. It was just what he too would have asked for. He fluffed up the tobacco between his clammy fingers, then packed the bowl of the gnarled wooden pipe as meticulously as he would his own. He tapped it down carefully, not too loose and not too tight. He could hear their twin heartbeats beating in rhythm again, though it sounded now as though he was hearing their echo from a great distance, just as the light of stars reaches us from many years away. With the candle he made the charring light, then tamped the tobacco back down into the bowl. He looked over at his friend, who was watching him carefully. At last, Paul made the true light and brought the pipe to his mouth, taking shallow puffs until the smoke spun out in curls and clouds.

Then he reached across, through the darkness, and without a word pressed the pipe into the painter's hand, the stem still misty from his lips.

# BEYOND THE SHORE
## 2291

It goes without saying that you and I are dead.

The painter and the doctor's graves too have been churned over many times, the soil dug up and reused before being reclaimed by the turgid black ocean that sleeps over the earth.

A layer of ash has settled on everything that is not sluggish sea, and those who see the world now see it as though through cataracts, a gaudy haze that makes everything mist. This book has decomposed, the digital copies lost on obsolete servers and buried beneath an incomprehensible number of other digital files that no human eye ever sees. The sun, too, is not the same as it was, or at least it seems that way, because of the fog.

To Ka-Li it looks like a whipped-up froth the colour of day-old mashed potatoes and just as thick. She has only been outside twice, and both times it was so blubbery it stuck between her teeth, made her tongue feel gummy. They had to have extra sessions in the Booth afterwards, hooked up so long she could feel it tingling through every pore like pins and needles gone full electric. She likes the rivers she can swim through in the sensory pod, the ones conjured from some history not quite her own and filtered through her senses for her daily Immersive™ experience, the silver fish and dolphins that appear joyously beside her as she dips and dives through the rushing green water – but she knows that the real water beyond her tribe's tetris is not the same. It is more sludge, that flow, a thing that strangles. Black foam and spray, a rage of scudding shadows. But none of it bothers her.

At T+3 she finishes up her session in the Sunbeam© and, after breakfast Easy Noodle™ with Ma and LaoMa and Tai-LaoMa she curls up on her bunk and uploads to the Stream. It is time for her lessons. As she connects, the program gives her the sensation of flying upwards, beyond her tetris and ever higher, and she blinks and sees her friends Lo-Bai and Jie-Shi soaring through the clouds beside her.

'Wei, hi!' She calls and waves.

They call back across the unbroken blue, and soon the three girls float through the portal and into the classroom. The Program Master greets them and guides them toward a choice of windows. The girls choose as one – the green window, their favourite: *Learning through Exploration* (they will save *Computer Engineering* and *Survival Emergency Procedures* for the two afternoon classes).

The Program Master bows and smiles as the pre-Ocean world loads. The landscape reconfigures around them and they feel that familiar sensation of a prickling in their fingertips, their toes arching up from the imaginary ground. They are gliding into history. They float past a star exploding, then families of apes in the trees, then a caveman hunting deer and bison on the plains.

'Zoom,' Jie-Shi says, and the scene fills out around them

They are standing in the steppes of the Hawash River valley, where a man-like creature is wading into the pulsing water. This is easternmost Africa, what is now Ethiopia, some two and a half million years before they were born. He walks with a hunched swagger, his back a dark mass of fur-like hair, his eyes beady and narrow as he searches through the curves of the stream. He bends down and thrusts his club-like hands into the water, picking through the pebbles, until he finds the weight and shape that best pleases his palm. He takes his pebble from the water and, back on the grass, he bashes it with the harder limestone cobble he has set aside until he has split the top so that it has a sharp, jagged end. As he works, the sound echoes out through the valley around them: clink, thwack, clink, bash.

'That is one of the first tools,' the Program Master says. 'A hammerstone. With this he will cut bone, slice through tangled roots, carve meat from the sides of wild ass, oryx, gazelle, or zebra.'

'Zebra is that horse with zigzags,' Jie-Shi says, pointing to a black-and-white animal in the distance. It goes without saying that there are no horses now, but it is one of the girls' favourite parts of the day's lesson to watch these multi-dimensional animal reconstructions moving through the Stream.

'Correct,' the Program Master says. 'Who knows what other tools aided mankind in progress from living in caves to the great and glorious dawn of the Biological Imperative?'

Ka-Li put up her hand, and the Program Master nods.

'Factories?'

'Correct. Zoom.'

The pixels refresh, and they are watching workers in the Industrial Revolution huffing and panting. All around them is a metal-on-metal din, the thwack and the bash of the workers at the furnace, ringing through the factory. It seems so hot inside that the windows are steamed and the bunched faces of the older workers are blushing with sweat. They look through blinding heat towards the rumble and snarl of the melting furnace that stands at the back of the factory floor.

Everything is a little brighter than it should be, a little too clearly defined, but they are used to the quirks and nuances of the program. As they drift between each scene, the Program Master runs through his speech about Natural Selection, about Global Warming, about Biological Imperatives, about the world-saving work of the Most Beneficent Prime Government.

'How did the Biological Imperative improve our existence?' the Program Master prompts.

All three of them can repeat the answer by rote:

'The Prime Government fixed our immune systems. Once we were broken, but now we are saved. The Biological Imperative protects us from illness, from antibodies, from age. All praise the Prime Government. We are better people now.'

The Program Master wants to show them the steam engine, explain causation and the beginnings of industry, the development of finance — but the girls instead begin to chat amongst themselves. They are there, but not there; moving invisibly among the ever-changing movie, and they are drawn as ever to the tiniest of details: the young man coughing and hacking into his hankie by the rumbling furnace.

Ka-Li lingers beside the coughing worker, watches him hunch over and then haul in another shovelful of coal. He has dark hair with a few streaks of grey, and patchy stubble from a rushed shave. His shirt is missing a button, and his eyes are the colour of bubbles. Ka-Li is fascinated. Not because there aren't any males in her tetris, but because of something she can't quite put her finger on.

'Zoom,' she says.

His face is streaked black, and though she knows he is not real she has the urge to reach out and dab away the dirt and sweat dripping down his forehead and welling up in creases above his eyelids.

'Funny kind of animal, weren't they?' Lo-Bai says.

Jie-Shi wrinkles her nose. 'You mean they were gross.'

'No, but...' Ka-Li says, 'but he looks funny.'

The PM intervenes. 'Before the Prime Government launched its initiatives, life was difficult. This worker's lungs are compromised. His main interface will soon expire and his harddrive will therefore be forced to power-down. This was common in the time before the Prime Government. Once we were broken, but now we are saved. All praise the Prime Government. We are better people now.'

Ka-Li watches his face crease into a frown, his eyes swim with light. The other students are bored, but she cannot take her eyes from this hologram.

'Does he know?' she asks.

'Yes. He is aware of his malfunctions. The knowledge of his impending loss of warranty engenders feelings of sadness. His work will be taken over by other labourers and then –'

'What do you mean *sadness*?'

The Program Manager is silent.

The other girls turn now too. This has never happened before. The Program Manager has an answer for everything. He is their teacher, their guardian, their guide. He is a part of the software.

'You were correct. They were a different kind of animal,' he says at last.

He raises his hand and the landscape reconfigures around them. Now they are in a thick rainforest surrounded by pouty orangutan, tree frogs the colours of bad dreams, cawing birds who strut and plume upon their branches. Usually, this is saved for last: a reward. But not today.

'Why did he look so funny though?' Ka-Li says. 'It can't just be his warranty, can it? Why did he look like that?'

Her classmates are more interested in a great speckled snake coiling from a branch, but she knows the Program Master has no choice but to answer.

'He is sad.'

'You said that before,' she huffs. 'But what is sadness?'

The Program Master blinks.

'It is an obsolete chemical reaction in the brain that the Prime Government has helped us fix. Once we were broken, but now we are saved. It is only a glitch in the system.'

'What does that mean?' she asks.

He goes on. 'Sadness is an archaic noun denoting a feeling that life is not as it should be. It is an anomaly that has been eradicated. Now we are saved. All praise the Prime Government. We are better people now.'

'I still don't get it,' she says.

Once again the landscape reconfigures and the sky begins to blur into a restless blue swirl. The girls rub their eyes – they are not used to this level of resolution. The sky is blue paint, the mountains behind them blue paint, the horizon nothing but haze.

'Malware!' Lo-Bai whispers.

Jie-Shi gasps. 'Uh, there's something wrong with the pixels!'

'It is not a virus,' the Program Master responds. 'You do not need to be concerned.'

But still the girls stare open-mouthed: they are in a painting. They are surfing on slick blue ridges, riding wild waves of blotted blue. And everywhere they turn an old man is sat at a table in front of them, his wrinkled face a mash of paint, his suit an ocean billowing in storm, his eyes burning with that same look she saw in the factory worker.

'There's something wrong with it,' Jie-Shi says.

'No,' the Program Master answers. 'It was created this way. This is a primitive form of a lesson.'

'But it's not even 5D. What's it for?'

'Your ancestors looked at it.'

'Why?' Jie-Shi says.

'Like a window?' Ka-Li asks.

'Yes. Like a window.'

'Does it move?'

'No.'

'Oh. What does it do then?'

'It is purely instructional. The file has been saved from the pre-Ocean. This is what your ancestors filed under "sadness". An aberration.'

Lo-Bai and Jie-Shi reach out, running their fingers over each smear, each running fleck. It looks to them distinctly lo-res, like something any newbie could rustle up in *Introduction to Programming*. Child's play. Not even multi-dimensional.

For a second Ka-Li feels something she has never felt before. Something that fizzes through her whole body, that makes everything around them seem out of time, out of place. Nothing can go back to how it was before. But in another second it is gone.

The other girls are losing interest – it is primitive to them, silly, no more real than this far-flung story is to you, reading it right now. We used to live in trees, then in caves, then in cities, then in tetris. So what? People used to die from black death, leprosy, cholera, pneumonia, sadness, old age. But they don't have to worry about that now. It's ancient history, so who cares? They are better people now. The pre-Ocean, the past, for them is nothing more than a story. And a boring one, at that.

Why was it uploaded to the system? (We must assume the real thing, unless stored in air-tight, temperature-controlled conditions that miraculously and against all the odds some-how escaped fire, flood, war and the countless other ravages of the new world, was lost long ago.) It is simple. It is a souvenir. Someone, sometime in the distant past, knew that they would need reminding. It is a memento of an animal life they have left behind.

But what is it?

Ka-Li is still puzzled. But not for long. They do not know what it is, but as with the Ocean and the ash outside their tetris, they know enough not to press. Once they were broken, but now they are saved. They are better people now.

Lo-Bai points to the flowers by the old man's hands.

'Zoom,' she says.

The flowers sprout, bud, bloom, and spread out all around them as the landscape reconfigures into a traditional English country garden. There is a fountain ahead, and a maze made out of neatly-manicured hedgerows. A sparrow making its nest in the nearest tree. The students spend the next ten minutes walking winding paths and learning the strange and tongue-twisting names of those long-extinct varieties: lavender, hollyhock, rosebush. The sensation that there is something else, something missing, is soon forgotten. None of it bothers them.

# ALL THE EYE MISTAKES FOR LIGHT
## 1909

On first glance it looks like our lives shrink. The boundaries draw in and we venture from home less and less. Possibilities diminish, plans deflate. And then there are our bodies. Paul's suits had grown baggy, and so had his skin. His eyesight had turned to rust, his ears to echo. One knee was seized up and useless, and the other was in mourning for its much-missed sibling. He could not remember when he had last stood without help. He sagged a little on the left side and could not open his claw-clenched hands to hold the palms flat. His bones creaked whenever it rained, and yet summer was no better, for when the sun grew too bright he was afflicted with migraines that made him feel as though the sharpest of splinters was being pushed slowly into the softest parts of his brain.

But on second glance, that is not quite right. It is not that our lives shrink. It is that they can no longer be held in. As our bodies wither, our lives spill over and go on elsewhere. Paul's life was no longer contained in the body of a feeble old man with a dribble-flecked mouth who spent all day hunched up in a chair, but instead filled those rooms. That old brass bed where his wife had once slept beside him, the masterpieces by his best friends hanging on the walls, the childish drawings from when the kids were young in his study, the fishing tackle in the cupboard, the medical books on the shelves, the scores on the piano, the medal from the war in the cabinet, the startling paintings by the troubled man who came to stay one summer up in the magic room. His life went on in every corner, and if he could not always remember it all then it did not matter, because it carried on around him regardless.

That morning his daughter had shaved him, had washed and dried his papery skin, as she always did, then dressed him and helped him into his chair. And there he had stayed all morning, his thoughts no more than flickers, stirring up the silt in a murky pond. Marguerite hovered around him, adjusting the blanket on his lap, dabbing at his chin, talking to him in a constant monologue that drifted in and out of his consciousness.

'I'm thinking of re-hanging the Renoir in the living room, Papa. You know what they say, a change is as good as a holiday. What do you think? Oh, and I sent Marie to the shop for some fresh bread, Papa, and after lunch I thought you might like for me to read the papers to you, about the latest opening in Paris, perhaps?' To each question, Paul nodded, his eyes closed. Marguerite had noticed how rarely he looked at her, but had not been sure whether to attribute this to the fact that she resembled her mother so closely that it caused him grief to see her, or simply that his eyes could no longer bear the light. But the truth was, as always, a little less romantic: for if Paul's memories were now somewhat askew, then his regrets still cut quick, and he felt something close to shame every time he looked at his daughter.

She used to be beautiful. Men used to come all the way from Paris to spend a little time with her. Half his artist friends were besotted, intoxicated by her wild looks and mocking humour. She was fierce and funny, and spent half the day with a smile twitching at the corners of her quick mouth. But now she had settled into the role of old maid. She had grown heavy-set in middle-age, her hair thin, her face haggard and tired. Men used to beg her to run away with them. Now they stayed away. Like her father, she rarely left the house.

It was the same with Paul Junior. He used to be an intrepid adventurer, bubbling with plans and schemes. He used to disappear from the house at dawn and only return at dusk, having spent all day building camps in the woods or fishing down at the river. Now he spent all his time upstairs, making copies of his father's favourite paintings. Brushstroke by brushstroke, line by line, he flexed and worried until he was satisfied that he had fathomed how it was done. He had no interest in creating anything of his own, only in learning the secrets of those pictures that so transfixed his family. And while he worked, he wore his father's old blue suit and cap.

In his more lucid moments Paul understood that it was his fault. After Blanche died he had held them as close as he could. He had tried to protect them from life, not realizing that seedlings protected from the fierce light of the sun will wither and fade. He had infected them. His grief had begot their own: it was a vine they had fed and fed until it had wrapped its creepers around their limbs and ensnared all three of them. And now it was too late.

Maybe this is why he looks the way he does in the portrait. Maybe this is where true sadness comes from: the realization that you have failed those closest to you, that you have let your hopes slip away, that in the end you have let down those who needed you.

I know what you are thinking. Why am I being so hard on him? He's a helpless old man now. I could have been kinder and finished the story somewhere else. I could have left him to his peaceful retirement in his comfortable home, surrounded by the paintings he loved, and skimmed over the rest. I could have focused on other details: how his loving family never deserted him, how they stayed together no matter what. There is something in that. I could have chosen another ending: the art lover in his garden, watching the sunset turn the hills to rust.

But that would not be true. I know him too well now, and I am certain his regrets caught up with him. He was a master neurotic, an expert at torturing himself about all the things he should have done differently. Yet consider his eyes in the portrait. They are unflinching, and so we ought to do him this same grace and not turn away. His face in the picture tells us this much: he has seen the future and knows how it will end.

That morning was one of those dips, where flickers of guilt strayed across his mind, and he could not shake free of them. Marguerite tried to draw him out, but she knew his moods better than to press him. Instead every hour she came through and moved his chair so that, one by one, he might face each one of his favourite pictures, and in this way she hoped he might spend an hour trampling through the snow beside the old church, an hour in the company of that stern girl with eyes full of feathers, an hour punting on the river at sunset, an hour in a carnival populated by dancers with doglike faces – though where he really was, she could not begin to guess.

Perhaps part of him really was somewhere else. Did he somehow sense that Johanna van Gogh – the widow of Vincent's brother – had now sold his portrait, so that his doppelgänger had already begun its strange journey through time and space towards us? It seems unlikely. But not out of the question.

It was a slow morning. Sometimes, people came to see his impressive collection, sometimes the nephews or children of his old friends stopped by to break up a journey and wish him well. A few and far between came to ask about that wild genius he knew for a couple of weeks. Occasionally, the postman, or deliveries from the grocer. But today, nothing. Not that it mattered to him.

For lunch Marguerite helped feed him watercress soup and daubed at his mouth with a napkin (his teeth were ground down to dust, his eyes folded into origami creases). After the plates and glasses had been cleared away, and Paul Junior had stomped upstairs to take up his brushes, Marguerite looked to her father and he gave a nod. That was their signal, and so she turned his chair to face the window and sat down at the piano.

It was a daily habit the two of them had grown fond of, and both had long since accepted that without the comfort of routine their lives might come adrift. The piano was the same brown beast that Van Gogh had painted her sitting at some twenty years before. It was a temperamental creature that Marguerite had to soothe and pet in order to earn its co-operation. She looked over at her father, before flexing her fingers.

Then she started to play. The melody was halting at first, something tentative and uncertain, but slowly it began to take shape as something more insistent. It was a tune at once both sad and uplifting, and as the noise washed over him Paul closed his eyes, letting his forgetfulness wash away his regrets.

Minute by minute, the music swam him back on its tides until he was carried to some distant shore. His gnarled old fists tapped against the arms of his chair to a creaky, stuttered rhythm, and when he opened his eyes again he could see from the window the trees in the garden, the trellis, the overgrown lawn, the flowerbeds, the coops and hedges; and in the distance the fields, the crows, the hills. It seemed now like a painting: all surface. But in the half-light of his broken sight he saw – or thought he saw (for there is now no difference between the two) – some shape upon the swirling hills, a young woman perhaps, though in the end it was impossible to say.

Let us leave him here, the last of his memories falling and flying to the strange melody that echoed round the stuffy little front room. He has a minute or two left, but time is even more elastic than usual when it comes to beginnings and endings.

Is he scared? Or will he welcome it? I cannot begin to guess.

But then again, these are not the right questions. Because he knows something that I myself have learned by writing this story down. I have learned this: I have been wrong all this time.

Wrong about what? The soul.

Now don't panic. I'm not going to get all preachy on you, I promise. Just bear with me for a moment. Listen: the soul really is just as we were told at Sunday School. It is something vital, something unbreakable, something unique within us. Our true self, if you like. And those Sunday school teachers were right too that it outlives the physical world, that it survives the decay of the body. But they were wrong about where it goes.

This soul does not spark like a flame dancing from candle to candle, to be born again in another form. This soul does not descend to hell, nor suffer through purgatory, nor ascend to Heaven. It is not immersed in the Divine like a drop of rain losing itself in the sea. It does not end up in the Gardens of Paradise, or some blissful sleep. But neither is it nothing, some archaic illusion that should splutter and fade in the face of more quantifiable wonders. No.

This is what I want to tell you: we've had it all the wrong way round. The soul is not something we keep with us and take wherever we go next. The soul is not the part of us that travels on. It is the part we leave behind.

It is something we give away so that others might find us – in a memory, in the words of a song we know by heart, in a borrowed trinket, in an old birthday card, in the smell of a particular perfume, in an ancient woolly jumper, in a battered photograph of a party from many years before. Or in the sad smile of a gentle old man in a painting. The soul is the part of ourselves we give to the world.

Your soul does not belong to you. You will not take it with you. You will leave pieces of it in every room you enter, in every person you touch, in every object you hold close.

Look again at Doctor Gachet. Look at him closely. He smiles back at you because you and he are the same. He smiles sadly because he knows it is all useless, and yet even in those darkest moments there is still that tiniest sliver of hope.

He smiles because he knows that wherever we go, there is always a part of us that stays.

## ACKNOWLEDGEMENTS

This novel was completed thanks to an award
from The Society of Authors' Authors' Foundation.
I owe a great debt of thanks to Dhruti Shah for her encouragement and feedback. I am also very grateful for the support
from Everette Dennis and Hariclea Zengos. For always stepping up to help, thank you TJ. Most importantly, this book
could not have appeared without the support, belief and
hard work of Todd Swift and the Eyewear Team.

# PRAISE FOR SAM MEEKINGS' PREVIOUS BOOKS:

'A powerful and mesmerizing novel,
both mythic and intimate. Sam Meekings has a maturity
of insight and theme not commonly found in a young writer.
This is a masterful accomplishment of imagination, insight,
and lyricism.'
Amy Tan

'Sam Meekings's remarkable novel – it's more than
interesting, it's captivating, and all the more so
for being real.'
The Scotsman

'Meekings is a bangup storyteller, and his easy handling
of rich and varied material – rustic splendor, class warfare,
profound anguish, drastic social changes – will keep readers
rapt.'
Publishers Weekly

'Utterly beautiful and memorable.'
Scotland on Sunday

'A story that is intriguing and well-written. A book
that feels highly original, has appealing characters and is
beautifully written.'
The Bookbag

 **EYEWEAR** PUBLISHING

Eyewear publishes fiction,
non-fiction, and poetry.

*Recent prose works include:*
*The Virtuous Cyborg* by Chris Bateman
*Eagles and Earwigs* by Colin Wilson
*That Summer in Puglia* by Valeria Vescina
*Juggling With Turnips* by Karl MacDermott
*Aliens, Gods & Artists* by Sam Eisenstein
*The Other Side Of Como* by Mara G. Fox
*Deeper* by J M Richards
*Tuscon Salvage* by Brian Jabas Smith

WWW.EYEWEARPUBLISHING.COM